BARON'S COURT, ALL CHANGE

Also from Cripplegate Books

Denizen of the Dead –
The Horrors of Clarendon Court
edited by Stewart Home
published 2020

The 9 Lives of Ray "The Cat" Jones
by Stewart Home
published 2021

The Bastardizer Polishes a Turd
by Chus Martinez
coming soon

BARON'S COURT, ALL CHANGE

TERRY TAYLOR

INTRODUCTION BY STEWART HOME

CRIPPLEGATE BOOKS   MMXXI

Published by
CRIPPLEGATE BOOKS
London

ISBN:
978-1-8382189-2-8 Paperback
978-1-8382189-3-5 Hardback

September 2021

Baron's Court, All Change
was first published by
MacGibbon and Kee in 1961
and by Four Square/NEL in 1965

This edition first published by
New London Editions in 2011

Introduction © Stewart Home, 2011
Graphic and text design by Luther Blissett

Cover photograph of Terry Taylor in Tangier
circa 1961 by Johnny Dolphin.

*For my
favourite
gym instructor*

INTRODUCTION

Many novels are forgotten and more or less disappear from circulation. The majority of books to suffer this fate more than deserve it. A handful of them are classics and eventually find their way to wide circulation. One of the most famous examples of this is *Les Chants de Maldoror* by Comte de Lautréamont, which made little impact on publication but became a canonical example of modernist literature after being rediscovered and championed by the surrealists. *Baron's Court, All Change* by Terry Taylor is a very different type of lost classic. It created a bigger splash than *Maldoror*, but by the late-sixties had faded from view and most people's memories. It provides an accurate account of the drug subculture in London at the end of the fifties. The realism and hep talk of *Baron's Court* shocked many readers when it first appeared in 1961, but would have raised far fewer eyebrows in the aftermath of the summer of love. That said, it is only more recently that it has become possible to appreciate its historical significance.

Now that *Baron's Court* is being republished there is little need to describe the novel or its plot. Instead I'll explain how I came across the book and why I've spent nearly a decade talking it up to almost anyone who'd listen. The first time I'd have come across Terry Taylor's name was probably when I read Tony Gould's Colin MacInnes biography *Inside Outsider* in the eighties. Gould devotes a couple of pages to Taylor because he was the inspiration for the unnamed narrator in the most famous MacInnes novel *Absolute Beginners*. Gould doesn't call Taylor the world's premier mod, but this claim might be made for him on the basis of his fictionalisation within the pages of *Absolute Beginners*. That said, one of

7

the crucial differences between *Absolute Beginners* and *Baron's Court* is that while MacInnes sympathetically portrayed youthful modernists without being a part of their scene, Taylor writes about them with an insider's eye and knowledge.

If I'd come across a used copy of *Baron's Court* soon after first reading Gould's MacInnes biography, I'm sure I'd have picked it up. Instead what Gould wrote about Taylor gradually faded and I'd forgotten it by the time I re-read *Inside Outsider* a decade ago. If Gould had written as much about *Baron's Court* as he did about its author, I'd have filed it alongside British youth culture novels of a similar vintage such as *Only Lovers Left Alive* by Dave Wallis and *Awake For Mourning* by Bernard Kops. Unfortunately a copy of *Baron's Court* failed to fall into my hands at that time, whereas pretty much every other example of the drugs and youthsploitation genre I heard about I picked up not only easily, but for a song. This was a period in which I was reading all the fiction I could find based around the counterculture and youth cults.

Terry Taylor came to my attention for a second time about ten years ago when I started researching the life of my mother Julia Callan-Thompson and her connections to the counterculture. I discovered she'd been close to Taylor in the 1960s, and as luck would have it, around the same time a very battered paperback copy of *Baron's Court* came into my possession courtesy of a book exchange stall. Reading the novel for the first time was a revelation. Here was a book about drug dealing first published in 1961 that not only mentioned LSD, but totally transformed my understanding of early mod culture. The smartly dressed working-class modernists in their Cecil Gee shirts smoked 'charge', while the middle-class 'trad dogs' in their ill-fitting sweaters were popping amphetamine pills. And making matters even better, the book just romped along. It was a great piece of story telling.

Having read *Baron's Court*, I wanted to know more about the writer. Although my mother had died in 1979, there were still people around who'd been acquainted with Taylor in the 1960s. Unfortunately no one was able to help me trace him and several of my mother's friends told me that they'd heard he was dead. I put Taylor's story together as best I could from both print and oral sources. It ran something like this. Terry Taylor had been born in Kilburn, west London, in 1933 and got into modern jazz and smoking 'charge' as a teenager. In 1956 Colin MacInnes got talking to Taylor in a drinking club in Berwick Street. At the time MacInnes was living above Gallery One in D'Arblay Street and Taylor was working as a passport photographer in Wardour Street. Gallery One was owned by Victor Musgrave, whose wife Ida Kar was an important post-war photographer. At this time John Kasmin (a famous gallerist in his own right in the sixties) was Kar's assistant. Ida had an open marriage with Victor and after MacInnes introduced Taylor to her, Terry became her lover – despite an age gap of 25 years between them. Meanwhile Kasmin became Kar's business manager and Taylor took on the unpaid role of her photographic assistant.

The atmosphere at Gallery One around this time was extremely bohemian – you could call it a little piece of swinging London a decade before the rest of the city started to rock. This atmosphere oozes out of a series of pictures Kar took of Taylor getting stoned after a photographic session for the little known jazz singer Judy Johnson. These extraordinary images appear to have been hidden from public view until I included them in the exhibition *Hallucination Generation* at the Arnolfini Gallery in Bristol in 2006. I guessed Ida Kar must have taken quite a number of pictures of Terry and I eventually found them in the archive of her work held by the National Portrait Gallery. At the time I was searching for these works the NPG hadn't included them in their online catalogue of Kar holdings because they had no biographical details for Taylor, which I have since been able to provide.

For a time, Taylor took to living at Gallery One, but eventually he moved on to Notting Hill. After this relocation, Victor Musgrave introduced Terry to Detta Whybrow when by chance both turned up in D'Arblay Street at the same time. In conversation Taylor and Whybrow discovered they lived close to each other in Notting Hill. Shortly afterwards Terry called on Detta at her home and they became lovers—an affair that continued from the late-fifties until the mid-sixties. *Baron's Court* was published in 1961 and from then onwards Taylor spent a lot of time in Tangier. In his memoir *Journey Around an Extraordinary Planet*, American beatnik poet Johnny Dolphin describes how he got heavily involved in a magic group formed by Terry Taylor and various Berbers which met in Tangier to materialise thought forms. The process combined smoking grass with magic and the practice was brought back to London.

By the mid-sixties Terry, Detta and the circle around them—including my mother—were very interested in LSD. Detta persuaded a chemist she knew called Victor James Kapur to make LSD for her when it was still legal. The acid is said to have been very pure and an intense tripping scene developed, as well as much street dealing. Of course, it wasn't long before LSD was banned and a series of police raids in November 1967 led to Detta and some of her friends appearing on the front page of *The Times* and at Bow Street Magistrate's Court over drug offences. Kapur received the heaviest sentence of nine years at the Central Criminal Court in May 1968, and was removed from the Pharmaceutical Register later that year. Both Terry and my mother were out of London when the busts took place, and as far as I can tell had left the UK before the drug became illegal. My mother was in Paris. Terry was still spending a lot of time in Tangier.

It amazed me that this circle of early countercultural 'freaks' and the first LSD manufacturing bust in the UK had fallen out of the history of the British underground. It was a major omission in the many books I'd read about the subject. I chased up the newspaper stories about the bust after first hearing it as oral history. I also clued up researchers such as Andy Roberts about this fascinating hunk of lost history — enabling Roberts to do further research in the police files and include it in his 2008 book *Albion Dreaming: A popular history of LSD in Britain*. I'd already written about Taylor on my website, and I'd also made a couple of hundred photocopies of *Baron's Court* and passed them around, since I absolutely adored the book and wanted to see it widely read. Incredibly the only person I came across who'd read *Baron's Court* before I slipped them a photocopy was the journalist Jon Savage. Even polymath novelist Iain Sinclair — who knows London literary obscurities like no one else I'm acquainted with — was unaware of Taylor's youth cult classic until I brought it to his attention.

I knew that Terry had left London permanently in the early seventies and it was there that the trail I was following in the hope of finding him pretty much went cold. I contacted Tony Gould who told me that although Taylor had helped him with his MacInnes biography, he no longer knew how to get in touch with him. My mother's address book contained a couple of entries for Taylor in North Wales. I fired off letters but received no replies. Next I used the electoral roll to locate everyone I could with the name Terry Taylor in Wales, Herefordshire, Shropshire, Manchester and a few other places I thought this elusive author might be living. Still I had no luck. By chance in January 2005 I met Johnny Dolphin, mentioned earlier, who was very keen to discover what had happened to him. Not long after this, out of the blue, I got a message from Taylor himself, via the email contact form on my website. Terry said he liked what I'd written about his book online. I'd established contact at last – and the chance to ask Taylor about the many crazy rumours I'd heard about him.

When we spoke on the phone Terry came across as a down-to-earth bloke, albeit one with many incredible stories to tell. Shortly after this I was lucky enough to find a first edition hardback of *Baron's Court* at a bargain basement price. Meanwhile, Terry provided me with a manuscript copy of an unpublished novel called *The Run*. It was set in Tangier and covered the same scene Esther Freud records in her book *Hideous Kinky*, but from the point of view of an adult insider. *The Run* was every bit as good as *Baron's Court, All Change*.

Returning to the early sixties, in Tangier Taylor had been hanging out with the likes of William Burroughs, and as a result he'd become interested in developing his writing in a more experimental direction. This didn't go down well with Terry's publisher when he offered them a book entitled *The Dancing Boy* as a follow-up to *Baron's Court*. His editor at Mac-Gibbon & Kee told him to rewrite his second novel as a conventional narrative. This advice was ignored and that's why Taylor currently only has one published book to his name. In the various personal upheavals Terry has gone through, he lost the manuscript of *The Dancing Boy*, but *The Run* from the early seventies still survives. Although William Burroughs picked up the nickname El Hombre Invisible, I think it fits Terry even better than the author of *The Naked Lunch*. Taylor might be a countercultural face but he can also blend into a background and look natural anywhere. On either side of the eighties and throughout that decade, Terry and his wife ran a highly successful sandwich shop in the seaside town of Rhyl, North Wales.

Moving forward to the twenty-first century, my efforts to create a buzz around *Baron's Court* by writing about it, and circulating photocopies, eventually began paying off. Nearly everyone I gave a xerox of the book was incredibly enthusiastic about it. I was also receiving abusive email from bibliophiles who were frustrated by their inability to obtain an original copy of *Baron's Court*. My favourite came from a used book dealer who told me that in twenty years of trading this was the first time he'd found it impossible to locate a commercially published title of such relatively recent vintage — and he begged me that the next time I found a novel I wanted to enthuse about and promote as a lost cult classic, would I please refrain from picking on anything as obscure as Terry Taylor's work! Copies did turn up occasionally but usually at quite at a price. When Repton Readers first offered a hardback edition of *Baron's Court* for sale on Amazon in 2009, they asked a whopping £238 plus postage for it!

So why did a far-out drugs novel like *Baron's Court* fall through the cracks and disappear from view for forty odd years? I'd see its main problem as being that it was at least five years ahead of its time. Nonetheless, it only needed a handful of cult fiction fans who'd been born after *Baron's Court* was first published to learn of Terry Taylor's life story, for interest in both him and his book to rocket. Add in that *Baron's Court* described mod and the counterculture in very early stages of their evolution, and that it was the first British novel to mention LSD, and those who'd heard about this were soon itching to get their hands on the novel.

The publication of a *Baron's Court* paperback by Four Square in 1965 is difficult to explain. Four Square bought the rights within weeks of Terry landing his hardback deal and he'd expected them to issue a mass-market edition in 1963. Perhaps they got cold feet about the subject matter but with the burgeoning drug culture of the mid-sixties considered it too hot a property to be allowed to fall completely out of their publishing schedule. By then 'with-it' editors were aware of a growing interest in drugs and casting about for books dealing with the subject.

With a little help from me, and a lot of word of mouth recommendations, interest in *Baron's Court* has been building for a few years now. With its republication this lost classic can finally reach a new audience who will be able to see its historical significance. Just as importantly, it is a fast and furious read that you won't want to put down. *Baron's Court* now has a longer and more exciting public life ahead of it than its stranger than fiction past! Among other things, it is a hipster Bible that remains forever 'younger than yesterday'. Which makes the book rather like its author. Terry Taylor is still pursing his interest in jazz and taking time out in places like Morocco and Goa. It may be forty years since he last lived in a big city, but he remains the hipster's hipster! Some are hip, while others write knowingly about being cool without being able to live that way themselves. Terry's accomplishment is to have done both brilliantly!

Stewart Home

Addendum: This introduction was written for the now out-of-print 2011 Five Leaves reissue of *Baron's Court, All Change*. Terry died peacefully from old age in 2014. It was a great privilege for me to meet Terry face to face and to see him get some of the recognition he deserved before he died. He wasn't just an absolutely fabulous writer and modfather, he was also a great and extremely charming conversationalist.

Stewart Home, 2021.

I

SQUARE

"IT'S ALL A LOT OF NONSENSE!" Mr Cage said, beaming at me from across the shop. "You'll have to buck your ideas up, John."

For the twenty years he'd been manager, every shop 'boy' had been given the name John.

"Because if you don't it's going to affect your work, and Down and Company wouldn't be very pleased about that, would they?" I carried on brushing the hat, pretending not to have heard him.

"Well, would they?" His voice a little louder this time.

"No, sir, they wouldn't, I suppose."

"Then, get all this tommy-rot out of your head. Soon you'll be bringing all those spirits into the shop with you, and then what would we do?" Annoyed at my silence, he added: "I'm sure you want to make this shop into a seance-room, like the ones you visit every night. I'm seriously concerned about you, John. It's not right for a young lad of your age to go on like this. I'll have to bring you a copy of the Bible to read. That's the best thing for you."

As he was talking, a customer came into the shop, and I felt relieved to get away from him for a few minutes. After I'd served the customer I thought that would be the end to our conversation. But no. He came over, his huge frame towering above me, and his small pink eyes looking as friendly as they could. He started again. "I don't want to lecture you, but it's for your own good I'm telling you this. Take up some healthy interests, like other fellows of your age. Join a youth club and mix with youngsters like yourself, instead of all those neurotic old fogeys at this Spiritualist Society of yours. Believe me, my boy, you'll be as mad as they are before long,"

He knew I wasn't taking any notice of him so he turned offensive again. "Well, make sure it doesn't affect your work," he roared, "or I shall have to report you to Head Office, and you know what that'll mean!"

At last five-thirty came. I felt like a butterfly breaking out of its chrysalis. Freedom at last. I hurriedly left the shop, wearing the dark grey hat I was forced to wear like all the other employees of Down & Co. As soon as I was out of hat-spotting distance, I took it off and carried it like I always did. Being only sixteen years of age I was self-conscious about it and knew that I looked stupid. Mr Cage had the same opinion, but it was one of the many rules of Down and Co.

At the bus stop the same old faces were queueing up. The same old faces, waiting for the same old bus, in the same old street, every day. To make it more sickening they were happy faces, too. They looked as if they felt privileged to work in dreary shops like the one I worked in. I tried to blot them all out of my mind. I wanted to forget, just for a few hours, that I was part of them. To kick them clean out of the old thinking box—pretending to myself that they had nothing to do with me.

"Good day at work?" I heard a voice behind me say.

"Oh, it's *you*," I said to a future zombie, that was about my own age, and worked in the tailor's shop next to the bakers.

"What's the matter with you? You look as though you've just been given the sack," he said with a bloody stupid grin all over his bloody stupid face.

"I wish I had," was my reply.

"You'd never get another job like that one if you had. Down and Company's one of the best firms you can work for. They're established, they are, and don't forget their pension scheme. It's one of the best in the country."

"Fuck their pension scheme!"

He looked shocked. His beady eyes glanced away from me, and he nervously fumbled with the button on his very square D.B. suit. Peasant's variety. "You don't have to swear," he said in a poofish voice, "If you don't like selling, why stick at it? Your old man has his own painting and decorating business, hasn't he? Why not work for him?"

"What's the difference? Selling hats in a morgue of a shop, or being lumbered with your old man climbing ladders all day? It's all the same to me."

The bus arrived and I made it very sharpish up the stairs to try and dodge this moron that was dragging me down double quick. But there was no escape. He planted himself on the seat next to me.

"Didn't your old man *want* you to work for him?" he whined on.

"Yes, he did," I heard myself saying. "But after a few thousand rows and arguments I had my own way. My own way! I told him I wanted to sell. I'd be the world's best salesman, travelling the globe for some super American company. I sold all right. In a poxy suburban branch of a hat company!"

The poor unfortunate youth sitting next to me tried to sound sympathetic. "Don't let it get you down. It's useless carrying on the way you are. I'll tell you what. Why not come to the Palais with us tonight? There's a crowd of us going. Lots of girls get there — we'll have some fun."

The Palais! An evening of quick-quick-slow and music to match. Of looking for that fabulous chick that you never find. Of 'the boys' talking about football and work and the current pop singers and their imaginary sex life.

"It's Tuesday," I said. "The night for our developing circle. I shan't be able to make the Palais."

"Do you still go to those Spiritualist meetings? You're a strange one. It's all a load of rubbish if you ask me."

"I'm not asking you!" I snapped back at him.

"All right — all right..."

"I thank God there *is* Spiritualism. If it wasn't for that and Jazz I wouldn't know what to do. While your old man forces you to go to church, I go on my own accord. I've been given proof of survival, while you just sit there in that crazy pew of yours and be told you *must* accept, without the slightest bit

17

of proof, mind you, whatever that old Bible Basher tells you. Man, you're way out of line."

"I think it's just your yearning for unconventional things that attracts you to it."

The bus arrived at Drayton's Garage, where we hopped off, leaving us a ten minute walk up the Drayton Avenue, the place I knew I could shake off the menace that was with me, as he lived in a turning off before I did.

It wouldn't have been so bad if he hadn't kept rabbiting so much. I'm not kidding, he went on and on, like those dreary houses and front gardens went on and on. He was going to France for his holidays, he told me. Fuck him and France, I felt like saying. He never gave me a minute's peace. The local youth club was having their annual dance next week, at the tin hut they call a dance hall, why not come? he asked me.

"I hate the youth club," I told him.

"What *don't* you hate?" he asked, with an "I-hate-*you*" sound in his voice.

"I don't hate freedom," I answered. "I don't hate truth or people that live their own lives, and I don't hate people like my sister Liz, who are so weak they can do bugger all about it. I don't hate you because you're one of those — I just feel sorry for you."

The poor fellow just didn't know what to say — you could see that from the expression on his face. He walked along, with his going-greasy mac, with all the buttons done up on, showing his highly starched white collar, that pulled so tight around his neck that I thought it was going to choke him any minute; his face was red from embarrassment, too. "I don't need any of your sympathy, thank you very much," he managed to get out. "It's right what Young George said. You're the original crazy mixed-up kid!"

"Not for long, don't you worry. I'll escape from this stagnated cesspool they call the suburbs! I'll ride out one day — and when I do, nothing will give me greater pleasure than to leave you and Young George behind, to your unreal life of television and peeping behind the curtains and your suburban respectability!"

"I think you're trying to be rude," he answered back in a small voice.

I couldn't stand any more of this idiot. "You bet I am! Why don't you wake up? You're dead before you've ever lived! You've had it, matey. And like the stupid fucker you are, you don't care. The suburb's bug will bite you if you don't watch out – and you're bit, boy! You've caught an incurable dose! But not me – oh no! *Me?* Never! I've had my inoculation against it! And I'll get away from this disease-infested land before long – so help me, I will!"

After reaching my old rambling homestead, I went straight up to the bathroom to make myself beautiful, which consisted of not only having a good wash to make the Down and Co aura scarper, but my weekly shave, which I carried out like some serious religious ceremony. Then I splattered myself with some of my dad's after-shave which someone had given him for Christmas but which he never used, and I tried not to notice the packet of contraceptives that he always keeps hidden behind his tin of constipation salts, because they always made me blush. Then, after putting on my non-working suit, I made it down to dinner.

My mum was in the kitchen – real busy she was, flying around the place in a double hurry, all hands and steamy face, no time and powdered nose. "Dinner won't be two ticks. I'm just waiting for the greens," she said, putting the plates in the oven to warm up. "Wish your father would turn us electric – can't stand these gas cookers." She poked down the bubbling greens with a fork, then went to a pile of ironing that was on the fridge and started to hunt through it.

"They say that the great advantage with a gas cooker – " I said, sampling one of her famous rock cakes, " – is that you can *see* the heat."

"Everyone's going electric these days. Even that scruffy Mrs Walsh up the road's got one. I saw a beauty on the tele — it had a posh glass door that you can see through as well."

"Watcher looking for?" I asked.

"Your father's underpants. Got to get them aired for the morning. Where can they... ah, here they are!" She then displayed a pair of men's underpants that came straight from the penny-loaf-and-twopenny-packet-of-fags era. They weren't just the woolly, dung-coloured, long-legged variety — they had a frayed hole by the left kneecap and bell-bottoms as well.

"Don't tell me he still wears those ankle-length, itch-making, monstrosities?" asked I, who is very broad-minded, but was unable to accept that even my old dad was that square.

"You know that he catches cold easily. Why, only yesterday — "

"But we're in the middle of summer. It's June not January."

"He can't take any chances with his fibrositis..."

"Fibrositis? It's a wonder he hasn't got prickly heat or whatever they call it, with those things on."

My big sister, Liz (who is ten inches shorter than me), came down from her room, looking as if she hadn't had a good dinner for months. She looked straight through me and said to our parent, "Dinner ready yet, Mum?"

Her mother wasn't pleased with this rather easily answered question. "You can see it's not! I've been put behind with your washing. I'll tell you one thing, my girl. If you think I'm going to wash your smalls as well, you've got another think coming! It's disgusting, it really is!"

Liz did a wise thing. She escaped into the dining-room.

I should have done the very same thing, because my mother then said, "I've got the tickets for the local ratepayers' concert on Saturday. Front row, as well." I was so taken aback that the rock cake nearly choked me.

I tried to figure out quickly how to inform my mother that yours truly would rather attend two dozen performances of

Chu Chin Chow than to be an onlooker to that mission of boredom. I'd had it all before, that was another thing: yes, *me*! I'd actually paid admission to witness this ratepayers' command performance in the past. Now don't get me wrong. I'm not saying it's not good value. Quite the opposite if you wanted a good giggle and managed to get a seat at the back so that your Michael-taking laughter couldn't be heard too much. They've been having the same performance for three years, maybe longer because I can't remember before that. There's always Mrs Burk, the woman that goes on the knocker for national savings, singing an aria from *Madame Butterfly* – you know, the famous one when the heroine is doing her nut because she thinks that she can see her old man's ship on the horizon, so she gets herself worked up into a right old state because she knows damn well that if it is, they'll have a ball and do the town that night. Well now, Mrs Burk is hardly the typical oriental heroine type. So she's goofed before she's started. She looks and sounds more like a pregnant gorilla who's due for a caesarean birth.

Then old Mr Goatly, the cat who dishes out the chickens' grub at the church hall every Sunday morning, gives forth with his mangy monologue, all about this green-eyed monster from foreign parts. The man in charge of the lights really goes to town on him because he shines a weird green spot right in the middle of his eye; and the kids scream, and if the censor were about he'd most certainly give it an X certificate. I think I've told you enough.

I braced myself for her reaction from the words I was about to say, which were: "I may not be able to go this year. Not till the second half, anyway."

She didn't take this too badly at all. "What a pity. Young George is doing his violin solo in the first half, and you'll miss it."

I couldn't keep a serious face. My cheerful chuckle could be no longer kept to myself; I had to share it with the world.

"And what are you laughing at, young man?" the woman that gave me life said to me.

"I can just see Young George fiddling with his Stradivarius now! He'll look a bigger poof than he usually does!"

My dear old mum put the brakes on and stood staring at me, her face a little whiter than usual. "What did you say then?" the words rolled out menacingly.

"I just said that he'll look a bigger poof than he usually does."

That's what I thought you said," she said in a louder than soft tone. "I won't have you swearing in my house, do you understand?"

Not having an earthly what she was rabbiting about, I decided to make some enquiries in that direction. "What do you mean—swearing? I haven't said a word!"

"*Poof!* That's what you said! I heard you with my own two ears!"

"But poof isn't a swearword, Mum. Why, poor Young George can't help it—he was born like it—I could have been born the same..."

"Don't say that swearword in my house, I tell you. And stop giving me a volley of abuse!"

She then departed into the garden to hang our Liz's smalls up, but before doing so, with a well-practised action she slipped the hair-net off her head because she couldn't be seen in the garden by the neighbours with it on, which would have been an impossibility anyway without the aid of a lunar telescope.

I decided to cool it in the dining-room. As I was putting a very swinging disc of the Bird's on to aid my digestion, my father looked up from his writing desk and said (I knew what he was going to say before he got a word out), "Do we have to have that noise on at mealtimes?"

"Yes, we do, my very square father," came my reply. "It's the only time I get to listen to some music on your splendid radiogram."

"You can't call Jazz *music*! It all sounds the same to me."

"That's because, unlike mine, your parents were too mean to give you a proper musical education."

He smiled and went back to the very complicated business of working out how much profit his paint brushes had earned him that week. He got as much of a kick from those books as I did from the sounds I was listening to. Work, money and television: that's what my dear old Pater had a ball on. But the fellow who'd really wise me up on the old man was my Uncle Jim, the communist. Least I think he's a communist because he wears a red tie and keeps talking about the workers and has one of those communist things that you cut grass with hung up on his wall. As I was saying, he told me volumes about his brother, naughty things, too: like him being a right bastard in his young days before they moved out to the suburbs. Come to think of it, I don't think the suburbs were even invented then. Used to knock my mum from pillar to post, he did, according to my Uncle Jim. And the women ran after him like mad, and he didn't complain, and he managed to get a couple in the family way. He must have been a handsome bastard, too, by the look of that photo he has of himself taken when he was about twenty. Sharp as a pin he looked in that Roman jacket, crazy cumberbund and stupid spats. Something like a middle-aged Teddy-boy. We liked each other though — probably the love thing came in it as well — but I don't think so. There was something missing, see. I'm talking about the real closeness that fathers and sons are supposed to have. You know what I mean, you've seen it on the pictures. The son going to his father's study and pouring his heart out to him, and ending up both crying on one another's shoulders.

But my mum's always made up for him. She's not a bad old girl, really. She makes a hell of a fuss over silly things but she's all right But you know what mothers are. You've always got to talk to them like mothers. Not human beings, but mothers. When I was at school and had a punch-up with the villain of the class, I couldn't go home and have my bruises bathed by her. I'd have to dodge her and nip up to the bathroom sharpish and get my sister Liz to do a Nurse Cavell, but if she found out there was murder because mothers don't expect *their* sons to fight. *Their* sons are supposed to sing in the choir and take piano lessons and join the Church Lads' Brigade. I'm sorry, not me, and not anyone else if they've got any bloody sense. Liz did, though. She did the lot except her mob was the Brownies. So our mum was ever so pleased and kept telling me what a little angel she was and what a right bastard I was.

All the same, I'll never complain about Liz. She's never brought up the fact that she's four years my elder, but I just couldn't get on her plane. She was on this: I want to grow up a healthy young woman and have loads of kids and rot away in a council house, one. Still — she was always nice to me, and she's quite sexy in a plain sort of way — if you like that sort of thing.

I mustn't go on about my family like this — because they're my family. They're all right — but they don't think. They take everything for granted. They read the *Daily Mirror* and go on their week's holiday and talk about their neighbours and display their television aerial in front of the house — but they're all right. It's only when you get hundreds of families like them all flung together that the trouble starts. You've got to act like your neighbours because your neighbours expect you to act like *their* neighbours and if you don't act like your neighbours — that wouldn't do, would it? It's fine keeping up with the Joneses but when the Joneses have to keep up with you it's a different thing. There was a rumour once that one old girl down the road didn't have a television set but still displayed an aerial on the top of her roof all the same. When the local witch-doctor found out about this it was bashed out on the tom-toms until every native in the district had heard about it. The poor old dear was sent to Coventry, or whatever they call it, and she had to leave the district in the end. I'm not sticking up for her — don't think that. She was a damn sight worse than those that did it on her — and you can't get much worse than that. What that woman should have done was this: she should have got a bloody great sledgehammer, gone to every house in the district, done a breaking-and-entering number, and smashed all the tellies to tiny pieces.

What would the neighbours have done then, without their magical machines? Not done to her—but what would they have *done!* Without them, I mean. What would they do with those precious hours upon precious hours, hypnotised by a savage eye that puts Svengali into the beginner's class.

I noshed my dinner like a madman so that I could make the developing circle bright and early, and as I was creeping out of the house my mum shouted me back. "Don't be late home tonight," she called from the kitchen.

"No, I shan't," hoping that would be all.

It was. I grabbed my copy of *Death Is Not The End* that I was reading, pushed it into my pocket, and was away.

It was an early summer's evening and the streets looked inviting but there wasn't a soul about. No kids even—and it was a shame. They were clean houses, not good ones; all painted well enough and some were even bright—but they were all the same—every one of them. Even the people were, somehow. They belonged to the place like a tribe. If the natives saw anything their eyes weren't accustomed to—say, for instance, a Spade with *his* native costume on—they'd all stop and stare and think he'd come from Outer Space. Yet, only a very few miles away, when you're free from this thing they call Suburbia (a good name for it, don't you think?) that same Spade could walk down the street with his pyjamas on and nobody would take any notice.

Down Drayton Avenue again I walked, taking giant steps to get me a train all the quicker; whistling loudly an improvised ten choruses of *Gone With The Wind,* until some old girl, her arms busy carrying some bawling brat, reached near me, so I had to let the imaginary piano take over, as the cries of this starving suburban bastard put me right off.

The developing circle took place in the main hall where we held our services. They rearranged the chairs in one corner to make a circle, and above us was a red light which made everyone look as if they were taking part in a horror film. The atmosphere was so perfect that if 'our friends from the other side' couldn't contact us here, I'm quite positive they couldn't contact us anywhere. On the walls were photographs of mediums with yards of ectoplasm gushing out of their mouths and nose and ears — they looked quite revolting — and on the wall nearest to us, framed for all to see, was the seven principles of Spiritualism.

I don't have to describe the other nine members to you individually, because although some of them were men and some women and some thin and others fat, really they were all the same. They were Spiritualists. If you haven't met one of this clan before, let me explain to you that although when speaking on their subject they have a perfectly plausible explanation for the happenings, and speak intelligently and all that, you can't help thinking that deep down inside they're all completely mad. Not dangerous, but mad. Nevertheless, they were my people. We had been fortunate enough to have been shown this great truth and we were thankful for it. This was the answer to everything. Science and religion could walk hand in hand to save the world. That is why if anyone talks about religious maniacs, I never laugh. Religion is a great kick.

As I entered, the eyes of the other members were upon me. I was the baby of the party, as it's usual to start your development at about the age of twenty-five. Because of this everyone took a great interest in me, and I think they were a little proud of me as well. They were convinced that I possessed great psychic gifts, that in a number of years would be developed fully. They regarded me as something of a child prodigy.

Although I met the same nine people every week for months, I hardly found out any of their names. With the exceptions of Mrs Diamond and of course Bunty, whom I knew then as Mrs Ryan.

Mrs Diamond was our leader; she was a teacher, too, and instructed us into the secrets of mediumship. She was typical of one of those dear old ladies that you help across the road at Eastbourne. I expect she was a very unimportant member of the community until she stepped across the threshold of our society. But now she was the star; and like all stars she posed like mad.

Bunty was different from the rest of the women and I think she was about the most unpopular. This chick didn't fit in with the scene at all. She had some very weird looks given to her when she turned up at the meeting with make-up on. Her bleached hair didn't help things either. That gave the old ladies of the circle plenty to talk about, but she didn't seem to care. So did her clothes: her short skirts really got them at it.

"It's disgusting for a woman of her age to dress like that," I overheard one old dear say to another. "She walks about like a teenager, and I'm sure she'll never see thirty again." I silently agreed with all that, except for the 'disgusting' bit.

Each Tuesday when the circle finished, we all made a habit of going to the coffee bar which was just a few doors from the society building. There we would sit around and kid each other how well we were progressing, and while the juke-box blared and the teenagers sipped their Cokes, we'd talk about someone's fat aunt who died fifty years ago.

That particular night the ceremony of the developing circle took place. We sat around in a circle and Mrs Diamond opened the proceedings with a prayer. How that woman prayed! She managed to get her enormous body standing up, and with her eyes tightly closed and her hands clasped together, her deep and powerful voice would fill the room. "Oh Great White Spirit (meaning God), we await your heavenly spirit messengers to come to us this evening. For we know there is no barrier between heaven and earth, as love conquers all barriers..."

We joined hands and sung hymns for a few minutes, so that the psychic power could accumulate, and then relaxed and meditated. Then a couple of the others whose development had reached an advanced state, went into trance. Their spirit guides (*you* might call them guardian angels) took control and spoke through them. This is a very strange sight indeed. As they are going under control their faces went through some peculiar contortions and their bodies would shudder a little. Standing up was a sign that they were well and truly 'under'. Then their spirit guides would speak, using the medium's voice, of course. For some unknown reason the spirit guide was usually a Red Indian or a Chinaman. Someone did tell me once that he thought this was because Red Indians practised some sort of mediumship when they were on the earth, so naturally they were best for the job. Next in line were the Chinese because there were some very wise ones amongst them. When I think back to what these wise old Chinese philosophers *did* say, I'm sorry to report that their conversation was very unwise indeed. Now I come to think of it, since then I've never heard a Red Indian or a Chinaman speaking with a French accent.

I suppose you're wondering by now what *I* did at these happenings. Well, I have to admit it was practically nothing, and it was because of this that I couldn't understand why everyone took the interest in me that they did. They told me that although I was goofing the mediumship thing at the moment, the talent was there, and sooner or later it would show itself. I'd waited and waited for something to happen and I soon got the feeling that it was later, rather than sooner, when I would see all these spirits that the others were supposed to see. They had faith in this hidden talent of mine, so I took it that they knew more about these things than I did.

Each week we took turns in closing the meeting with a parting prayer. It was my turn that week and I dreaded it. On my previous attempts to pray in public I'd always dried up halfway through and felt a real schmock. This week I wasn't going to take any chances, so I learnt a prayer off by heart from a prayer book, did a Laurence Olivier, and it went down big. Mrs Diamond congratulated me afterwards, telling me she saw a nun guide (another firm favourite with them) behind me, inspiring me what to say. I was tempted to tell her I hadn't received my inspiration from a nun guide from the spirit world, but that I'd stolen it off some west country vicar who was still very much alive.

We must have looked a strange party on our way to the coffee bar. Led by seventeen-stone Mrs Diamond, followed by myself, six foot and thin, in front of a collection of characters that could probably earn themselves a place in the Chamber of Horrors, and in the rear there was Bunty — who could have stepped out of the cover of one of those sexy-feeling-making publications.

For some reason or other the coffee bar was closed, so we decided to skip the coffee orgy until the following week. I walked a couple of hundred yards down the road to catch my bus home, and as I was nearing the bus stop I heard the delicious sound of high heels behind me. I turned around (I can never resist it!) and it was Bunty.

Across the road Mrs Diamond and the medium of the unwise Chinese philosopher were standing at the bus stop, and when they saw Bunty's tight skirt running towards me they shook their heads in disapproval. Jealous bitches! Just because their tight skirt days were over. She was now next to me and said, "Just take a look at those two over there. What's the first principle of Spiritualism? The brotherhood of man, isn't it? By the looks they're giving me they want to practise what they preach." I glanced across the road pretending that I hadn't noticed them before. She pushed back the mop of blonde hair that was falling over her face and continued, "I'm so disappointed that the coffee bar was closed as I do look forward to our little chats every week. Why don't you pop back to my flat, which is just down the road, and have coffee there? My car's just around the corner and I can easily drop you home afterwards."

As we made our way to the car, two pairs of eyes were watching our every movement. I wondered if the unwise Chinese philosopher objected as well.

She lived in a large block of flats, and as we entered a uniformed night porter gave her a very pleasant "Good evening". She mumbled something to me about her wanting to move down to the ground floor as we entered the lift. At the third floor we got out and walked along a passage which smelt of floor polish, and arrived at a door that had on it a neatly printed notice with her name on it.

As we entered the flat the smell changed from floor polish to perfume. It was dimly lit with concealed lighting and it was quite obvious from the start that she was proud of her home. She gave me a conducted tour of the whole place, which consisted of two bedrooms, a lounge, kitchen and bathroom. Every now and again she would tell me how much she paid for something or other, and I could tell she wanted to impress me. She did as well. My sixteen-year-old mind really lapped everything up. Two different coloured walls; pink and lavender, well, that was really something. Contemporary furniture — man, this is living. The radiogram! Black and gold. She must be a millionairess! Even a real chandelier. (Yes, I did say contemporary furniture!) Her proudest possession was a large and colourful abstract painting, which she gazed at as though she was hypnotised, with her eyes half closed. When I asked her what it was supposed to be, she gave out with a very complicated spiel, with such words in it as aesthetic, action and texture, which I didn't understand at all. This really sounded gone to me, but I nodded as if I understood. She must be a real intellectual, I thought.

I sat down and did a lot of thinking while she went into the kitchen to make the coffee. Why didn't my father have different coloured walls, contemporary furniture, a black and gold radiogram and a real chandelier? He could afford them, so why didn't he have them? The answer was simple. He preferred his flowered wallpaper and dark oak three-piece suite because everyone else had them. Like a flock of sheep they copy everyone else. Why wasn't there more Mrs Ryans in the world? I made up my mind I must be very careful what I said to her; most important of all, I mustn't sound childish. She treated me like an adult so I had to act like one.

She came in with the coffee and sat next to me, looking in my face as though I was the most interesting person in the world. "This is better than that old coffee bar, isn't it?" she said. I agreed. Man, this was a lot better. This was *me*. I felt really at home here.

Keep the conversation going, I thought. "Have you been a Spiritualist long?" I asked.

"On and off for years," came the reply. I didn't dig this at all. Either you were a Spiritualist or you wasn't, so I asked her what she meant. Her reply surprised me. "It's like this. I've always been interested in seances and things simply because they're different from the everyday happenings. I get very bored with life and people. When I look out of my windows on to the street below, all I see are lines of men with bowler hats and briefcases and women carrying shopping and pushing prams, and I could scream. Everyone wants the same things out of life and they're always the most uninteresting things. That's why I like Mrs Diamond and that crowd. I know they hate me but that doesn't matter. At least they enjoy themselves in a different way to everyone else." She paused for a moment to have a look at her painting, then: "No, I'm not a Spiritualist in the true sense of the word. I've nothing against them for believing in it, and I'm convinced they're sincere, but I think all these spirits are a figment of their imagination."

Bewildered by all this, I asked, "But why do you go to the meetings?"

"Because the whole set-up is so interesting. Here are these very ordinary people living in a world of science-fiction. And they're sincere—that's the most important thing. Even that Mr what's-his-name who has that Red Indian guide speaks through him, really believes that Chief Thundercloud, or whatever it is, really exists." She gave a searching look into my eyes. "I expect that you're disgusted with me now," she said, looking like a guilty little girl.

I didn't dig the scene completely, but I looked as if I did. But as her words buzzed around and started to register in the old thinking box, I began to understand what she was getting at. Perhaps I wasn't a true Spiritualist either, and the more I thought about it the more convinced I was that really my interest in it was for the same reason as hers. Yes, man, of course. It was my own personal little dream world, where I could hide away from all those ordinary things like selling hats and going to the Palais and...

She must have been reading my thoughts, because she said, "That's why I took an instant liking to you. I knew you always felt the same as myself. That you were in all this for amusement and not for salvation or to get in contact with some great aunt who died years ago. I could probably tell you more about yourself than you could tell me, because I've observed you closely these last few months. I'd bet anything that you're bored with people of your own age as I am with people of mine. That you want to escape from those football and pop singer lovers that surround you in the local youth club. But where are you to go and hide from them? If you think that trying to break into the adult world will do you any good, then, my friend, there's a terrible surprise in store for you. For no sooner than you've arrived in the so-called adult scene, you'll find that you're right back to where you started, because in that world they're as big a bores as they were in the world you've just left." She paused to light a cigarette, then: "But don't despair, there is escape, simply because, thank God or the Devil, there's other people in this world that think like us, and together, like a secret society, we make our own world. You're already in that society in a way because you attend our dearly beloved Spiritualist Church. But that's just the start. There's a hundred different paths to travel that have nothing to do with crying babies, football pools, watching the tele, and Saturday night at the local."

I sat back taking in these words like wine. It was like a sermon that hit right at the truth, or a head shrinker that had really got to the bottom of your problem, because he'd found out the cause of your madness, but even more important, was offering you a cure as well.

The more we talked the more we seemed to have in common. She even had sounds in the gaff, too. A fair sprinkling of all the names, but Diz and Kenny Graham with their Afro stuff seemed to be favourite. It wigged her like mad to know that I was already on the Jazz scene. It's the only music that I've ever been enthusiastic about. Ever since I heard Tito Burns' *Bebop Spoken Here* (which is now very unhip, but at least it was a start) on a jukebox in dear old Canvey Island, I decided that, at last, I was interested in music.

For those amongst you who do not care, or haven't bothered to care about Jazz, all I can say is that you're missing a great deal out of life. I suppose the highbrow stuff is satisfying to a degree, but the thing is, you know what's coming next. In Jazz, most of it's improvised, dig? And you never know what's up the musician's sleeve. He takes you into his own world, and through the sounds that he blows, tells you all about himself, and when you can manage to get on his plane, there's hardly a kick to beat it.

Before long the weird mixture of Jazz and Spiritualism took up all my spare time. One night it would be a Jazz Club, the next a Spiritualist meeting.

I realised sooner or later Bunty was going to ask me what I did for a living, and when telling her I would be embarrassed. I shouldn't be, I thought; she's an understanding person, but I still wished that the way I earned my bread was a little more romantic. Just as I was thinking of the best way to tell her, she came out with it.

"What do you do for a living?" she asked, without any warning.

"I sell hats," I stammered, watching her face for the reaction. It wasn't good.

"Sell hats?" she said, looking horrified. "Do you mean to tell me that an intelligent and gifted young man such as yourself is wasting his time as a shop assistant?"

What did she expect me to be, anyway? An arctic explorer or an M.I.5 agent? But still I could feel myself blushing and I wanted to get away from her and her flat. I suppose she was trying to give me a boost, but she was doing just the opposite. I felt really brought down. I felt like kicking her in the teeth and telling her that being a shop assistant wasn't the end of the world, and to mind her own bloody business.

"I don't intend to keep at it. I'm looking for something better all the time," I said weakly. This didn't sound very convincing, but at least it was something to say.

"We'll have to see what we can do about that later on," she said, sounding concerned.

Icebergs went on the atmosphere for a few minutes after that, because she tumbled that I didn't like her reaction to my working scene, but she soon got things swinging again. In fact she should be awarded an Oscar for the number one swinging atmosphere-maker.

I was getting a bit nervous about the time, as I couldn't see a clock about the place and I didn't possess a watch myself. You see, my mother liked to go to bed early, and as she wouldn't let me get my hands on a key, she'd have to wait up for me if I was late in. That didn't wig her at all. After opening the door for me, she'd turn straight around, walk hurriedly back to the sitting-room, and plant herself on her favourite armchair. This was your cue to follow her into the room, and I usually stood at the door. Then she'd say, of all things, "So you're in then?" What else could you answer but "Yes"? Then, living up to her reputation as the world's most talented worrier, she would relate to me the thousand and one things that she thought had happened to me. Everything from being run over by a bus to being murdered by an escaped lunatic from the asylum which was near our home. But dig this: this wasn't an act, but the real thing. She really did believe what went through her morbid imagination.

"Would you like a drink?" Bunty asked. "No thanks, I've already had two cups."

She smiled at me sympathetically. "No, silly, not coffee, a *real* drink."

She opened the cocktail cabinet, which was far from empty, and asked, "What's it going to be?"

I've never been interested in the lush, even to this day. At that time I'd hardly ever had a drink at all, with the exception of the occasional glass of cider with some cats from the Jazz Club, and that was only to appear hip, as the Vintage Merrydown was the drink of all the sharp ones in Town. Once I had too much of that, and had to quickly alight from the tube train about three or four times on my way home, in case I spewed all over the other passengers.

"Anything will do. Whatever you're having," I answered in my most adult voice.

"You *do* drink, don't you?" she asked, with the words coming out very slowly.

This seemed a direct challenge; as if my answer would make a big difference to our friendship. As if suddenly she'd thought, perhaps he's a square after all, and that my refusing the drink would prove the point.

"Of course," I managed to get out. She poured me a large glass and to show her what sort of an alcoholic I was, I drank the lot down in one gulp. It tasted like a mixture of petrol and rubber.

"I underestimated you. That's certainly a big swallow you have there," she said. I grinned like a mature old Daddy of the World. "Have another one," she said, as though it was an order, and she started to pour some more of the poison into my glass. The second one didn't taste too bad, and the third was even pleasant.

Sarah was singing on the radiogram like only she can, Bunty was sprawled on the divan like a film starlet, and I was stoned as hell. As my Uncle Jim would say, I was pissed as a newt.

"Mrs fat old Diamond should see us now," I said. "What would she say if she saw us now?"

"You're both a disgrace to the cause, she'd say. Don't ever darken the doors of this society again. Go to the Christian Scientists, or to hell, if you like, but keep away from us, 'cause we don't want you."

"She wouldn't. She wouldn't really, would she?"

"You bet she would."

"But that's not even Christian."

"She wouldn't think twice about it. Out we'd both go. She wants to get rid of me, anyway. Don't like the way I dress or something. Well, if she thinks I'm going to dress like her, and look as if I've come out of the ark, she's got another think coming."

"There's no harm in people enjoying themselves now and again. It's not right for people to think religion all of the time. It must do something to their brain. And anyway—I'm enjoying myself."

Bunty looked across to me and put on a Joan Crawford face. "I am, too. You're a real tonic to me, honest you are. I'm glad you came here tonight."

A clock outside struck ten, and there was an awkward silence as I was concentrating to count the chimes. I thought of mum doing her nut at home. Perhaps Liz was waiting up with her and helping her out with the worrying. 'Maybe it's a double act tonight', I thought.

"Don't worry about the time," Bunty shouted. "The night is young and so are we." She took a glance into the mirror. "I mean, so are you."

I could see now what she meant by action when describing that painting of hers. When I took another look at it, it seemed to be alive; all the colours going into each other and shooting out again, really enjoying themselves. Then forms came to life in it. First I thought I saw a bloody great lobster, then a naked woman with her arms outstretched, and then of all things, Mr Cage, staring right out at me, and giving me a 'wait-till-I-get-you-at-work-tomorrow' look.

Bunty was helping herself to another drink. "I expect you think I'm a drunkard, don't you?" she slurred. "I'm not really, but I couldn't care less if I was. I couldn't care less about anything. Life's too darn short." She raised her glass. "Here's to Dolly Diamond and her spooks! I wish her luck with her clairvoyance, psychometry, direct voice, levitation, transfiguration, materialisation and all the other 'ations' she gets up to. Have another drink."

36

"Thanks. I will. How about your husband? Won't he be coming in soon?"

She gave out a girlish giggle. "My husband doesn't exist any more."

"Passed over?"

"No. He doesn't exist for *me*. It's funny but I can't even remember what he looks like."

"I'm sorry."

"Don't be sorry. Good riddance to bad rubbish, that's what I say. He was all right at the time, I suppose. He looked very handsome in his uniform, as far as I can remember. You know, the usual army officer type." I couldn't think of anything more unattractive than an army officer type, but I didn't make any comment. "But all this was a very long time ago." She must have thought twice about her last sentence, so she added, "I'm making myself sound like an old age pensioner, and I'm not really, believe it or not. Guess how old I am—I mean, how *young* I am."

"I don't care. A person is as old as he feels. I think all birth certificates should be destroyed at birth."

"So do I. Good for you."

I managed to stagger out to the carzy, which was the bathroom as well. There were all sorts of perfume and powder boxes on the shelves, and it smelt more like a French brothel than a carzy. Then I found that I was talking to myself. Since then I've discovered this is the best way to find out if I'm pissed on the lush or not, because as soon as I am I start to talk to myself, not anywhere, mind you, but only in the carzy. I usually say things like, "I'm having a ball tonight, and so and so is really hip," and all that sort of thing. Then I want to whistle. I pretend that I'm a famous Jazz musician and that I'm not whistling at all but playing trumpet, and I might add that my whistling improvisation isn't bad at all. Then I laugh and say to myself, "Man, you're pissed," and look around, if it's a public carzy, to see if anyone's heard me.

I looked out of the window, which was behind all those kinky bottles and boxes, and looked down on to the street below. A couple of cats (the ones that mee-owwww) were screaming blue murder at each other, their coats shining like mad, and the Tom saying, "I'm going to have you tonight, pussy gal, if it's the last thing I do," and she replying, "No, you're not, because I don't fancy you," and then they ran like mad into some bushes to have their little bit in private. Then, looking across to the shops on the other side of the road, there, with its neon lights reflecting in my face, was the local branch of Down & Co. Fuck, I thought, you can't get away from the horrors of life even for one solitary evening. I slammed the window together, and went back to Bunty.

"Come and dance," she said, holding out her hands to me.

I've never liked dancing, as I could never see the point of it, unless you were trying to make a girl, and then it would be a good excuse to get near her and breathe in her ears and all that nonsense. But dancing for dancing's sake, I could never understand, especially at Jazz clubs. It's always been a mystery to me how musicians can blow well when they have a crowd of morons jiving around them, not even listening to the music.

"I can't dance," I said. I wasn't sure if I could even get up, let alone dance in the state I was in.

She wouldn't take no for an answer. "Everyone can dance. Just grab hold of me and walk," she said, pulling me to my feet. That's exactly what I did do, to Sarah singing a very slow *Loverman*. Her voice had some of the feeling of Billie and the ideas of Ella. She sang:

I don't know why, but I'm feeling so sad,
  I long to try something I've never had,

Never had no kissing, oh what I've been missing,
  Loverman oh where can you be...

Bunty's very close, I thought. She's getting carried away.

The night is so cold, and I'm so all alone,
  I'd give my soul just to call you my own...

Our hands and arms had forgotten where they should be for dancing; she had hers around my neck.

Got a moon above me, but no one to love me,
Loverman oh where can you be...

Her face was against mine now and she had her eyes closed. I couldn't make up my mind if this was sobering me up or not.

I've heard it said that the thrill of romance
could be like a heavenly dream,

I go to bed with the prayer that you
make love to me strange as it seems...

Then it happened. It was like a bloody great magnet drawing me to her, because before I knew what I was doing, I was kissing her smack on the lips. You silly great cunt, I thought, now you've done it! She'll probably kick you out of her flat and report you to the Chief Spiritualist by return of post. It wasn't like that at all. She hung on like mad, and I must admit I wasn't complaining, either. It's funny what comes into your head in moments like that. All I could think was, how different it was necking with her, to necking with that ginger-haired chick at the youth club, the one with no tits. Just as I was thinking about that she grabbed my hand and put it on one of hers, and before I could do anything about it we'd lost our balance and went sprawling on to the divan. After about five minutes of trying to carry on where we left off, we came up for air.

I felt a bit of a schmock because I didn't know what to say after all this, but Bunty wasn't lost for words.

"Do you have to go home tonight, darling?" she said, coming straight to the point.

"Yes, I do. My mum will be waiting up for me." I realised that this sounded as if I was a baby just being weaned, but what else could I say? I couldn't tell her that I was going on a big business meeting, or was escorting a film star out to dinner, or any of that crap. Anyway, the whisky, or whatever I'd had to drink, made me feel as though I couldn't care less what I told her.

"Couldn't you tell her that you were at a friend's all night?" Bunty said, looking at her scarlet red face in the mirror.

"She'd have the police, the army and even the fire brigade out searching for me. You don't know my mother," said I, putting my jacket on again, which I'd lost in the struggle.

She looked a little bit annoyed. "Haven't you *ever* stayed out the night?"

"I have once or twice when a friend of mine has a party or something, but I have to give her plenty of warning," came my reply.

"Very well, then. On Saturday next your very best friend is having a party, and you won't be able to get home. Tell your mother that."

"Right. I'll tell her that."

There was an awkward silence.

"I'll have to be going now, I really must."

"Take this card and give me a ring Saturday morning, just to confirm. Okay?"

"Okay."

"Well, aren't you going to kiss me good-bye?" I kissed her on the lips.

"You're only a child, really, aren't you?"

"You don't seem to be complaining."

"Stay with me, child, and I'll make you into a man."

I didn't wait for the lift, but ran like mad down the stairs, praying to God my mother hadn't had a nervous breakdown.

"Meet Dusty Miller — it's his pad," said Danny, taking his non-imitation suede jacket off and throwing it on to a pile of clothes on the bed. He turned to Dusty. "A nice place you have here, man. Very stoning indeed."

"It suits me," was all our host said. Then he gave me one of those 'who-are-you?' looks. Danny noticed it so he pulled him to one side, and in a quiet voice, but not quiet enough for me not to hear, he said, "Don't worry about our friend — he's cool enough. Just met him in the Katz Kradle. Crazy sounds they're dishing out there tonight. Bill Higginwell must have enjoyed my deal. He was blowing that tenor like a madman. Block-up to hell, he was."

Dusty Miller looked me straight in the eye from behind a pair of Brubeck spectacles. Just for a second he hesitated, then he offered me his hand. "Welcome," he said, and by this time his eyes had made a conducted tour all over me. "Haven't seen you about before."

Stupid me felt embarrassed. This cat sounded and looked so sharp it was a shame. "I go to the Katz Kradle every week, but I haven't been going too long," I said. "That Bill Higginwell was certainly blowing tonight. He was really great. I still can't get over it. Really inspired tonight—he was."

Dusty's short little body shook with laughter. "He was inspired all right: Harry was with him strong!"

I said: "Harry? Who's he? I don't think I've met up with him."

The few people that weren't actually in our group but were in hearing distance, turned around sharpish when they dug what I'd said, and they and Dusty and Danny laughed like that crazy laughing record my Dad plays at parties. I think it was Dusty that said, "So you haven't met Harry, eh? Well, you will, man, you will and before very long!"

I took off my coat and walked it over to the bed to escape from their laughter. I wasn't sure what the cool thing was to do after that but the radiogram came to my rescue, because by it in a huge red plastic rack was the greatest collection of hip records that I'd seen outside Dobell's. Everything was there—well, nearly everything, anyway—not only the obvious ones, but the lesser known west coast musicians and the better John Bulls, that most people don't buy. I started digesting a couple of sleeve notes.

"I haven't seen you here before," I heard a chick's voice behind me say.

"I haven't been here before."

"That probably accounts for it. Well then—a newcomer is amongst us. That calls for a drink. What will you have?"

"A cider will do."

"A horrible drink—that. I never indulge in jungle juice unless it's really necessary, but every man to his own poison."

She went to the table that displayed a stone keg of Merry-down, and started to pour a largish one into an earthenware mug. Her pleasantly plump body swayed slightly and she kept raising the mug up and down from the tap, in time to the King Pleasure disc that was playing on the gram. I tried to make out her age; she wasn't old, I mean she wasn't thirty, but if she'd told me she was I'd have believed her. She came staggering back to me and her blurred but sparkly eyes (I hope you dig) half-closed, stared at me wisely behind long lashes. Her face was cute – a bit worn – but with character.

"I thought you never indulged in cider," I said, pointing to the glass of vintage she held in her hand.

She gave me a charming smile that developed into a gig-gle. "Only when it's necessary," she said. "And tonight it's been really necessary up till now."

"It's not necessary any longer?"

"No."

"Why not?"

"Because Danny's arrived. You know – the cat that came in with you."

"Oh, I see. Is he your boyfriend?"

She must have found this terribly funny because she laughed out aloud. "Good heavens, no. No, no, a thousand times no!"

"What difference does he make then?"

She didn't answer straight away; instead she looked at me for a moment with a puzzled expression. Then, "If you don't know – we'll leave it at that."

There weren't too many people about us, but the small room that we were in made them look more. They were mostly just past the teen stage, and definitely a Jazz crowd, but there was something decidedly different about them to the mob that congregate at the Katz Kradle. They were more relaxed and minus the innocent look despite their young age. They didn't look like villains, mind you, but like my mother says: they were little old men cut down. A young Spade was in the corner, beating time to the disc on a gleaming new pair

42

of bongos; stripped to the waist, his well-developed chest glistening with perspiration like you see in those jungle films, and he was looking at the chicks in a confident Spadish way.

The chick had refilled her glass and she came back with another one for me. "Cheers," she said and knocked it back all in one go. She saw me staring at her. "Don't mind me. I'm a trainee alcoholic. What's your name?"

I told her.

"Mine's Miss Roach. Don't think I'm being formal — everyone calls me that — it's rather fitting. How come you meet up with Danny, anyway?"

"I got chatting with him in the Katz Kradle Jazz Club. You know it?"

A wave of her perfume hit me as she said, "Do I *know* it? I should say I do."

"It's great — yes?"

"It's great — no! I've nothing against the music — but otherwise — negative. So Danny invited you along here — right?"

"Absolutely."

She seemed interested in me and it wigged me. "And what do you think of the set-up? Approve or not?"

"Approve, most definitely. I haven't many friends, what you can call friends, anyway. Where I live everyone seems dull — held back somehow — even the kids. I can't stand it."

She offered me a cigarette. "You've only two things to do. Either carry on standing or sit down."

"Man, I want to sit down, and I'm going to, don't you worry. By hook or by crook I'm going to get away from all of it."

Her face went slightly serious. "Let's hope it's not by crook."

A young cat, just a few years older than myself, was sitting away from the rest, looking as remote as anyone could in a crowded room. "What the matter with our friend over there?" I asked, pointing to him.

"That's Popper," she said, still a bit serious. "He's sick."

"What's he doing here then? Why doesn't he go home or see a doctor?"

She stared at me, just for a second, before answering, then she quickly said, "No doctor can help him."

Things were getting warmed up by now: the voices were becoming louder, and that thing called atmosphere was poking its head around the corner. A couple were dancing by the gram. Not jiving like they do at the Kradle, but with much less energy and with mechanical-like movements. The chick with her eyes closed seemed more interested in the music than with her dancing, and the cat spinned her around now and again, but he made sure that he didn't do any of the work himself, although he was right with the sounds, his head nodding in perfect time with the drummer's cymbal. They danced floppy.

Miss Roach had refilled my glass again. "Do you smoke?" she asked me.

"What sort of a question is that?" I said, showing her the fag I had in my hand.

She gave a girlish giggle. "No, silly, not straight ones. Charge."

"Charge?"

"Yes, Charge — Pot — Shit — Tea — Gunja — Tampi — Reefers — Weed — or if you want me to be really square — Indian Hemp!"

"No, I don't. I mean, I've never tried. Do you?"

"Of course, Doll. We all do. That's what I meant about waiting for your friend Danny to arrive. He's a dealer."

"What's that?"

"He sells it."

This nearly knocked me out. "You mean he's a dope pedlar?"

She really did laugh this time; a hearty laugh that echoed around the room. "Don't let's get dramatic," she managed to say. "Dope pedlars are people that you read about in *Life* magazine. It's nothing as serious, or come to that, important. He just supplies us with our little smoke when we want it. Why don't you try? It'll turn you on, and you never know, it may wig you."

Dusty Miller came over to us, his eyes full of interest. "Enjoying yourself?" he asked me in a friendly way.

"I certainly am," I told him truthfully. "You have some great records there," I said, pointing to the box.

"You like Jazz then?"

"It's the only sound for me," I said in my sharpest voice.

"Nice. We'll have to have a rabbit about it some time. There's not much happening in Town—not like the old days—so we have to make our own amusement. We have these little get-togethers all the time. We take it in turns for whose pad we use. You have your own pad?"

"No. I live with my parents," I said quietly.

"That's a drag," he said. "I pity you."

I felt I could talk freely with him. "It's not so bad living with them. It's where we live that bothers me. Middlesex."

"Oh fuck, that's worse than the sticks. You have my sympathy."

We were interrupted by Danny. "Ready, Dust," he shouted from across the room. "I've made six spliffs up."

"Fine," Dusty shouted back to him. Then he made an announcement to the whole room, sounding like an eccentric millionaire: "The first one's on me, people. Danny's here to accommodate you if you want more."

Miss Roach pulled me to one side. "Stay by me, sweetie. It's best not to let the others know that you don't smoke. I'll give you a crafty draw on mine."

Dusty came around the room distributing the spliffs to the various groups that were ligging about. He came over to us and gave Miss Roach one, which looked longer and thicker than the usual cigarette.

Everyone seemed to light up at the same time, but before they did they closed all the windows and Miss Roach informed me, like an expert, that this was to stop the smoke escaping, as the smoky atmosphere helps your highness. A few seconds later the room was full of a smell that I'd never come across before. It was something like the stink of Turkish cigarettes, only more so. Then I saw Miss Roach inhaling deeply on hers; concentrating like mad — everything else kicked out of her mind — finding room for only the thing that she held between her fingers. When she drew on it she closed her eyes, and she gave out a weird sound when she inhaled; she took as much air down with the smoke as she possibly could, and the hissing of the air hitting her teeth reminded me of the noise that steam trains sometimes make when they are standing in a station.

"That's better," she said quietly. "Now it's your turn." She noticed the uncertain look upon my face. "Don't be 'fraid," she went on, "it's not going to kill you."

Without thinking I took the spliff between my fingers and drew on it. "Not like that," Miss Roach instructed. "Take it right in, as deep down as it can go and *keep* it in, that's the main thing. When you've had a blow, don't let it go, but keep breathing in air to send it right downstairs to the bargain basement."

I did what I was told. It didn't taste half as bad as I thought it would. In fact it was quite pleasant. It went down a lot easier than tobacco would, and before long I was inhaling hungrily at it.

"Not too much for the first time. We don't want you cracking up," Miss Roach said, taking it away from me.

I wasn't concerned with her voice, because already I'd realised I was feeling different. Everything was happening so quickly. At first I wasn't sure exactly what it was. Then it came to me that the scene was going out of focus like it does on the tele when you turn the wrong knob. But not everything. Some of the scene was still as clear, in fact, sharper, but the rest was in a fog. Certain things stood out in the room like they had a searchlight trained on them — Miss Roach — the spliffs — the clock on the mantelpiece — but most of the other things weren't bright at all. My heart was breaking the speed limit — thumping away like mad it was, and I felt hot although the sweat on my forehead was icy cold. Then the scene became terribly unreal, and it frightened me. The people's voices seemed far away, and the smoky atmosphere wasn't helping things, either. So this is what it was like to be high, my mind kept telling me. It's different to what I read in the Sunday newspapers. I should be flying high and feeling wonderful and sexy and all nice things, but the things that I was feeling weren't nice; they were dream-like and I was afraid to go deeper into it—I was fighting but it was no use. They were unreal and the unreality scared me, because I didn't know where it would take me. I think I heard Miss Roach say, "Are you all right? It's always a bit weird the first time." And after she'd said it I couldn't make up my mind if she *just* said it or if she'd said it minutes ago. I said something to her and I heard my own voice like I'd never heard it before; as if it had echoed back to me and I was hearing it like you do on a play-back from a tape recorder. I wondered if anyone knew how I felt. Were they hip to what was happening? They were laughing—were they laughing at me? I was suddenly terribly hot and I felt sick. The taste of the Charge was in the back of my throat, and I was still breathing that same taste in because the smoke was thick around me. Someone cracked an amyl and I wondered what the hell they were up to: were they all mad or something? And the smell of it mixed with the Charge was about all I could stand. I found myself on the landing. Miss Roach was next to me. I think she asked me not to leave or something like that, but I told her I had to go. And go I did.

II

TRIANGLE

WHEN MY SISTER Liz wasn't at the breakfast table, I knew there must be something wrong.

She's one of those strange people that *likes* getting up early, so that she can stay about three hours in the bathroom and take as much time over her breakfast as I would over a four-course dinner. The cornflakes didn't taste the same without her useless chatter that always accompanied them. To make matters worse I had to prepare them myself, *and* collect the milk from the doorstep and pour the sugar over them. Not that I'm one of those dreadful people that likes convention, but when you come downstairs and find that you have to prepare your own breakfast when you're still half asleep, it's a bit much, isn't it?

Dad always left the house hours before I ever thought about getting up, and mum had some weird ideas about shopping early so she wasn't on the breakfast scene, either. That left my beloved sister and myself both trying to kid each other that we weren't miserable in the mornings. In fact Liz wasn't, and it always made me as mad as hell to think anyone could be happy at 8.30 a.m. So after eating the cornflakes which I ruined by pouring too much milk over them, I decided to make a full investigation of the disappearance of my dear old skin and blister.

I wondered if she'd gone out on one of those crazy queueing-up marathons at the sales that she couldn't resist, or if she'd gone in early to work to catch up on some of that insurance she was always raving about. When looking in the letter box I found there was a letter for her, and as the post is delivered at an unmentionable hour in the morning, I took it for granted that she must still be in the house. There was a letter for me as well, which was very unusual, because since I got sick of writing to some dozy pen friend who lived in Salop who was always raving about building model airplanes, I hardly ever received one. It was from Dusty Miller, and it just said: See you Katz Kradle tonight (Wednesday). Important. Dusty.

This was rather a strange message to receive because since my first meeting with him at his party, we'd become firm friends and hadn't missed a Wednesday night at the Kradle for about six or seven months. Dusty knew I'd be there as it was the night when we always had a serious discussion on about two million subjects ranging from girls to Jazz. It must be important, I thought, else he wouldn't have squandered the postage money. Don't get me wrong, Dusty's not mean, that's the last thing his enemies could say about him, but everything he does is for a purpose. He thinks about his every little action, but usually fucks it up anyway. But I liked him all right. The main reason I suppose was that he'd brought some action into my life. I admired him too, sort of hero-worshipped him, I guess. He had educated me in the gentle art of Hemp appreciation; oh yes, I soon became an admirer of it—it's easy when you have a bit of practice. Not that I could afford much myself, but Dusty always managed a turn on and I was never left out. I admired him because although he hadn't got far in this crazy world, he was trying. You can't believe all he says, but he does try. He's a philosopher, too, there's no doubt about that, and although he shows off all the time you've got to listen to him. It's strange how you get on best with people that are so different to yourself.

I knocked on the door of Liz's room, and sure enough her squeaky little voice called out, "Is that you?"

"Right first time," I answered, going in.

I must tell you something about Liz's room because it's classic, it really is. It's so tidy you feel uncomfortable. I always felt she kept it that way so that she could show her boyfriends what a marvellous wife she'd make them. Not that she had orgies with her boyfriends in the room every night, or made a habit of taking them up there at all, come to that, mum made sure of that, but I'd noticed that if she could make some excuse to get one of them up there just for a minute she'd be pleased as Punch about it. How can you get worked up over a room? That's what I wanted to know. A room's to sleep in and somewhere to keep your clothes and all that, but Liz would treat it as though it was a sanctuary. As I've already told you, my old man is in the decorating game, but Liz insisted that she decorated it herself. Can you beat that? I wouldn't mind if the reason for all this was because she wanted some weird coloured walls, like purple for instance; but no. Red roses on a white background. Honest. Above the bed was a signed photo of Frankie Laine grinning at her like a great big ape, and on the other wall was Kay Starr who wasn't quite so bad but a bit mumsy. Another crazy thing: out of her own personal pocket money, twice a week, she'd buy flowers and have them on the dressing table alongside her bottle of Californian Poppy. That was about the end for me as she was never in the room to see them, except at nights when she went to bed.

As soon as I saw Liz lying there in bed with her very un-sex-making pyjamas on, I knew she wasn't well. She gave me a 'I-want-your-sympathy' look, as she pulled the bed sheets high over her shoulders. Her face was even paler than usual, and believe me that's very pale, and there were tiny beads of perspiration on her forehead, looking as if they'd been put there for some weird decoration. The room was so clean and tidy it reminded me of a hospital ward complete with patient.

"What's all this, my Lizabet, feeling unhealthy?" I said, sitting myself on the edge of the bed.

"I'm all right. I shall be fine in a minute, once I get up," she answered, sounding like a movie heroine after being taken to hospital following a car crash.

"Surely you don't want me to put on the big brother act and tell you that you shouldn't get up at all and all that nonsense. You take it easy and I'll bring your breakfast up here and you can have it in bed, and don't ever say I don't ever do anything for you." She lay there not saying a dicky-bird. "Does mum know you're not well?"

That woke her up. She half shouted, "No, and don't you tell her, either. She's got enough worry without me making things worse for her. Now clear out of here quick. I want to get up. Well, go on, don't just stand there — scram!"

Before I knew where I was, I was lumbered out on to the landing. I went downstairs to the kitchen and was putting the kettle on again when I heard the key go in the door. Mum came into the kitchen carrying about two dozen shopping bags and looking exhausted. "What on earth are you doing," she said as though she'd found me chopping up our dog Rinty into little pieces.

"All right — don't rub it in, I know I don't usually make the tea, but I'm quite capable," I said, lighting the gas.

"Miracles will never cease," she said, putting the shopping away. "Where's your sister?"

"She overslept this morning. She'll be down in a minute."

I went back to the dining-room and relaxed in the armchair with a copy of *The Other Side,* my favourite Spiritualist newspaper. Now I must admit that my religious kick had nearly worn out. Dusty and all that went with him was taking practically all my spare time, and I had left Dolly Diamond's developing circle. She had a right go at me and told me that I was a very silly young man for doing so, as she expected me to develop into a really talented medium; a second Estelle Roberts. I hadn't neglected Bunty quite so much; the sex kick was definitely in the lead from the religious one, but I wasn't seeing quite so much of her either. But I hadn't stopped reading *The Other Side,* because it's a gass, it really is. It tells you all this crap about how Sir Arthur Conan Doyle and a whole load of other educated guys were Spiritualists, and spent their lives fighting for the cause, and as they're educated and everything they've got to be right, and it isn't up to us uneducated morons to argue with them. Of course, all these cats died hundreds of years ago, or nearly that amount of time anyway, but they never let you forget about them.

Then it goes on to tell you about how successful the propaganda meeting was that was held in such and such a hall, and that the medium was right on form that night and told twelve people that their pet dog who was run over last year is still barking away in his own little spirit world. The classified ads would knock you out. 'See your dearly beloved Grandma that's passed over, with the Psycho-Ray Goggles' or 'Middle-aged lady wishes to meet middle-aged gentleman to form a circle.'

When Liz arrived downstairs for her breakfast she looked like one of the patients from *Emergency Ward 10*. She's thin at the best of times but she looked a real Belsen number now. Her clothes didn't help any. I couldn't understand why she dressed so damn badly. I'm not saying I'm a fashion expert, but fuck, she didn't have any idea at all. She was wearing that unpleated skirt of hers, the one that makes her look like a Russian peasant woman gone wrong, and her shoes couldn't have been flatter if they'd been plimsoles. I couldn't see anyone really fancying her, unless they were on some kinky little nine-year-old girl with thin arms and legs and blushing and innocent kick. The look she gave me said, "'you-breathe-a-word-to-mum-and-I'll-throttle-you." I glanced away pretending not to have noticed it.

"What's the matter with you this morning?" mum said, bringing the breakfast in.

She didn't look up but carried on staring at the woman's magazine she had in front of her. On the cover was one of those lamp-post-looking models whom I'm sure don't exist in real life, but I could tell she wasn't reading it. "Nothing," she answered casually.

"It's not like you to be late for work. You ill or something?" mum went on.

"Of course not," she blurted out. "Why the inquest? He'll tell you that my alarm didn't go off. Go on, ask him."

Our mother turned to my direction but didn't say anything.

"That's right. I had to wake her up," I said, sounding very disinterested. I received a nice you're-very-faithful-look from Liz and I returned it with a you-can-always-rely-on-me one.

"Well, I'd better be going. Down and Company couldn't carry on without me," I said, picking up the bag of cakes for my elevenses which was on the table.

"Hold on a minute and I'll walk up to the bus stop with you," said Liz, gulping down her tea.

"You two sound unusually affectionate this morning. Usually having a glorious row by now," mother said suspiciously.

We both gave her a son-and-daughter-kiss and were off.

The quietness of the street was unreal because the scene wasn't exactly deserted. The few people about on their way to the graft seemed to be walking on tiptoes in case they woke the neighbours up, and the milkman seemed half afraid to clink his bottles. I felt like shouting at the top of my voice. "Wake up! This is the world! The place where your time is limited, so it's up to you to make the most of it. Don't think — live!"

The sun was already quite warm and it promised to be a glorious day, but I couldn't have cared less if it had been snowing, as all I could think about was the fact that it was half day closing and I'd be free from work at one o'clock. Liz walked next to me with her eyes glued to the ground as if she was a tramp looking for dog-ends, not saying a word but humming something from *Salad Days* to herself very quietly. She looked pathetic walking there in the sunlight with such a morbid expression on her face; like a little girl lost.

"Well, what gives?" I said, as it was the only thing I could think of saying.

"Nothing," she said half-heartedly. Then, "I've got to talk to you."

"Go ahead and talk," I said, getting interested.

"No. I mean, not here. Look, can you meet me somewhere after I've finished work?"

Now I must explain that my sister Elizabeth isn't the dramatic type; I mean she doesn't make mountains out of molehills and all that, so by now I was feeling a little bit disturbed.

"It's my half-day today and later I've got to go up west to the Katz Kradle, so I could meet you up Town if you like."

She didn't say anything to this but stopped in the middle of the pavement, fished a pencil and paper out of her frowsy-looking handbag, rested it against a garden gate and started to write.

"This is the address. It's just off Piccadilly. I'll be there at five-thirty, so wait outside," she said, handing me the paper.

Then I remembered the letter of hers that I still had in my pocket. I took it out and gave it to her. She looked at the envelope and said, and she really said this, honest, "Oh fuck!" I was so embarrassed I didn't know where to put my face.

And that was that. She didn't say another word until I left her at the bus stop, and then it was only, "See you later," and as I took my seat in the bus and watched her tiny figure walk towards the station, I felt, for the first time in my life, a real brotherly feeling come over me. My sister Liz, who I was always having a go at and calling a drag and a square, was unhappy and I felt concerned.

The morning at work was like a hundred others. Wait outside the shop for Mr Cage to come along and open up. "Morning, Mr Cage, sir" — sweep the shop out while the zombie they called a senior salesman pretends to dust the shelves, serve the cap customers because you don't earn much commission on caps, and get the tea and pour it out while the other two watch you as if you were a slave.

The zombie is a middle-aged jerk who lives with 'Mummy' in a toffee-nosed block of flats complete with mod. cons. 'Auntie' left him the flat when she pegged out two years ago, and he's raving all the time about some poxy television personality who lives in the flat below him, and he gives us all the news and scandal about this poor chap that hasn't done him any harm; especially the bits about how he brings all those effeminate young boys into the pad, and they make such a lot of noise, and I know he's only jealous because his effeminate young boy's days are over.

Oh, man, I could scream!

Then the important news came through the telephone, that Mr Pilkington, the shop inspector from Head Office, was on his way. The very first time I saw him I could have sworn that Hitler didn't really commit suicide, but escaped. The way that Mr Cage obtained this news was brilliant (so he thought). The manager of the branch up the road let him know that old Pilkington had left his shop, and as he always came to our shop next, he would pass on the news. Brilliant, Mr Cage, brilliant!

"All right, men," Mr Cage would say, as if he was addressing a battalion of troops, "Pilkington's on his way!"

This was a sign for us to get busy, and if we didn't have anything to do we'd better find something. Through the mirror that was in the shop's doorway, we could always see Mr Pilkington approaching, and as he came through the door it was up to the zombie and myself to rush forward and pretend we had mistaken him for a customer, just to show him that our branch was on its toes.

"Everything all right?"

"Yes, everything's fine, Mr Pilkington, sir," I would say, lying like mad.

"I'm hearing some good reports about you from Mr Cage. Keep it up — keep it up."

"Thank you sir, thank you," not caring a fuck about Mr Cage's good reports.

"Any chance of a relief manager's position this summer, sir?" the zombie asked Pilk.

"Yes, there are chances. Oh yes, quite," he answered, knowing that he had as much chance of being a relief manager as I did.

And so it went on. Each of us trying to kid each other that running a shop, a hat shop at that, was a very important thing. Like it was U.N.O. or something. These cats *lived* this hat shop thing. They weren't pretending—it was their life. Just think of it. They gave their *lives* up to keeping peasants' heads dry. If they were musicians, yes. If they were priests or doctors, yes; if they were poets or painters—but hat salesmen: oh God—no!

I was so browned off with Down & Co when I walked out of the shop at one o'clock that I felt sick. I started to walk home instead of catching the bus, because I wanted to get the Down & Co smell off my clothes and off my body. It has a smell you know. Like age. I couldn't even stand to be seen carrying my hat, so I pocketed a paper bag before I left the shop, and once I was clear I put it in that. As I walked down the street I watched the other shops closing and the other Mr Cages and the other zombies coming out, and they all looked really pleased with themselves. Automatically I went into a pub and when I pointed to a crazy-looking bottle with something green in, the barmaid gave me an "Are-you-old-enough?" look, but served me all the same.

Then I went into the park, that has a big house in the middle of it which always reminded me of a castle. It was owned, so someone told me once, by a very rich cat, an eccentric millionaire, I think, who left it to the Air Training Corps or something mad like that, so instead of looking grand and royal like, which it should have done, it had these enormous canvas notices right across it saying: Join the A.T.C., which made a fool of that poor old castle. I sat down on the grass and smoked a cigarette and watched the kids playing; they looked very happy and I wondered if any of these poor little bastards would work at Down & Co one day, and if they did would they grow into another Mr Cage? It didn't seem possible but it frightened me all the same.

I wandered into the gardens and saw a gardener on his knees pulling out weeds amongst the flowers. He wasn't exerting himself but doing everything very slowly, and there was a wonderfully contented look on his old leathery-looking face, and I envied him. I crossed the wooden bridge and went down to the pond which was very still and had great water lilies floating in it; they looked so strong that it made you think you could walk on them. This was the pond that when I was at school we fished for newts in. We tied a worm on to a piece of cotton and gently put it in the water, and along came a poor little newt and swallowed the worm. Then we pulled the cotton out with the newt dangling on the end of it. The alarm would go up and we were chased out of the park by the gardener.

I thought to myself: Come off it, boy, you're getting sentimental — and buggered off home.

"Wipe your feet before coming into my house!" my mother called out as dad opened the door to me.

He gave me a crafty wink, nodded in her direction, and whispered to me, "I'm dreading the winter coming. What's it going to be like when there's snow on the ground?"

"Home for lunch?" I asked him.

"Working round the corner. A lovely roof job, restacking the chimney. Don't mind those in the summer," he said, as though he'd been commissioned to paint Buckingham Palace. "Mother Manley's in there."

"Oh no!" I just said.

Mother Manley is a friend of my mum's that has lived opposite us since the family moved into the house twenty years ago. There's nothing wrong with her really, except that she talks. I mean she never stops talking and it's always a lot of nonsense. If you try and start an intelligent conversation with her she has a gift of turning it into something quite different. As I approached the dining-room I heard her lifeless high-pitched voice at work.

"... and I told George, I said, it's the change that makes all the difference. Here I am seven days a week, fifty-two weeks a year, without going any further than the Black Horse, so it's about time I went away. It'll do Young George the world of good as well. Looking quite pasty he is these days. I'm not like Mrs Walsh up the road, trooping off to Spain and the continent every year. There's plenty of beauty to see in our own country without all these expensive holidays abroad..."

She was so wrapped up in her rabbiting that she didn't even notice me come into the room, until I'd seated myself down behind her. "Good Lord, you *are* growing," she cried out when spotting me. "I don't know who you take after, I'm sure, although your mother's brothers are on the tall side..."

I wasn't taking any notice of what she was saying as her conversation about holidays was still in my mind. At this point I think I'd better let you in on an orgy my family take part in for two weeks in every year. I'm talking about their annual rave to Canvey Island. For fourteen days they pack their bags and troop down to this suburbanites' heaven, and usually I tagged along with them. The depressing thing was that they were due to go again on the following Saturday. I hated the idea because for me it would be like fourteen Sundays at home with the sea in the background. The only pleasant thought about it all was that I'd saved a pound a week out of my wages for this holiday, so if I didn't go I could have a ball with it. I'd been saving for a year, so fifty pounds meant a hell of a good time.

Mum came in with my fodder on a steaming hot plate which she held with a cloth. "Eat it while it's hot," she ordered me. She never missed saying that at every meal-time. Then she seated herself next to Mrs M.

"Well now," mum said, "we've got some news for you. Mrs Manley has managed to get the bungalow next to ours, for the same fortnight when we go to Canvey. She's bringing Young George, too, so he'll be company for you."

As you've probably guessed, Young George is Mrs Manley's offspring, about the same age as myself, but thank God that's about all we have in common. He's learning to play the violin, and he practises every day, and he's a boy scout. Rumour has it he's over-friendly with the scoutmaster, but I couldn't care less about that part; what he gets up to is his own business. I went to school with him. He was a prefect and the milk-monitor and top of the class and never late and I hated him.

Dad said: "The weather forecast says we're going to have some good weather next week."

Mrs Manley said: "Young George is *so* looking forward to it."

Mum said: "We haven't missed a year at Canvey for twenty years, except during the war."

I said: "I'm not going."

They all said: "What!?!"

"I'm not going. I'm sorry if you counted on me, but there's a very important concert I've got to see and I just can't miss it," I lied.

The funny thing was, they didn't start having a go at me straight away. No, they played it cool at first, and told me not to be a silly little boy and give my holiday up just for a Jazz concert that lasted only a couple of hours. The change would do me good. Sea, sand, fresh air, ice cream, and to crown it all—Young George!

"I'm sorry, if I've disappointed you," I said quietly.

"So we're not good enough for you, is that it?" my mum shouted at me. "Your own family not good enough. I expect you prefer those tearaways at that Jazz Club of yours. Well, I'll tell you this much: you've *got* to come. I *order* you to come, d'you hear?"

I stood up and shouted back at her. "I'm not coming and there's nothing you can do about it. I'm not a snotty-nosed kid any more, and I'm too big to give a hiding to, so you'd better face the fact that nothing you do or say will make me go to that God-forsaken hole!"

"But what about Young George? He was so looking forward to you being there," chimed in Mother Manley, determined not to be left out of it all.

"I couldn't care less about that poof of a son of yours!" I screamed out at her. I left my lunch and walked with a big theatrical exit out of the room.

It's no use denying it, I regretted this little scene as soon as I'd escaped up to my room. I expected mum to come up and tell me what an ignorant rude young bastard I was, and make me apologise to old Mother Manley, but I didn't see any more of her until I was leaving the house on my way to meet Liz, and then it was only a glimpse of her in the kitchen, and although she saw me too she didn't say anything, and I felt a right cunt.

The place where I lived comes under an area they call Greater London, which is such a ridiculous name I shan't make any comment on it. So to get to the London which isn't so great but a bloody sight better, you have to board a tube train which goes on a twenty minute journey above ground till you come to a station called Baron's Court. Just as you leave Baron's Court station the train goes underground, and this never failed to give me a little thrill. At that point, when the train first goes into the tunnel, you are leaving Greater London, where the natives starve themselves to buy a new car to show off to their neighbours with, and enter the manor of the real Londoners. The ones the whole world have heard about and respect, and when you cross this border the people seem to change from puppets into human beings. I know they still look miserable (you can't fail to on the tube somehow), but they definitely change for the better. From Baron's Court on you start hearing foreign accents and languages, and you see people that interest you (including the natives) — the scene starts to change from black and white into technicolour.

I got off at Piccadilly Circus, which you can't fail to mistake because of its neon lighting, up the escalator where the people that are going down stare at the people going up and the people going up stare at the people going down, and out with the rest of the mob into the street.

Looking at the slip of paper Liz gave me, I found I'd come out of the wrong exit which I always managed to do somehow, so I crossed the street, passing Eros and all the hundreds of people staring at it. I never gave it a second glance because I've always thought that London's statues are a complete wash-out, or most of them, anyway. Take Nelson's Column, for example: all that column like a great big giant, and at the top there's poor little Nelson that you couldn't even see without the aid of his telescope. The steps and surroundings of Eros are the same; very impressive, but when you look for Eros himself you can hardly notice him.

Liz was already waiting when I arrived at our meeting-place. Without saying a word we started walking back towards the Circus. I was waiting for her to make conversation. I expected her to start rabbiting away in her usual excited manner, but she didn't, not a word.

"Good day at work, Liz?" I asked, trying to get things going.

"As well as can be expected," she said coldly. Then silence again.

The streets were crowded with people all leaving work and going home; walking in a confused but orderly mass. Relieved that it was all over for a few hours but knowing that they'd be doing the same thing, at the same time tomorrow and the next and the next day after that.

"Where do you want to go? For a drink? I'll buy you a Babycham, if you like. Do you remember you had seven last Christmas, got drunk and sang six choruses of *Mother, I Love You* while mum sat down and cried her eyes out?" I said.

"I'd rather have a coffee if you don't mind. This place will do," she said as we came to a respectable-looking place of refreshment.

I chose a quiet corner where we could sit and talk without having an audience and ordered the coffees. I was just planning the best way to get Liz talking, when who should I see in another dark corner of the coffee bar but Danny the Dealer, the cat who'd first introduced me to Dusty. He saw me at the same time and beckoned me across to his table. I asked Liz to excuse me and found my way over to this Irishman whom I'm sure is as English as I am.

61

"What happens that I find you in such a square and respectable joint, Danny boy? The waitress buying or something?" I said, sliding on to the form next to him.

He looked far from happy. "Man, I'm finished — *really* finished — washed up and kaput!"

"What do you mean, Danny? What gives?"

"I've been nicked, and lumbered at that!"

"What? I can't believe it! It's no good telling you how sorry I am, that won't help you, but how on earth did it happen?" I asked him.

"Man, it hurts me to talk about it," he said, but I knew he was dying to tell me all the same. He continued: "They've known about me for a long time and I knew there was going to be trouble soon. I got the tip-off from a very reliable source of information. A few days before I found this very depressing fact out, I'd been on my usual expedition to that fair city of Liverpool, and picked up a very swinging two pound weight, which I might add, was Congo Matadi. So what did I do? I sold the lot at a ridiculous price just to get it off my hands. Then I waited for Mr Law's visit feeling very pleased with myself, as I'd have the laugh on them. But... oh man, I can't go on!"

After a few minutes of pissing about giving him all my sympathy and all that nonsense, he carried on with his tale of woe. "Well, eventually they arrived. I opened the door, welcomed them in — six of them there were — and they pulled the place apart. I gave them all the help I could, opened drawers for them, the lot. And guess what happened, man? When they realised the gaff was clean they took some out of their pockets, right in front of me, mind you, and asked me where I got it from. Man, I swear by all that's holy, that they put it there, and when I called them all the dirty bastards under the sun they told me I'd better be quiet or else they'd show me how rough they can get. Man, this has finished me. I've lost faith in human nature. British Law and Justice be fucked!"

"Man, that's bad," I said. "It's not only bad it's frightening. That means all us cats that have a little harmless smoke aren't safe. No matter how cool you play it, if they want you they'll get you. So what happened, did the magistrate take a lenient view and let you off?"

"Let me off? I'm on a fortnight's remand on bail, and come up tomorrow. This is it, man, they'll sling the book at me this time. I'm already on two years' probation for the same thing. The first time's okay, but the second innings they throw the book at you. You'll have to buy your little smoke off someone else now."

I was mad. I wasn't only mad at the deal the law gave to Danny, but I was annoyed he was out of business. Although he pulled a few strokes on you now and again, Danny was a very reliable pusher. You couldn't call his deals huge, but you could always rely on him for quality. He never lumbered you with any duff gear, and if you were lootless any time you fancied a smoke he'd always give you credit. Danny would be missed.

I said my farewells to him, wished him luck for his performance in the morning and returned to Liz.

"I know that fellow from somewhere," she said. "Who is he?"

"No one in particular," came my reply. "Just someone I know from the Katz Kradle."

Her face seemed to be deep in thought. "Just a minute. Doesn't he sell reefers?"

"No, he doesn't," I snapped back at her, "and don't call them reefers, you sound so square."

"I hope you're still not smoking them, anyway. If mum found out it would finish her."

"Don't start having a go at me. I wish I'd never told you now."

"You wouldn't have done if you hadn't been so high. You looked absolutely stupid that night. If that's what it does for you you can keep it. It can't do you any good."

I was losing patience with this very square sister of mine. "It certainly doesn't do me any harm. It's a lot healthier than drinking, anyway."

63

"How can you call *drugs* healthy!"

"They call them drugs just to give them a name. Aspirins are drugs but everyone takes them. Don't you realise some drugs do a lot of good?"

She always found an answer to everything. "Indian Hemp doesn't."

I wouldn't give up. "It certainly doesn't do me or anyone else any harm."

Stubborn cow. "Why do they ban it then?"

"Why did they ban alcohol in the prohibition days in the States? Look, understand this. I smoke Charge because it agrees with me. Everyone has their own stimulants, if it's a cup of tea or a glass of whisky. I don't like drink, so I smoke Charge. I don't suffer from hangovers with it, I don't get violent, and I'm not doing anyone any harm, including myself, from smoking it, so mind your own business!"

She did, too. She sat there looking like a scolded child, without saying a word. She's always been the same; argue like mad and then stop and sulk. But you'd like old Liz. You can't help feeling sorry for her even when there's no reason to. She draws sympathy out of everyone, even when she's happy. I mean, you look at her and you say to yourself, "she's a nice little girl, poor thing". You can't help it. Of course, you can't get to the bottom of her at all. There seems to be a million things ticking away in that little head of hers; all sorts of things, and you feel like knocking on her forehead and saying: "Open up there — let's have a peep inside," but she won't let you. I think she suffers with an inferiority complex like mad, but then don't we all? I mean, the people that obviously do you take for granted, and the ones that seem as if they don't, you swear blind they're putting on an act to hide their complex.

"You'd better tell me why you dragged me all the way down here to meet you. What's it all about?" I asked Liz.

She went even more serious than she usually is. Her eyes glanced away from me and I saw a thousand thoughts cross her mind. She moved uncomfortably on her seat and said: "I don't know whether I want to now. I've thought it over and I can't see any point in telling you. It wouldn't make things any better."

"Come off it, Liz. Surely you haven't brought me all this way for nothing? Anyway, it'll do you good to talk about whatever it is."

"All right," she said very quickly. "I'm pregnant!"

This knocked me right out, it really did. My *Salad Days* sister, the one that was always preaching to me, was in the pudden club. I could hardly believe it. But then they always say that the quiet ones are the worst.

"Does mum know about this?" I asked in my most sympathetic voice.

"Of course she doesn't — and promise you won't tell her. Come on — promise."

"Of course I shan't tell her if you don't want me to. But all the same she's got to know sooner or later. How far have you gone?"

She blushed like mad. "Three months," she said in a tiny voice.

"You'll be showing soon and then she'll find out. Look, why don't you tell her? You haven't robbed a bank. You'll feel better when mum knows."

"She's not going to so don't keep on," she snapped back at me.

"I don't want to keep mentioning this but she'll have to know sooner or later. I'll tell her for you if you like."

"Oh no you won't. I'll handle this my own way. A friend of mine's going to help me."

I didn't get that last bit at first, then I tumbled.

"What do you mean — *help* you? Now listen, Liz, you've got to be sensible about this. You can't start doing things to yourself. It's very dangerous, do you understand?"

She started to get up from her chair. "I wish I hadn't told you now," she said. "Forget I ever told you. I'll see you later." She reached the door before I could even get up from behind the table. In my rush I knocked a cup and saucer flying which made a hell of a noise, and everyone looked around at me. I caught her up a couple of yards up the road but before I could get a word in she beat me to it. "Leave me alone, do you hear? I shouldn't have told you in the first place. Just let me think."

I just didn't know what to do for the best, so I let her cross the road and lose herself in the crowd.

The Katz Kradle's considered the best Jazz Club in this country, but I hate it. Although I go there week after week, I think it stinks. The music's great, and they've spent hundreds of pounds on the decorations (I'm not kidding either, Jazz is big business), but it's the members that spoil it. They behave themselves well enough, there's never any punch-ups or anything like that, but they're such drags it's a shame. I'm sure half of them can't tell the difference between a trumpet and a trombone, and go there for a change from the Palais. There are exceptions, of course, and some of the cats do go there to listen to the music, but we're definitely in the minority. The others congregate at the Kradle just to show each other how sharp they dress, it's a sort of weekly Easter Parade, and to make it with the delightful Jewish chicks that get there. There's a war on between our battalion of music lovers and the great army of jive fiends at this club of ours. There's never any trouble but it's what those politician cats call a cold war. I wouldn't mind if these morons admitted to the world that they don't understand or appreciate our sounds, but they don't. They crowd around the stand beating time to the music with their feet, making as much noise as the drummer, and when the soloist plays something they *can* understand, say, for instance, a couple of bars of *Rule Britannia* in the middle of *Fine and Dandy*, they go into ecstasy, but if he played something subtle instead, it would leave them cold. All right, so we don't dress as sharp as they do, but instead of squandering our bread on drag, we invest it in LPs.

The club is owned by a dapper little Jew by the name of Harry J. Waxman, who mixes freely with the members, and asks them how they're enjoying the music, and tells them who he's got blowing next week, but—as goes Phil Seaman's great philosophical conclusion—he doesn't know a crotchet from a hatchet. We're forced to patronise his club because there's nowhere else we can hear sounds like they are at the Kradle—for that we're very grateful to Harry J.

We get our kicks, though. If it's not a friendly discussion it's trying to lay a chick, and if it's not that it's probably having a good old smoke up in the carzy. And there's always something happening at the death. One of the cats that has his own pad will give an impromptu party where we all get stoned and have a ball, and if we're lucky we managed to lumber a dealer back with us and get him really block-up so that he starts to get generous and brings out a dirty great ounce as his contribution to the gaiety.

As the Katz Kradle is such a big club, it took a time to sort the wheat from the chaff and find the cool school. The dim lighting didn't help either, and I had to do a complete tour of the gaff before I found Dusty and the crew. It was very crowded but not too hot as Harry J. had invested a packet in air-conditioning gear.

On the stand the musicians were all ligging around and looking bored as hell, while the drummer, who was sweating like mad and getting himself worked up into a right old state, was doing his solo. Bashing every drum and cymbal for all he was worth and making a bitch of a noise, while all the musical morons called members were shouting and clapping and making it sound more of a row than it really was.

There were only a couple of cats with Dusty. Buttercup, a professional wrestler who doesn't wrestle now because he's not in his top physical condition owing to his drinking about ten pints of Merrydown a night, and Popper, the sick man at Dusty's party. Since then I'd found out that he was a junkie— so, I suppose, he had every right to be sick. As soon as Dusty spotted me he left them and pulled me over to the Coke bar and ordered two.

"Why can't they get a lush licence in the poxy place?" he said loud enough so everyone around the bar could hear him. "These kids spoil the whole scene."

He led me to one of the many corners in the club (there seem to be corners all over the place), and gulped down half of his drink in one go.

"Why the dramatic correspondence, Mr Miller?" I asked.

"I had to see you, man. Very important. Just to make sure you'd be here." He gave me a typical Dusty Miller look: 'I'm hustling, I'm nervous, but not scared, and everything I do is for a purpose.'

The Radio-Luxembourg-type voice of the MC blared out from the loudspeakers that were all around the club. "Don't forget Saturday night is rave night at the Katz Kradle. Not one, not two, but three swinging groups will be playing for you. Our two special guest stars will be Spud Tate and Hank O'Rawe those two great tenor men, who will be featuring the exciting 'Battle of the Tenors'. Don't forget. Next Saturday at Harry J. Waxman's Katz Kradle Club."

"You've heard about Danny, I suppose?" Dusty asked me.

"Yeah, I met him about an hour ago. Bad luck, eh?" I answered.

"Bad luck? It's fucking disgusting!" He pushed his pair of thick-lensed spectacles that he wears closer to his eyes. "Man, this is nothing but a police state. They talk about Russia and their secret police, they talk about Germany and their bleeding Gestapo, but we're no better off than any of them. The law is a business like any other, and the men who work in it want to get on just like a bank clerk does, and they know the only way to do it is to nick as many people as possible. They've got to make arrests to survive—it's their bread and butter. And if there's a bright young bogey who's talented enough to be a bigger bastard than the average, they shove him into the narcotics squad. Danny's plant isn't the first time it's happened and it won't be the last. Do you realise that they can pull *anyone* from the street and whip him along to the station, search him and inform the poor unfortunate cunt that he's got Hemp in his possession? They don't even have to show it to him. And who's the magistrate going to believe?"

Dusty pulled a packet of cigarettes out of his dirty suede jacket and offered me one. He always said that suede jackets or shoes looked wrong unless they had a bit of dirt or grease on them. It gives them character, he says. His pasty white face that always wants a shave went back as he inhaled deeply on his cigarette, and his small, piercing eyes glared at me from behind those thick lenses.

"Now to come to the point. I wanted to see you tonight for something really special, that—without sounding too dramatic—may alter your whole life," he said, pushing the mop of black curly hair back from his forehead. "I want you to answer a few simple questions."

"Fire away," I said.

"Firstly, you're going on some weird vacation with your Mater and Pater, I understand?"

"Wrong first time. I've changed my mind."

"Good. Very good. Sensible boy. Now then, you did inform me a couple of weeks back that you'd saved a paltry sum of one pound a week from the fabulous earnings so kindly bestowed upon you by your employers—for this said holiday. The total accumulation of this, I believe, comes just past the fifty nicker mark."

I chimed in very sharpish. "Listen, Dusty Miller. You are definitely quite positively, not getting your dirty maulers anywhere near my hard-earned loot!"

He gave me a shocked expression. "My dear boy, realise this. You are four years my junior, and also, I think, my friend. For these reasons I wouldn't take liberties with you. I want to make it clear from the start that I don't want you to part with your life savings unless you are a hundred per cent—I repeat—one hundred per cent crazy over this quite extraordinary clever idea of mine."

The army of dancers were getting dangerously close to us, and I could see that Dusty was getting ready to pounce on the first one that touched us. He was looking at them from the corner of his eye, and I could tell that he loathed the idea of all these squares prostituting our music. He got up suddenly from his chair and bawled at the nearest couple to us. The fellow was about my own age, with a college-boy hairdo that must have cost him at least half a note, "Do ya want *all* the fucking club to yourself?" he screamed at him. "Why don't you go and do your jungle dances at the village hall in Clapton Pond where you come from!"

"Where were we?" Dusty asked me. "Ah yes, your fifty quid. You realise of course, that now Danny is not on the scene any more there will be a lot of hungry mouths to feed? But who's to feed them? There's a bomb to be made by someone who knows Danny's territory, and who knows it better than us? Yes, man, we'd make a great team..."

"Just a minute," I interrupted. "What d'y mean we'd make a great team?"

"You and me, dig? Oh man, I can see it now. Money, chicks, as much Charge as we can smoke..."

"... and the law! Six months each!"

"Don't be a cunt, man. We're too sharp for all that. Danny trusted too many people – strangers at that. All kinds of faces he'd serve. Not to get greedy, that's the secret of success. I tell you, man, we can't miss!"

"I suppose you want my holiday money to put up for the Charge?"

"It'll be the best fifty pounds you've ever spent. What an investment! It'll double and treble before you realise you've spent it. And, my boy, the important thing is this: You can tell Mr Cage and Mr Pilkington and Mr Bloody Down and Company himself to put those hats exactly where they won't go!"

The musicians were really swinging now. Throwing out the last choruses right at us. Smashing it against the walls and the doors and the people. And behind it all a feeling of We-know-you-don't-know-what-we-mean, but-we-do-and-that's-the-important-thing. Bill Higginwell the tenor player was on the stand bending forward, knocking the hell out of *The Girl Next Door.*

"The snag is," I said to Dusty, "whoever makes the scene has to get in quick before the rest of the dealers come nuzzling in and take over Danny's round. Where are we going to put our hands on enough Pot to start up business?"

Dusty looked pleased with himself.

"That's *my* contribution to this little partnership. I know where I can buy a one pound weight—yes, sixteen wonderful high-making ounces—for the fantastically give-away price of fifty pounds!"

"Thank you, *Bill Higginwell!*" the Radio Luxembourg voice boomed out.

"All right, Dusty, we'll do it!" I half shouted. "It's my only chance to stay on the right side of Baron's Court! Good-bye, bowler-hatted men and pram-pushing women! Farewell Down and Company, farewell!"

Half an hour later we were climbing the stairs of The Man's house. He lived on the top floor. There was nothing but light and shade and it reminded me of a staircase that I'd seen scores of times in thriller films.

He was younger than I expected him to be. A handsome Spade from Africa, about Dusty's age, who reminded me of a gazelle the way he glided around the pad.

"This is it, gentlemen," he said while bringing out the Charge which was in a large plastic bag. He sounded like a compère introducing a variety act. "All the way from Africa. Real Congo. The best Gunja you're likely to smoke for a very long time."

We sat down to taste for quality. Dusty took an amount of it from the middle (in case our newly found friend had planted some stoning stuff on the top only) and made us all a fair-sized spliff instead of the customary one you usually share.

"If we like it we'll buy it," said Dusty, lighting his up.

I did likewise.

Nothing. There's nothing happening to me. I know it. I *can feel* it. I can feel it? Has nothing got a feeling? I suppose *it* is making me feel nothing.

Remember *all* things are important. You've got to get to know of their existence, and in time appreciate them. For they are everything. The thrill of being aware of them is wonderful, and when you get over that you can advance to even higher realms of feelings which are new and interesting and explorable.

Everything is important. We mustn't ignore anything. Everything can be and is interesting. Everything—cigarette packets—glasses—cats—clocks—wallpaper—everything.

Time is something. It's *happening.* But it's happening slower than we realise. We want to fasten it up but it's very slow really. "Come with me," Time shouts. "Don't hurry on with the rest but wait for me, it'll be worth it. You'll appreciate me much better—and you'll discover that I *exist!"*

Sitting is nice. To relax and *feel* your tiredness going through your arms and legs and head is all right. Not wearying mind you, but enjoyable. Pleasant peace. Peace is pleasant.

Warmth in your chest and throat. A warmth that makes noise. The noise of electricity. Buzzzz...

Oh people, whom I can talk to—where are you? I'm glad I met you because you can come in with me, too. Let's be a team and think alike. Tell me of the things I can't quite get into focus and I'll alter my rangefinder and join you so that we can dig the scene together. For that favour I'll turn you on to mine. My scene, like a Cinerama screen, unfolds before me. I've been used to village hall film shows, but now I see Cinerama...

And all that Jazz.

A few things had to be sorted out.

Saturday had come before I knew what had happened. There was movement in life now. Mum and dad had really been brought down because Liz had pulled out of the holiday rave as well. There was quite a bit of drama with mum doing her nut and crying and telling us she'd brought us up the best she could, given us everything we wanted, yes, even spoilt us, and the only way we could repay her was to back out of the holiday and spoil it all for them.

I helped them on the last minute rush on Saturday morning, while Liz conveniently stayed in bed out of the way. They both got panicky and neurotic while they buzzed around the place in case they left behind their money or raincoats or contraceptives or something. And then they finally left. "Cheerio, Mum and Dad. Have a good time and get plenty of rest. Don't forget to send us a card. Cheerio!"

I lounged in the chair thinking about the day ahead. Dusty and I had to go over to the gazelle-like Spade's pad, whose name we'd found out was Ayo, that evening, to collect that bag of happiness in exchange for the necessary loot. Ayo was giving a party for a girl friend he wanted to impress and he invited us. We couldn't refuse an invitation like that one; I mean, the man's a dealer so you'd be barmy if you did.

The house seemed very strange without mum and dad ligging about in it. Empty rooms and a quietness I'd never noticed before. I felt it was my house for a whole fortnight, and I put my feet on the mantelpiece which I would never have dared do with my houseproud mother about. I put on my noisiest Stan Kenton record, turned the volume full on, and his fabulous brass section echoed through the house. The intricate web of sounds were too much for only two ears to listen to, you need a dozen at least because so much is happening.

The garden outside looked great. Better than I'd ever seen it. Come to think of it, I don't think I'd ever really seen it before. The sunshine and flowers and even dad's tall ladders looked all right. Rinty, our Alsatian dog, was having a ball catching wasps in his mouth. He's marvellous at it. Quick as lightning he snaps them up. before they know where they are. Then he gets stung and rubs his nose on the grass like mad, but he don't care. He's off again to a minute, looking for the next unfortunate wasp to come his way.

Dusty came over at half past ten. Very pleased with himself he was as he came through the door. He had his best clothes on and he looked quietly sharp; he didn't look as if he'd dressed himself up but he looked good.

"Good morning. How's it feel to be independent?" he asked, going straight to the gram and putting on the M.J.Q. Then, "Got the loot?" he asked, lounging back in my dad's armchair.

"I picked it up from the post office yesterday. I hope we're doing the right thing. This is the most money I've ever had in my life, so I don't want to goof with it."

Dusty looked hurt. "Goof? How can we goof? I tell you, man, this is the surest thing I've seen for a very long time. I only wish I'd had the money myself. I don't mind telling you, I wouldn't have cut you in if I had."

"You're such a friendly friend," I said.

"You just relax. I've brought a little present for you."

"I've been dying for a smoke all the morning," I said, taking it from him. "I've got the skins in the drawer."

I took the cigarette papers out of the drawer and made a nice long but thinnish spliff with three skins. Not too much tobacco mixed with the Charge, but with the end of a straight cigarette as a filter.

"This is the position," Dusty said, inhaling as much air with the smoke as he could so that it went right down to where it would do most good. "I think we'll get rid of the first pound weight in a couple of days, because at the start we'll only sell in ounces. We'll get eight quid an ounce easy while this drought is on, and this'll give us a good start to get a bit of bread in our pockets. I've got all Danny's musical contacts lined up, I know them all. I've been on the blower this morning to about half a dozen of them and they're all dying to pick up. I tell you, man, there's good times ahead."

I found a half-full bottle of sherry which had been left over from last Christmas, so I poured the two of us a drink while Dusty kept himself busy by making another spliff.

"Ayo phoned me this morning," Dusty said without taking his eyes from the papers he was sticking together. "He wants us to bring our own chicks. I've already phoned Ruby — she's crazy about coming."

"Trust her if there's plenty of Pot on the scene, nothing would keep her away."

"That's what I like about her. She's really hip to the happenings. Who are you bringing? Miss Roach?"

I told him I didn't know whether to take her or not. I'd taken her out a few times since our first meeting, and I liked her, mind you, I'm not saying I didn't. She was great in a crazy drunken way. I use the word drunken because that's how she was most of the time. She wasn't content with the Charge on its own — oh no, she'd want the lush as well. As you know, lush is intoxicating, so may I add is Charge, perhaps even more so; so you can guess that Miss Roach wasn't the ideal type to take to a party where you want to relax and enjoy yourself, without having to worry about the possibility of having to carry a drunk home. She was like that cat I read about once, who kept changing his personality and now and again he'd go all ugly. Mr Hyde, I think, his name was. Well, anyway, she was like that. One minute she'd be all serious and the next she'd be as high as a kite. She *could* be serious too if she wanted. She was an artist even. Painting it was what she was having a go at. The most abstract abstracts you've ever seen. She's not the Chelsea type of art student. The one with baggy skirts and sandals and dirty feet, and on this, I want to be weird one. No, she's cool. Cool in the nicest way to be, that is, not realising you are. To make matters perfect for her, her old man who lives in Yorkshire, sends her down a nice monthly allowance, but that's to keep her out of the way, I'm sure.

"I don't know whether I should bring her," I told Dusty. "She can become a number one drag at times, and could easily nause it all up."

"She's the only one. You *must* bring her. I tell you, man, she'd be a big hit at this jollity tonight."

So I phoned her.

"Hellou," came her dreamy voice at the other end.

"Hello."

"Oh, it's *you*. How are you, precious one? Hold on, I'll turn the sounds down. There, that's better. Well, what's been happening?"

"Everything," I said in my coolest voice. "A friend of mine's having a little get-together tonight. I wondered if you'd like to come."

"*Like* to? I'd *love* to. I'd never refuse a little get-together with you. Where shall we meet?"

"I'll pick you up at your pad. Look, Ruby's going with Dusty. Why don't you bell her and tell her to be at your place at eight? We'll all meet there, and don't be too stoned, else I shall leave you at home. See you then."

"See you."

Dusty was looking really comfortable by now. He'd pulled another chair up to put his feet on, he had a pillow to support his head, and his foot was going up and down like a baton beating time to the music.

The M.J.Q. sound came out as if it was solid, forming shapes around the room; first one shape and then another, and like it was one man making it, not four.

Dusty raved on, "That's the great thing about Mother Charge, you never know which way she's going to take you. You think after a tune you know all the different paths you can travel on, but you soon find out there are others. Monday, a laughing one. Tuesday, a serious one. Wednesday, a working one. Thursday, a lazy one. Oh man, isn't it exciting? A thousand paths to travel on and each one different. But it's rather frightening at first. I remember the first time I was turned on, you can't forget it really, can you? It's like having sex for the first time, stays in your memory forever. It's the feeling of not knowing what to expect that's the drag. And when it creeps up on your brain and starts to perform, it's a bit frightening because you don't know where it's going to take you. But when you know, it's great. You can sit back and go along with it and you're not scared at all. I remember a little Greek cat I turned on for the first time. An intellectual type he was; a poet or something. Worried me for months to turn him on, he did, wouldn't give me any peace at all. So one night when I'd just come into a bit of loot and bought half an ounce of that very stone-making brown Rangoon stuff, I took him along to the pad and made him a nice fat zeppelin-shaped spliff all to himself. What a raver he turned out to be! He stood in the middle of the room and described all of his sensations to me as they came to him, one by one. 'A golden band is going over my forehead and pulling tighter and tighter,' he said. Then he saw the scene flicker like a television does when it goes wonky, and he raved on for at least an hour, and I had the whole episode taped on my Grundig. It's a gass, man, it really is. I'll have to play it for you sometime. He wasn't sure of himself after that. He couldn't make out if the Charge had wigged him or not, but I told him that the first time is usually a bit dodgey so he tried again. And, man, it became his best friend. But to top everything, guess what happened? He asked me where this stuff comes from and I told him it grows in quite a few countries but the best brand comes from the Belgian Congo. Believe me man, this is what he did: he packed a haversack or something, and decided there and then that he'd hitch-hike all the way to the Congo! Honest. And no one's heard of him since!"

I managed to get a word in. "I bet he's having a ball now."

"You telling me! I can just see him now. Sitting under those ten feet Charge plants just picking it off and making a dirty great spliff one after the other, and cuddling a fourteen-year-old Spade chick. What a life, man! I only wish I had his courage!"

I suppose we got carried away a bit talking about the kind of life we'd have if we were in this Greek cat's position. We built it up until we were practically convinced ourselves that we were there. Showing conjuring tricks to this crazy tribe that hadn't even seen a pink man before and really knocking them out with all this magic of ours. Yes, they'd make us some sort of Gods and wait on us hand and foot and we'd live the ideal life. Nothing but one big ligging, smoking and fucking session. What more could anyone ask for? And we'd send all our friends a postcard and tell them all about it, the news would soon travel and we'd be the talk of the town. We'd even grow into a legend and be discussed in all the hip circles, and after a few years we'd return and they'd hold parties in our honour, and we'd tell them that we couldn't stay long as we'd have to be off again back to where we came from, and they'd ask us thousands of questions and want us to take them back with us, but we wouldn't. But why not? Yes, we would take a few characters back with us, only a very selected few, though — serious smokers only — no junkies, we couldn't stand that carry on in our little jungle. Miss Roach would be at the top of the list, she'd be very welcome. She could get as block-up as she liked there. A few home-grown Spades must be taken also. They would get the natives really at it, seeing their countrymen dressed up sharp and speaking in a Cockney accent and everything. We'd all have our own little jobs. I'd be entertainments manager and organise the orgies, Dusty could be the Charge Inspector and see that the larder's always full, Miss Roach would be the official taster, and Buttercup could be chief roller because there's no one that can make such perfect spliffs as him. He can make them to look like genuine Pall Malls, or if there's plenty of pot going, a full size Corona Corona; eight skins he uses sometimes. Africa would soon get their independence if we were there, and when they did, who'd be in Government? Right, first time! The laws of the land would be changed, of course. Hemp smoking would become compulsory, and if anyone broke that law they'd be liable to a heavy fine or imprisonment or both. We'd soon deport the die-hard British imperialists and set up the friendliest government the world has ever known. After the population had heard something about our plans for their country they wouldn't even want an opposition. We'd have to be very careful about immigrants. They'd have to pass a very sticky test to see if they were hip enough to gain citizenship to our country.

"It would soon become one big Ventree," said Dusty, looking as relaxed as Dean Martin singing a slow pop.

"Ventree? What's that?" I asked my semi-stoned friend, who was obviously on a talking one.

"You've never heard of Ventree? Oh man, what a place! It's an institution which caters for a selected few that are in need of mental readjustment," he said, sounding terribly educated.

"You mean it's a nut-house?"

"No, not in the true sense of the word. It's an establishment that uses highly modern methods for mental recuperation with the accent on group therapy."

"Where did you learn all those long words?"

"Stop butting in," Dusty said, helping himself to one of my straight cigarettes. "Well, anyway in this place all the inmates sit around in a large circle and tell each other what sent them mad. That's supposed to cure them. But the important thing is that they can do as they damn well please. They're given a warm, comfortable bed, good food, if they want to paint or write or sculpt they're given all the necessary jaba juntz, and even if they want to come to Town they're welcome. Now, man, as you can imagine a large number of layabouts, who are fed up with doing skippers and living rough, are only too pleased to spend a few months there, until the head-shrinker realises that they're not really mentally unbalanced, but just plain lazy. I took Buttercup there once to visit Charlie the Chargehand—I don't think you know him—he's a bit older than the usual crowd, but very young in heart and a right raver. So much so that he convinced the head-shrinker that he was an Indian Hemp addict. It was the big laugh everywhere we went. This cat had pulled the biggest con trick of the century, because they even allowed him to smoke in there."

I butted in. "This cat *must* have been a right one to get away with a stroke like that."

Dusty wasn't pleased with the interruption. The Charge was making him talk as much as old Mother Manley. "You telling me? Well, anyway, he messed himself up at the death because he started to turn this chick on who was supposed to be an Indian princess or something impossible like that. The Charge made her even more mad than she really was, because she went around the gaff telling everyone that she visited a strange new world every night with the aid of Harry the Hare, the patron saint of Indian Hemp. Then they finally caught them in bed together and told them that that wasn't included in the group therapy, so they must go."

"Where is this place, anyway?" I asked getting interested.

"It's in Surrey, man. I never forget the first time I went there. Snowing like mad it was, and as Buttercup and me was approaching the main entrance, we saw this cat in shirt sleeves outside in all the snow, everything so very white, tearing chunks of scarlet red jelly from the packet, holding them high above his head offering them to the seagulls. He was a junkie and went in there for a genuine cure and I think they helped him no end. He was the one that wrote a series of articles in a Sunday rag about two years ago, entitled "I Am A Drug Addict And Have A Monkey On My Back," etc etc, or some crap like that. We met this Indian princess just as we were leaving and she took set on us, asking if we'd got any of that naughty tobacco on us, and it was up to us to spread the gospel of Indian Hemp among our fellow men. It all ended in Drama. Buttercup goofed like mad because he asked this nut case if she'd care to meet him when she was let out on parole, and she went berserk, shouting out aloud that she wasn't a prostitute or an easy woman, and how dare he suggest that she should climb into bed with him, which the poor fellow hadn't done at all."

80

We finished off the bottle of sherry. "Where are we going to keep the Charge after we've collected it from Ayo's tonight?" I asked Dusty.

"That's up to you," he answered quietly. "It's your bread we're buying it with so you've every right to keep it. But I shouldn't have it here if I were you. Number one, it's dangerous, because mothers have a gift for finding things in their own house. And number two, we must have it handy where we can get at it any time we want."

"So where do you suggest?"

"I don't particularly want it in my pad. I'd have a lot of explaining to do if Mr Law found a pound weight in my little home."

"Well, if I'm not going to keep it and you aren't, where the hell's it going to go?"

Dusty looked very wise. "In someone else's pad," he said.

"What?" I shouted. "They'd nick it. I don't know one person in this whole wide world that could be *that* honest. Honest."

He gave me a sly smile. "They couldn't nick it if they didn't know it was there."

"What d'y mean?"

"Come now, use your imagination. Suppose we hid it in someone else's pad and they didn't know anything about it. Then, if anything unfortunate *did* happen, we'd be laughing. It's a foolproof scheme. A Dusty Miller special."

"Just a minute — wooow, back there. Let's get this straight. Are you suggesting that we stash it in someone else's pad so that if anything *did* happen they'd take the can back for us?"

Dusty dug that I wasn't keen on his idea. "Let's put it this way: if someone else minds it for us, without knowing of course, then the chances are ten million to one that the law would ever find it."

"And whose pad do you suggest we use as a storehouse?"

"I think the lucky person will be — Miss Roach."

I didn't like it one tiny little bit. "Oh, no, not her. She's out. I like her too much to pull a dirty trick like that on her. Think of someone else."

"But it's the ideal place. Bayswater's very handy to get to if we want it in a hurry. And remember, friend, that it mustn't appear strange when we keep showing up on the scene. Someone else might sus something, but not her. She's very sweet on you, so it's up to you to return the amours. Play up to her and start going steady, then she'll *expect* you to spend a lot of time around there. I've found the ideal place to stash it away as well. Her toilet has a lovely cupboard in it that houses a hot water tank which was made for the job."

"Are you sure there's no risk involved — her getting caught with it, I mean?"

"None at all. I tell you, man, it can't fail."

Liz came downstairs shortly after that. She came into the room fully dressed but I don't think she'd washed; there wasn't a trace of lipstick on her chalk-white face and her hair looked like a bird's nest. She sat down without saying a word, holding a cup of cold coffee in her hand, then she sniffed the air suspiciously.

"I don't think you've met Dusty," I said to her. "Dusty, this is my sister Liz."

She looked over to him but didn't even smile. He got up from his chair and said, "I'm very pleased to meet you, doll. Your brother's told me a lot about you."

She gave me a filthy look and I could tell that she thought I'd told Dusty about her being up the spout. Then she said, "If mum came back now she'd kill you. I think you've got a damn cheek smoking that stuff here as soon as her back's turned. You ought to be ashamed of yourself." She didn't raise her voice when saying this so it drove home all the more. If she'd have shouted it out to me I could have shouted back, so I had to play it cool.

"Don't be silly, Liz," I said laughing. "It's not Charge you smell. It's Dusty's special asthma cigarettes. He has to take them for his bad chest."

Dusty didn't like the idea of putting it all on to him, but he coughed all the same. "Yes," he said confidently, "it's the weather. It seems to affect me more than the cold does." Then he overdid things with a noisy fit of coughing that must have lasted a full minute.

This didn't impress Liz at all. She raised her voice this time and the deadly serious look on her face frightened me in a way. "Why don't you grow up? You all think you're very sharp and hep or hip or whatever you call it, but you're nothing more than a couple of overgrown schoolkids. All this stupid Jazz talk which you force yourself to say, you can't kid me it comes naturally, and to smoke these reefers is very clever, isn't it? To waste your money on that rubbish so that everyone thinks you're real cool cats is enough for you in the tiny world that you live in. But don't you realise the seriousness of it all? I couldn't care less about the harm it might do to *you*, but don't you ever think about mum? What would happen if you were caught with this stuff by the police? You'd probably get away with probation, but what about mum? Think of all the trouble you'd cause her when she thought that her son, her only son, that she idolises and loves more than anything else in the world, was nothing but a drug addict!"

"Don't give me all this drug addict nonsense, Liz, for Christ's sake," I snapped back at her.

"All right, so you're not drug addicts," she went on, "but mum wouldn't realise that. Don't you understand what she'd think if something did happen? It would finish her, you know the type of person she is. She gets worked up over nothing so I dread to think what would happen if she found out about this. She'd be lucky if she came out of it alive. You're nothing but a stupid, ungrateful selfish little bastard!"

As you can imagine I wasn't very pleased about this. She was showing me up in front of my best friend, someone who had some respect for me and whose respect I wanted to keep. But deep inside I could see that there was some truth in what she was saying. Not all this bollocks about drug addicts and acting sharp, but the bit about my mother. So as it often happens when someone is told the unwanted truth, I did my nut.

"You're the one to talk about bringing worry to mum. That's very funny, very funny indeed," I shouted back at her. "I don't suppose you stop and think about yourself for a moment. Elizabeth, the good and quiet girl of the family, the one that's always preaching to me and telling me what a naughty little boy I am. How about when mum finds out about *you*? Haven't you stopped to think of the worry that you're going to cause her? And don't call me a bastard, either. You can save that title for the child you're going to have!"

Her face all twisted up, she started to cry but couldn't and she looked really pathetic and a bit horrible. She stood in the middle of the room, her shoulders forward like a hunchback's, and she took big breaths of air in, or I should say, tried to, and I thought she'd stopped breathing or something. Her hands went up to her poor untidy hair, and man, I really got the horrors.

I looked over to Dusty just for a second and he was transfixed to his chair, staring at her as if he was getting sadistic pleasure at seeing her in the state she was in.

"I'm sorry, Liz. I really am," I said, going towards her. She gave me a look of hate, yes, man, *hate*! I'm sure it was hate, and she managed to get out, "Don't come near me... you can't be my brother... You're horrible..." Then she was away out of the room before I knew what had happened.

The M.J.Q. were still playing busily away on the gram. I even remember that it was *Concorde* they were giving out.

"Make another spliff, Dusty," I said. "For Christ's sake, make another spliff."

It was raining like mad when we left the house to meet the girls. The weather had lasted out for two weeks but now it was pissing down. The sort of rain that challenges you to put on your most rainproof raincoat but always wins in the end. We hung on at home waiting for it to stop, but when it got to quarter past seven and we saw there was no chance of it

84

giving over, we decided to brave it. Dusty hadn't brought a mac so I gave him an old plastic one of my dad's to borrow; he also collared one of his paint-smeared caps to keep the wet off his hair-do that had cost him three half crowns that morning.

The evening promised to be swinging but I was far from that way in spite of the fact that we'd knocked out a tola's worth of Charge that afternoon which should have brightened up anyone's day.

Liz had cleared out shortly after the drama and when I heard the front door close I felt like rushing out after her to pull her back and get on my bended knees if necessary. You see, a little bit of excitement like that perhaps wouldn't affect you or I too much, but Liz is different. I knew she'd take it badly and wouldn't forget it in a hurry. The trouble with her is that she takes things far too seriously and she won't fight back, that's another thing. Even when we were kids and I nicked a toy of hers or pulled her hair or something, she'd go straight to our mum and make a great issue out of it and treat it as something that I meant. It got me in such a state I was frightened to do anything in case she took it too seriously. And because of this you felt sorry for her but dare not show it because that would make her a bloody sight worse. She's not got out of that way yet, but now and again when she's relaxed, and that isn't often, I can assure you, she'd open up just a little and let you into her world. Take this *Salad Days* lark for instance. When we did have a talk, you know what I mean, a *real* talk, and I'd tell her, or try to anyway, about Jazz and what an exciting healthy thing it was, she'd rave about this musical play that she'd seen seven times (yes, I did say seven!), and in her way I could tell that this show, or the idea behind it, wigged her as much as Miles on form does me. She'd rabbit away like mad and get really excited like a little girl telling another little girl about a fairy story she'd just been told, about this crazy piano that made all these cats dance like mad when they heard it play. It was great to see her show so much enthusiasm, and no one could say that I took the mickey out of her, in fact I tried my best to get her at it because it was great to see her get worked up over something as she's so couldn't-care-less. She must be really gone in her own way to get carried away with something which you must admit is nothing more than a glorified version of *The Pied Piper of Hamlin,* or wherever the cat came from. If she'd been the biggest square on earth, which she wasn't really, you couldn't blame her for it. After all we were brought up in the suburbs and if anyone gets away with that without turning into a zombie then they must consider themselves a very lucky person indeed. I knew that Liz hated the suburban scene as much as I did, but she wouldn't revolt; the disease had its roots firmly planted in her, and although there were corners of her mind that yelled out for help against it all, she couldn't fight. I suppose she didn't have the guts. Although she was having a go at me all the time, I'm sure she envied me because I was doing something about it and she couldn't. When we were having those talks I was telling you about, I got to know more about her than she wanted me too, and if I managed to get her down to the Black Horse and get a few Babychams down her, then it would be easier still. I'd have a smoke before we went in, then sip a glass of cider while I lushed her up. Believe it or not she'd soon be on a level with me, and start smiling and everything and even get a bit affectionate. The people in the bar that didn't know us stared like mad because I'm sure they thought that she was a girl friend that I was trying to get plastered so I could snatch a bit in her doorway when I said good night. But anyway, deep down Liz is real good. Truth. You'd say the same if you met her.

The rain slashed down on us as we made our way to the tube. Dusty's high was in a better state than mine so he was raving about how great the rain was and wasn't it marvellous sensation when it hit against your face? Sort of woke you up, it did. "Come on, rain," he shouted to it, "splash against my face. Oh lovely, marvellous, splash rain, splash!" But it made him annoyed to think I wasn't as high as him—that didn't help him at all. He wanted me to be with him, to pool conversation so as to help each other's highness, but I wasn't having any, and he didn't like it.

"Lovely weather for ducks," the ticket clerk at the station said. I felt like telling him to shut his bloody filthy mouth up and think of something a bit more original to say.

Baron's Court! Thank God for that. Thank God also for letting us get away from back there for a short while. I wondered if mum and dad was missing it all yet and perhaps getting a tiny bit homesick. You bet they would be. Dad would be missing his sports programme that's on the tele tonight, he never misses it, mustn't miss it, spoil his whole week if he did. I expect mum is missing that same old routine that she's always grumbling about. Yes, she grumbles about it all right, but you just try and keep her away from it for a couple of weeks and then see what happens. What's Liz doing? At home in bed trying to cry herself off to sleep, or at her lover's house begging him to marry her, or in church asking for forgiveness? And where's Bunty? At a seance getting her kicks seeing hip squares having a ball, or seducing some poor unfortunate teenager who's a virgin and can't cope with her?

We went through a terrible performance changing trains. Dusty got really involved with the porter asking him which train to take for Bayswater, and as usual when you've had a smoke, things became a bit vague to him, so in the end I had to go to the rescue because we'd have been all night getting directions. Then he drew my attention to one of those very swinging posters you see on tube stations. This one was a huge flower covering the whole of the giant poster, except for a few words at the bottom advertising something, but you couldn't see the words as you were hypnotised by the flower. Dusty said: "Isn't it a gass? The flower comes right out of the poster as if it's coming to get you. Man, it eats you. It draws you closer and closer, then eats you!" He suddenly laughed out aloud, then started to sing to the tune of an old time music hall song:

I was eaten by that flower on the wall,
I was eaten by that flower on the wall,
I know I'm not too fat,
But that flower don't mind that,
I was eaten by that flower on the wall.

"Shut up, you drug fiend," I said to him.

Miss Roach lives in a basement in a something or other terrace in Bayswater. It's a thoroughly respectable street so they say, with an old ladies' home in it, so it must be. In fact they're all proper houses with proper people living in them. Even Spades live in it. No, there's no colour bar here — as long as the Spade is a student and carries a rolled umbrella, a badge on his blazer and a briefcase to prove it. When you stand outside the house that Miss Roach lives in you'll say to yourself, this is a very respectable house, that is until you look down into the basement. Then you can't believe you're in the same street; you must be in a different part of London, you think. Then you realise that Miss Roach lives there, so you need no further explanation. We fought past the rusty pram, crates of beer bottles, half finished piece of sculpture and dozens of empty wine and spirit bottles that were cluttered up outside the door, and knocked.

She greeted Dusty with a giggle, and myself with a giggle and a kiss.

"Come in," she said huskily. "I've got loads to show you."

After saying hello to Ruby and taking our dripping wet coats off, she showed us her latest artistic efforts.

This is the one," she said, taking off the piece of sacking that was around it. "'Viper's Dream' I call it. Didn't know I'd painted it till I woke up this morning. What do you think of it?"

"I can't actually understand what exactly it's supposed to be," I said.

"It's not supposed to be anything *physical*, it's a feeling, a mood."

"What mood?" Dusty asked sarcastically.

"The eternal torment of the junkie. The longing that never ends. The completeness that's never there. Can't you feel it? Can't you *see* it?" Miss Roach said, getting all worked up.

"I'm afraid not," I said. "But then I'm only a square as far as art's concerned."

"Don't say that. You have it here," she said, pointing to her head. "It's only got to wake up and it will, too, one day. Suddenly it'll all come to you in a flash and you'll see things that you've never seen before. It happens to everyone like that."

"At least I've got something to look forward to," I said, sitting myself down in a chair that didn't have too much rubbish on it.

The room was a replica of the basement outside except that it looked lived in. It wasn't dirty, but everything was lying about the place as if it had legs and could get up and find another place for itself when it wanted to. But the important things were in the right places, so it balanced somehow.

"See, I'm not block-up either. I've been on a fast for your benefit. Aren't I a good girl? I can even walk a straight line, look," Miss R said, getting up and performing. She walked her imaginary straight line perfectly. She'd made herself look younger than I'd seen her for a long time, but then I expect the reason for this was that it had been two or three months since I'd seen her as sober as this. Her famous large block-up eyes were wide open for a change, and her new blonde hair (it was dark last week) was unusually tidy.

Ruby was puffing nervously away at a cigarette till the lipstick was thick at the end of it, and her brown, beady eyes were shifting from one of us to the other, determined not to miss anything. The nicest thing about her was her hair; gingery-red it was—natural, too. She wasn't much older than myself but had certainly got around owing to the fact that she'd been carted about by a musician who was nearly twice her age; a very good musician who played at the Katz Kradle regularly, and had initiated her into the hip circles. He'd got tired of her now and dropped her, but she didn't seem

89

to worry about this as she could find her own way around now. But she'd never let you forget that she'd been his chick, and she'd always talk about him by his Christian name, and she got this crazy idea in her head that she must be very hip indeed just because this musician cat had chosen her to go to bed with. Her face was whiter, her shoes more pointed, her skirts a little tighter, than most of the other chicks.

"Do you know Ayo?" I asked her.

"Yes, I've known him for ages. A great friend of Ronnie's he was. He used to come around my pad regular. I remember he once came with a couple of other Spades when my mother was there, and when they'd gone she said what a nice friendly race they must be to share their last cigarette like they did."

"What have you been doing with yourself lately?" Dusty asked Miss Roach.

"Gardening," she answered. "Gardening's my latest and greatest hobby. Come and look," she said, pushing up the window. "I'm confined to window boxes at present, but when I become famous and rich I'll buy a farm miles from anywhere and grow things to my heart's content. There, what do you think of them?"

There were two long, thinnish window boxes on the sill and in each of them were three plants that looked something like the tomato ones my dad grows in his garden. They were about eighteen inches tall.

"Whatever they are they're nearly dead," Ruby said.

"What are they? An exotic flower from the east?" Dusty asked.

"No, my friends, they aren't. They're *Cannibus Indica,* alias Indian Hemp. The home-grown variety, grown from a few seeds that I had left over one morning about six months ago. Aren't they beauties? They'll be ready for smoking in a month's time, then I'll hold a party and invite my special friends only. We'll try the harvest, and, I pray, get high as kites."

"I hope I'll be invited," I said.

"You'll be invited to anything special I have up my sleeve," said Miss Roach, squeezing my arm.

"I bet they took some growing," Dusty said, showing some interest now.

Miss Roach sounded like a middle-aged lecturer. "They did indeed. But I persevered. Watered them every day — never a minute late — cared for them, *felt* for them. I practically worshipped them because I could see the whole operation growing before me. They were alive — Hemp growing on my window sill — getting *bigger* every day. What a happy thought!"

Then she gave us something from a milk bottle that certainly wasn't milk. When we asked what it was she told us it was something special she'd mixed that morning but couldn't remember what she'd put in it. Whatever it was it tasted alcoholic.

"I've got something else to show you. A new member to my family," Miss Roach said, bringing out a box that had been hidden by a million things in the corner. In the box was nothing less than a guinea pig.

"What's that for?" Ruby asked, with a 'I-hate-guinea-pigs' look on her face.

"He's my guinea pig. I call him Weep because he makes a noise that sounds like that all the time. He's company for my cat Wardell Gray, too. And guess what? He eats paper. He's absolutely crazy about it. So anytime it's Sunday or something special or I want to please him, I give him a whole magazine all to himself, and he has a ball. He likes the shiny covers best, don't you, Weep?" Miss Roach said all in one breath.

"But what's he for? What use is he?" asked I.

She seemed to be losing her patience. "He's *my guinea pig*. Any time I have any new tablets to try out that someone turns me on to, I try them on Weep first. If he doesn't get ill or die, I take them myself. That's what guinea pigs are for, aren't they?"

When the girls had gone out of the room to the carzy or somewhere, Dusty reminded me that I mustn't forget the Romeo act with Miss Roach, as planned. He gave me a long spiel with instructions all about the noble art of making a girl, and I thought he was going to draw diagrams as well.

"It's up to you," he told me. "Don't forget we'll need to come around practically every day, so we don't want to get her suspicious. Play up to her, marry her if you like, but don't let us down, we've too much at stake."

"But she's bound to know I'm pushing, sooner or later," I argued with him.

"That's all the more reason for her to sus something. I tell you, it's the only way."

"Where does our dark friend's party hang out?" Miss Roach asked me, coming through the door.

"Not far from here. We'll be there in about ten minutes," I answered, looking out of the window to see if the rain had stopped. It had.

"I hope they're not *all* Spades there," Ruby said, admiring herself in the mirror. "Spades are great in their mannish way, but they're not neurotic enough to get high with for me. The British ones, that is. The Yankee ones are too neurotic."

Miss Roach followed up with, "I know what you mean, but it's only the way they look upon this Charge thing. It's not a kick and something that's very naughty to them. They're used to it, it's sort of natural to them, something they take for granted, a part of them. That's why they take it so cool."

We finished off the milk bottle which did wonders, really, because there wasn't much of it left and I already had a buzz on from it, and after last minute touches to the girls' make-up, we were away.

When we arrived at Ayo's pad I found a much different set-up to the one other Spade party I'd been to. I took it for granted there'd be a sea of black faces, all sitting around very quietly and coolly, smoking their Tampi like Woodbines, an African record on the gram full of drums and dozens of high-pitched voices in strange harmony, and a fair sprinkling of blonde chicks who'd caught the colour bug. No, it wasn't what you could call a Spade party at all, in fact, apart from Ayo, there was only one African there, and much to my delight there were faces that I knew well.

Buttercup was busy helping everyone to drinks, pouring glasses of vintage cider from the stone kegs that lay on a wooden table, and obviously getting his kicks from making himself helpful. His should-be-white tee shirt, that badly needed the aid of one of those miracle soap powders that are advertised on the tele, showed up his once good physique that was now turning to fat. As soon as he spotted us he turned us all on with a full glass of Merrydown, sitting us on a sofa in the corner and asking us how we all were with that wonderfully pathetic look on his face.

"Giving all this up soon," he said to me. I'd heard it scores of times before as it's his usual greeting to you. "Going to wrestle again, man. Fifty quid a fight, that's what I used to get. Just think of it: fifty quid a fight! Don't you worry, I'll soon be on my feet again. I'm giving up the scrumpy 'cause it's doing me no good. Won't be able to fight properly if I carry on with this stuff. Makes you lose your memory, you know. Can't remember a thing these days."

His dry, unemotional voice came at you with a ring of pity in it, and although he was all of seventeen stone and could more than take care of himself if he was forced into a punch-up, and wasn't what you could rightly call handsome, you wanted to look after him somehow, because that feeling came to you that he couldn't look after himself and everyone was taking liberties with him.

I took a quick look around to see what the evening promised, and I was pleased to observe it was plenty. Just a swift glance around told me that the party wasn't exactly in its early stages, as everyone looked well on the way to being stoned. There were about a dozen people there, and you could tell that Ayo had gone to the bother of making sure there were an equal number of chicks, to make things even more swinging. We said hello to everyone at once, and I noticed Popper was there, so was Algernon Fliewright, a writer who could never get anything published because it was too far out, so because of this, and the fact that he chewed benzadrine tablets like sweets, he was always brought down, and never failed to tell you so. A couple of half-caste girls that had immigrated to London from Tiger Bay were jiving in the corner together. Really attractive chicks, with black straight hair flying all over the place in time to the music, and a sun tan that an English peasant woman would have to spend a bomb on abroad to pick up. They'd collected the best from both races; they knew it—and made the most of it.

We settled ourselves comfortably on the sofa preparing ourselves for the happenings. Dusty gave me a sly wink that conveyed a lot. The wink told me there were good times ahead, and for a brief period we could forget the world outside and the life that had been forced on us by the poor unfortunate cunts that were out there planning it all.

As soon as we got settled down our host did his duty by presenting us with a couple of king-size spliffs which we blew away very quickly and greedily between us.

The atmosphere was marvellous. That's the only word I can use to describe it. A sort of atmosphere that can make you high by itself. The air was filled with smoke, and the acrid smell of Hemp was everywhere, like it was in everything, making itself crawl into every little nook and corner so it was there for always, reminding you about it all the time. An atmosphere that made a noise without you having to talk or play records or anything; a silent noise that you felt in your brain telling you there were good times ahead. An atmosphere that shouted in your ear that you were going to get block-up. That whatever happened it would do its duty and send you to niceness. And if Harry the Hare, the patron saint of Charge that the Indian princess raved about *was* a fact, then he was most definitely here, jumping and skipping about the place, pleased that he was in the company of a few of his most sincere disciples that were glad of him; yes, worshipped him for the happiness that he brought them. Never letting you forget that it was him and him alone that was helping you on your way to contentment; so never let it go out of your mind for a second that it's Harry, and be grateful to him, and when he's thirsty, which he soon will be for sure, send him down some liquid refreshment, because after all, he's been good to you, so it's your duty to look after him.

The faces were there on the scene before you, all there, but very far away, like you were looking at them from a distance. But now and again one comes up big before you, right in front of you and you see a scar on that face that you've never noticed before, and you hear a voice as though it came from an echo chamber, ringing down a long funnel, telling you they're having a good time and they haven't seen you for ages and where have you been? Then a hand with a spliff between the fingers, offering it to you, and you see the joint burning badly because there's too many seeds in it, and you take it and wet the side that isn't burning right to try and get it better again, and then you smoke it as if it's the last spliff on earth (heaven forbid!) and feel and *see* it going down, right down inside you as far as it can go, exploring new parts of you which it has never seen before, turning them on to the joys of the weed.

Then you survey the scene, of saucepans on gas stoves full of fish soup, with pepper so hot it burns not only your mouth but your inside, and promises to give you a reminder of it next day when you have to do the usual thing. Of mantelpieces full of photographs of grinning Spades, famous ones, great ones, ones that blow those man-made instruments that make those heaven-sent sounds. But the photo in the largest frame isn't of anyone famous to us, only Ayo, because it's obvious that it's of his mum and dad back home. No smiles on *their* faces, but a look of inner happiness and pride. I wonder what they'd think if they saw their son now? A lot different to the little boy they knew before he set off on his great voyage across the seas. A drug pedlar and a good time boy, that's what he is, Mrs Ayo. Different to his many friends that came over here and studied and qualified and returned home all proud and happy and victorious.

A congo drum in the corner, the skin well worn from times that black hands had beat the hell out of it. When the drummer, accompanying a record, would convince himself that he played a damn sight better drum than the professionals on the disc, just because he'd been smoking the water pipe. As you think of that a water pipe appears before you like magic. A nice one, well made, with the mouthpiece staring out at you like a cobra ready to strike. As you suck and draw on it that lovely sound of bubbling water (in this case it was cider) fills your ears. Then you look down to the glass stem and see the thick white smoke rushing through it straight down to your lungs. Your head whirls for a second, then most of it leaves your head, but don't despair because all is not gone, some is left to stay with you to comfort you.

You put your shades on because the bare lamp in the room is getting stronger than the sun ever could and you can't stand this squinting because it hurts your eyes, but now it's better. Oh yes, a vast improvement. Peaceful now, even Buttercup's shirt doesn't look dirty. But weirder. Can't keep these glasses on for too long — get block-up too quick.

Popper's in the most comfortable-looking chair, sitting a thousand miles away from everyone else, but then he's always been the same; most junkies are. Junkies fascinated me from the start and I found out all I could about them. I wondered why he mixes with us lot instead of his horsy friends. Like most of them he's always complaining about us; says we're too sociable and talkative. "Relax, man, relax," he always says. "The trouble with you lot is that you're looking for kicks all the time." His thing isn't a kick, it's a way of life. His works were neatly arranged on the card table beside him, complete with spoon and a candle stuck to a saucer to heat his jacks up with. He went through the fascinating ceremony of having his angry fix, prodding his bruised arm with the blunt point of the hypo, desperately searching for a vein to send the poison in to a mainline station to go on its journey.

Not an expression on his face, forgetting the people around him, alone with himself and the thing he has with him. Has with him to his grave, yes, perhaps for always. His young face and tired eyes went through me as if I wasn't there, and his lifeless black hair fell across his face, and with a dirty nail-bitten hand he pushed it aside, only for it to spring back again.

"What's happening?" I shouted across to him.

His glazed eyes looked up and over to me. "Things not so good, squire. Lady Devalera, the psychiatrist that I'm under, is cutting up a bit rough. Wants to cut my prescription and send me to a nut-house for a cure. She thinks I'm selling some of my ration, the old cow. It's all down to these kids that think they're hooked and want to get on her books. The parasites! They spoil it for everyone.

Then he glanced away from me as if I were a stranger.

Miss Roach sat next to me working away on the pipe. How that girl can smoke! How she seems at home with it, as if it was made for her, but then I expect it was. She's even getting admiring glances from Ayo and his countryman on the way she handles it. Sucking down the smoke until it explodes inside her, then comes rushing out of her mouth and nose all at once. Then she inhales again to try and win back some of the lost smoke. Her eyes were closing up and she looks half Chinese the way they're just slits, with big bags at the top and bottom of them. She was with the music, swimming and splashing about, the sole thing in her mind, and now even in her body as it shook gently to the rhythm. Her neck did strange twists to the music, and now it was becoming sex-making. As she shook her shoulders, double time right on the beat, the tops of her breasts that were showing above her low-cut sweater shook too, and now and again she'd say out aloud to the musician, "Don't do it!" or "Do it!" and it sounded as if she was saying these words to her lover, not the man that was blowing on the record. The grin on her face never altering, saying to you, "I don't want to come down, I want to stay like this forever." She looks as if she's not taking any notice of the happenings, but you just try and pass the spliff so that she misses her turn. She'll soon wake up and tell you not to be so naughty. When she gets it between her fingers, that grin breaks out to a great big smile, and she says something like, "Hello, spliff, where have you been? I've missed you!" and you remind yourself that here is a genuine hipster of the female variety.

Things flashed through my mind; all sorts of things, good and bad. But the bad things were bad no longer, I could see some hope or something funny in them. Even old Mr Cage; I couldn't help smiling. But the fact remains that I've had enough of you, Mr Cage, all the same. You must go out of my life forever, because, let's face it, you're in a different world to me entirely. Although we work together side by side every day, we're a million miles apart. You were born into slavery—I wasn't. And in a couple of weeks I'm going to make a visit to your precious shop, my very last visit, and tell you so right to your face, and you won't be able to threaten me then because my chains will be broken from you, and I'll tell you exactly where to put those snap brim, homburg and bowler hats of yours, the all fur felt and velour ones as well! I'll have a few things to say to the zombie too. I'll tell him that the very best thing for him is to leave 'Mummy' double quick, and find himself a navy stoker, perhaps, then, life wont be so mixed up for him.

I'll study hard at my new profession. My mind's crying out for knowledge about the art of drug peddling. It's a complicated business, with the law as your rivals, like a fox surviving in an area where hunting is the chief pastime. Sure there'll be difficulties and hardship and anxious moments, but there'll be excitement as well. And if you do your job properly the rewards will come. Not only the bread and material things, but satisfaction that you're winning a battle against one of the biggest organisations in the country, even in the world, who have on their side brains with lifetimes of experience, men who spend years learning their job, that's just a cog in a huge machine.

But even more important, it's a passport to freedom from plane number one in this world of ours. It reminds me of the belief of my Spiritualist friends who are convinced that there are seven different planes starting from number one, which is the earth plane, leading up to number seven which is the Christ plane, the one that's the true heaven. Man, I'm going to aim at number seven. I've got a long way to go yet, but Hallelujah! I'm on my way, I've nearly forgotten about number one already, so look out, here I come!

Two American servicemen came into the room, coloured boys, who without wearing their uniforms told you they were Yanks, as if they'd had the stars and stripes held high above their heads. They had with them clothes that go to the cleaners every week, the confidence of a senator, the smell of Old Spice, a bottle of Southern Comfort in their hands, and a I'm-away-from-base-for-a-few-hours-so-I'm-going-to-have-a-ball look on their faces.

"Where's the shit?" one of them asked loudly, with his eyes shooting around the place looking for a chick that took his fancy. "Let's blow our doggone heads off! In Chicago (it's funny how none of them ever come from the South) we smoke this stuff twenty-four hours a day. We take it seriously over there. Man, you ought to meet some of the smokers in that great little city of ours. You'd say, Glory be, that can't be a man smoking that Pot, it must be a steam locomotive!"

"Try the pipe," Ayo's countryman said with a trace of sarcasm in his voice.

"Ah sure will," he said, taking off his jacket as if he meant business.

They both had a turn on the pipe, not very expertly but well enough to do the trick. It did. They coughed and spluttered but it was too late. The Congo was upon them. As soon as they'd put the pipe down one of them asked why we didn't have a window open to let some fresh air in the place, and when Ayo told him we didn't like the idea of letting all this precious smoke out of the room they looked puzzled and said they'd better be going as they had to look into another party before they returned to base. Then they swallowed it.

The eyes of the walls were studying us with amazement and ignorance. They'd seen lots of things: volumes of comedies and dramas and even pantomimes, but never this. You want to talk to these peeling, cracking walls for they seem wise to you—silent, observant, but not critical. Wise from embraces, fights, love, hate, tears and laughter—all to be lost one day when they pull this old house down, or someone drops a bomb and murders it. But that's not yet, wall, so join with us now and make the most of it. Remember, we too have to be pulled down one day. Join us and travel the million paths of intoxication, never knowing quite where we're going or where we shall end. Learn the art and science of getting high. Fight for your degree! It will help you to solve some of the snags in life, even all of them. Have it all in your brain, ready to be tapped when required—the complete answer to everything.

But, wall, never forget we respect you, for yours is a mind of experience that we can never get. The people that you must know, as we never can—their bodies and feelings stripped naked before you. We only see ourselves that way, and then we aren't an onlooker so how are we to know even ourselves? The sounds you must have heard, *had* to listen to—Bach and Brubeck, Jimmy Shand and Sonny Stitt, Word Jazz and Mrs Dale's Diary...

I could have sworn I'd been sitting next to Miss Roach for hours, so much had happened, but nothing you could talk about. But my mind had absorbed everything, not taken it in so it could be stored away forever, but pounced on it, observed it, thought about it, then chucked it away. The clock told me another story: that I'd only been there a couple of hours. It made me think about time. That it was rationed so we mustn't think about it lightly, but if we try and rush it and go berserk, putting all our energy into making a million things happen in an hour, then it would play funny tricks on us and disappoint us. Let it have its own way, putting the responsibility of ourselves into its hands, giving us the experiences that it wants to—one, five, or a hundred to the hour—*then* it won't disappoint us, I'm sure.

Dusty had his arm behind Ruby, running his hand up and down her back, trying to help the Charge out on the passion stakes, but he seemed clumsy; he was doing it all wrong, somehow, and I bet you anything you like he wasn't even fazing her. It obviously didn't wig her but he'd been kind enough to ask her to the party so she had to put up with it.

It must be a real drag being a woman. All kinds of male specimens making passes at you all the time, and you having to sort them all out like a card index, deciding who to give the red light to, or the amber one, or green. To those selected few who you shine the green light to you automatically have other problems: how far to go—a kiss? An evening in the back row of the pictures? Or to whip it on them. A very complicated business indeed.

Dusty glanced up at me. He could see that I could see that Ruby could see nothing in what he was doing, so he gave her a look, in full view of me and for my benefit, which put the blame on her somehow. Then he lay across Ruby and Miss Roach to say to me, "See me outside in a couple of minutes." He straightened up, puffed away on a cigarette for a while, got up and left the room. I followed him out on to the landing, and without saying anything we went down the stairs into the street.

I needed the change of scene badly. I'd been getting sleepy in that very stoning atmosphere but the fresh air, which had turned very cool because of the rain, I suppose, did the trick. Don't think it sobered me up or anything horrible like that, but it's great to make a different scene sometimes because if you're on the same old one for too long you're liable to get carried away and get too far out and end up not knowing where you are. There's no complaints about that when you're in your own pad, but when this happens in someone else's and you've got to be capable of getting home, it's different.

The street was quiet and dark, and an out of tune vamping piano could be heard from a pub down the street; a pub full of people getting stoned on gin and limes and stout and milds, having a perfect evening which comprised of not only their beer but a singsong and a punch-up and then a good fuck at the end of it. The perfect evening.

"They're having a ball," Dusty said, looking towards the pub.

"Yes, I think they are," I said.

"People everywhere trying to forget what and where they are. It's funny. It's a racial thing as well, you know — I mean the way they do it. China, it's opium. The States, the junk. Africa, the weed — yes, they've all found out what suits them best."

"How about in this country?" I asked.

Dusty looked disgusted. "We've no imagination here. I suppose you'll have to chalk up mild and bitter for us."

"I got carried away in there a bit," I told him. "I thought of so many things my mind got confused."

"What sort of things?"

"A million different ones. Including the doubt about if we're doing the right thing or not."

"What right thing?"

"About buying the Charge."

Dusty put on his wise voice. "It depends on what's bothering you about it. If the moral thing comes into it, then you can relax. We're not doing an ugly thing selling Charge. *You* should understand that. It's only the peasants that could think like that. Sure they'd say that we were corrupting the minds and bodies of our customers by starting them off on their journey to eternal doom and torment, that before long they'll be sampling every drug that man has discovered because the kick in ours had worn out, but we know different to that. We know the majority of junkies fall into the trap because of ignorance. That they don't realise the danger of it until it's too late. But the people that smoke Pot first get a knowledge of the *dangerous* drugs by mixing with smokers. You'll hardly find a junkie that smokes."

"I suppose you're right," I said.

"You bet I am. Think of what we're doing. We're letting people forget their troubles in the nicest, cleanest, healthiest, and cheapest way. How many double Scotches would you have to buy before you felt the way you do on one good joint? That's if you could ever feel the same on Scotch as you do on Charge. I tell you, man, we're doing a service to the community."

A service to the community. The service of getting you high. Roll up! Roll up! We sell the best Indian Hemp in the whole of London! Stay higher, longer, on our great little cigarettes! We'll send you to places that you never dreamed existed. To shining new worlds of peace and contentment, where the sky's always blue and everyone's smiling. Where you can do what you want to do even if it's just sitting on a chair. But we'll guarantee that you've never enjoyed a sit down like that in your lives before. Roll up! Roll up! Buy our Indian Hemp! We're doing a service to the community!

Then Dusty asked for the money. Fifty pounds. A fortune. Ten fivers that I'd been through hell to save. A pound a week out of that little brown envelope that Mr Cage gave me every Friday with a look on his face that told me he didn't think I deserved it. The reward from fifty-two weeks of him. Oh Christ! I couldn't stand another fifty-two! Here, Dusty, take it! Do anything you like with it but save me from another year of misery!

He folded the notes in two neatly, then put them carefully into his hip pocket. He did this operation in a confident and determined way as if he was used to doing this every day. There was a satisfied look on bis face.

"This is just the beginning," he said. "You'll see. Just the beginning of a brand new, shining, radiant life for the two of us. Remember this night, man, keep it clear in the old thinking box because we're going to talk about it for a long time to come. It's like the generals in the last war planning for the second front or something that changed and won us the war. I bet they think back to the night when they were planning it all and just about to put it into operation. I bet they're at the old regimental club right this minute talking about it. That's how we'll be."

Plan the operation carefully! Every little detail is all important. Don't goof with them there plans! Win the war! Down with the law! Ride through the streets of London — victorious! The enemy is defeated! Mr Cage has been blown out of existence forever!

"This is what we'll do," Dusty said, with a ring in his voice that told me he liked giving orders. "When we're ready to leave, I'll give Ayo the bread and collect the Charge. I'll give it to you in a carrier bag. Now don't try and hide it whatever you do, just think of it as if it's shopping. (Was he kidding?) Go back to Miss Roach's pad with her, stay the night if she'll wear it, and hide it in the cupboard I told you about."

"All right," I said.

"And by the way — good luck!"

The party was very much the same when we returned except for the fact that Ayo had done a disappearing act and come back with a newspaper that must have had all of an ounce to it which he soon made into giant spliffs, distributing them about the room to people that were grateful and people that were scared, but all of them high, so they smoked it just the same in case they offended their host who must be the most generous dealer in London if not the whole world.

I sat next to Miss Roach who hadn't moved an inch since I left her. Now I don't mind telling you that I felt a bit disturbed about having to play up to her. I'll tell you why. She's very attractive, you can't deny that, and if it came to a push I wouldn't kick her under the bed, but she's not the type of girl that inspires me to try my talents on. I mean she's great to be with as a friend but going to bed with her promised to spoil something between us. In other words she was a different sexual type to me, if you know what I mean without sounding too much like Dr Kinsey. This wasn't because I thought I didn't have much chance and was just making excuses for myself, as she wasn't backward in coming forward as far as giving me encouragement was concerned, but there was that little something there that stopped me from getting carried away on the boudoir scene with her. But I gave myself a long lecture on getting these ideas out of my head as it would hinder everything if I started getting neurotic about it.

"How are you feeling?" I asked her.

"Delicious," came the reply. "There's a nice warm sponge all around me and I'm surrendering myself to it. I'm floating in it and I feel delicious. This is marvellous shit, man, it really whips it on you. I was just pretending to myself that I could afford an ounce of it. Life would be a lot more bearable then."

"If you're only pretending, why stop at an ounce? What would you say if you had a pound weight?"

Her grin broke out into a smile again. "I wouldn't say anything. Words wouldn't be necessary. I'd just have a ball."

"I bet you would."

Her eyes looked up towards the top of her head as if she was looking for a thought. "With the aid of a pound weight I'd paint pictures that would even surprise *me*. I'd have one long smoking and painting session and if I didn't paint anything worthwhile after that I'd give it up forever and ever amen."

"Would you paint better pictures than Viper's Dream?"

"I don't know if they'd be better, but I'm sure they'd be a darn sight happier," she said, laughing aloud.

Her head started to nod to the music, she was really concentrating, registering every note that the musician gave out with, and as he came to the climax of his solo she shook her head a little like she was congratulating him on a job well done.

Dusty was rabbiting away with Ayo, looking important and pleased with himself, then after a few minutes they left the room together to do the final exchange. Bits of paper for something that grows in the ground. For a moment it all seemed unimportant.

I hadn't noticed before but Ruby was getting a bit over-stoned. Her eyes were practically closed, her head was drooping forward, and although she always wore pale make-up you could see this was the real thing. Not only her cheeks but her arms and hands looked unusually white. Her eyes weren't though; they were red. She pulled herself to now and again just for a second, but she couldn't focus the happenings at all so she went back to closing her eyes again. I could see Buttercup and Algernon Fliewright talking about her and obviously enjoying seeing her in the state she was in. Then she managed to get up from her chair, stagger into the middle of the room, and then in a loud voice, that I don't mind admitting really startled me, she cried, "I'M CRACKING UP!"

There was a mixed reaction to this. Someone shouted in a mocking sort of voice, "Don't crack up, Ruby. Hang on. Don't crack up!" I think it was Buttercup that said, "Where's Dusty? We'd better get Dusty."

Then one of the coloured girls went over to her and tried to lead her back to her seat but she wasn't having any. Ruby pushed her away, and man, she had a terrible, terrible look on her face, and she screamed at her, "Keep your dirty black hands off me!!!"

The atmosphere froze so you could practically see the icicles hanging off the ceiling, and everyone felt embarrassed for everyone else, but the Spade chick didn't do anything but walk calmly back to her seat. You see, no one knew what the best thing was to do really. I know what I *felt* like doing but then that would have probably landed me behind bars, so I slipped out of the room and found Dusty coming up the stairs with Ayo. I quickly told him what had happened and when hearing it he practically ran into the room and grabbed her coat double quick, went over to her and said, "Come on, Ruby, it's time we were leaving. Put your coat on."

"I don't want my coat on—I don't want to leave," she blurted out.

"It's time I took you home," said Dusty very coolly, knowing this would stand a much better chance of getting results.

"*You* take me home? You've got as much chance to sleep with me as Julius Caesar has. Leave me alone, leave me alone—d'y hear?"

Dusty was trying his best not to be shown up in front of everyone, so he tried the tiniest bit of physical persuasion to get her out of the room. He grabbed her by the arm and tried pulling her, very gently, mind you, but it was no use.

"I told you to let go of me. You're hurting me!" she cried out as if he was putting a half nelson on her. "If Ronnie could see you now he'd certainly teach you a lesson." Then she wrenched her arm away from him very quickly, and quite by accident Dusty received a blow to the side of the head.

I'm sure it surprised him more than it hurt, but that did it. He stepped back and shouted at the top of his voice, "You ginger-muffed whore! Get out of this pad before I knock you out of it!"

She didn't need any more persuasion. She was out of the door in a flash, and she must have got the horrors from Dusty because I didn't see any more of her nor did anyone else.

We said our goodnights and apologised for bringing such an ignorant cow with us, but everyone understood, and the Spade chick smiled and told us she hoped to see us again soon, and for a moment I wished I'd have kicked Ruby's teeth in when I had the opportunity.

When we got outside Dusty handed me the carrier bag, whispering in my ear to take good care of it, then he made some excuse to leave us saying he had to see a man on business.

Miss Roach suggested we walk home instead of catching a taxi, and as we did so the wind started blowing up and it felt great against our faces as we walked through the near deserted streets hand in hand. We didn't say a word, it wasn't necessary, we were both feeling marvellous despite the dragging down episode with that musician's moll, Ruby.

The rubbish outside Miss Roach's front door looked different. It was the man in charge of the lights that did it because now the moon could work out on the scene things began to happen. It was like a photograph by one of those arty photographers who have a ball with nuns and dirty washing and have their snaps covered in grain and not too well in focus. Sort of romantic and dramatic, if you know what I mean. The piece of sculpture looked really great like her soul come out at night. But so disappointed that she wasn't completed, you could tell by the look on her face, honest you could, man. I started giving myself the horrors about how it would feel to be a half-finished piece of sculpture. The pram became a cave — a real cave — all dark and secretive, welcoming you in if you dare. Complete with sea in front of it as well. A cat amongst the bottles, crouching low, with its heart pounding, praying we wouldn't see him because he didn't like the look of us, so I pretended I didn't because I didn't want him to run away from us like only cats can.

We entered the room and Miss Roach took my coat and put it on a hanger in the wardrobe which was an invitation in itself to stay longer than five minutes. She always looked relaxed but in her own pad she was even more so. The way she got about the room, the way she sat in a chair, poured out a drink or lit a cigarette, told you she was in her own little kingdom where everything was under control and she could deal with everything that came her way.

"I'm going to get something for us to eat," she said. "I know you must be starving — I am. I've only got spaghetti though, but it's home-made not that terrible canned variety. You can always tell when you've smoked really good Charge, because it makes you hungry, thirsty and sexy." The look she gave me when saying that last naughty word was far from sister-like.

I saw to the sounds while she heated up the contents of a large saucepan that gave forth a very handsome smell. I was anxious to get the Charge into its new home as soon as possible but I was a bit nervous about rushing it in case she became suspicious. I put on an up tempo disc of the Jazz Messengers with Mr Blakey pushing the others for all he was worth, but she told me to change it because she wasn't in the mood for races at that time of night and to put on a pile of LPs that were on the table by the box. I noticed that they were all dreamy vocals by Anita and Miss Christie and a few of the others of that clan.

After we'd eaten Miss Roach went to a cupboard and brought out a bottle of VP which she displayed with pride. "See what I've held back just for you? It took all my self-control to save it but I managed it."

"It's very thoughtful of you. Thanks a lot," I said.

She raised her glass. "Here's to you, Harry the Hare and me. The greatest threesome in the Land of Oo-bla-Dee."

After drinking a glass or two I decided to get the Charge out to its rightful place, so when she was busy looking for a packet of cigarettes she'd mislaid, I took the opportunity and left the room taking the carrier bag with me. When I got to the carzy I opened the cupboard that Dusty had told me about and there it was, the cleverest little hiding place that you ever did see. Like it was specially made for the job. I took the plastic bag out of the carrier and before putting it away I gave my eyes a feast on the naughty stuff inside it. It was most definitely green. Not as green as the Cyprus kind but more mature like. Not too many seeds and quite leafy and the stalks weren't over-thick so it would be easy to mince up. Before putting it away behind the hot water tank I stole a big pinch of it and took it back to the room with me.

Miss Roach was sprawled out on the sofa looking very contented indeed, so I sat next to her, held her hand and said, "I've held something back for you, too. What do you say about this?" I showed her the contents of the envelope.

"I say you're an angel," she said, giving me a child-like kiss which was wet and loud. "Where did you get it from?"

I decided to tell her everything. I did too. I told her about Dusty and myself going into partnership and taking over Danny's round, but omitting where the Charge was, of course. I'd taken it for granted that she'd be pleased because I don't have to tell you how handy it is when a friend of yours is a dealer. I mean you can always get a turn-on on tick or for nothing which is a comforting thought even for a would-be suicide.

Her face went very serious. "I think you're mad," she said quietly,

"Mad? What do you mean?" I said.

"You should have better sense than to start selling. It's an entirely different thing to smoking, you know. The law aren't all that concerned about smokers because they've got to put all their efforts into finding the dealers, and they find them, don't you worry. It's the most dangerous crooked profession to enter. I can tell you that and I'm no criminal. The trouble with selling Charge is that too many people have to know about it and no matter how careful you are the wrong person will find out sooner or later and turn you into Uncle Charlie of the narcotics squad for protection against their own little fiddle or for a few quid. No one lasts very long at it without Old Mother Luck is on his side strong."

"But Dusty's in it with me. He knows what he's doing, Dusty does."

"I think you have too much faith in that friend of yours. If he's so sharp why couldn't he raise the fifty pounds himself? And anyway, I don't completely trust him either. He's a laugh and all that but there's something that's sly. I don't like the way he looks at people sometimes behind those glasses of his."

I was getting a bit annoyed at her running my friend down. "Dusty's all right. Don't you worry about that. Anyway, I've made up my mind. I'm going through with it whatever happens."

She took the glass in her hand again. "If you've made up your mind there's nothing I can do about it. I wish you luck anyway."

"Thanks," I said, taking a drink. I then made a lovely four-skinned joint that knocked you out just by looking at it.

Oh man, don't some chicks get you down? Here I was, in Miss Roach's bedroom (which was also her living-room and kitchen as well) alone with her at one o'clock in the morning, with sexy sounds on the box, a supersonic spliff in my hand, and she goes and nauses things up by telling me I'm a naughty little boy for wanting to become a drug pedlar. The trouble with her is that she always sounds so sensible when she talks about serious things and you can't argue with her because everything she says seems so *right* somehow. I was never any good at arguing, anyway. I suppose it's because I'm so easily led. I mean, I start off fine with my ideas clear in my mind and determined that nothing my opponent says or does will alter my point of view, but then when you're against someone like Miss R who sort of sounds wise in a casual sort of way, you know what I mean, sensible without trying to be — then I'm lost. I say to them, "I see what you mean — but..." Then I discover I haven't a leg to stand on. It makes me so mad. It's like when I used to argue about Spiritualism with an atheist or a Catholic. I'd start off fine, then get complicated by bringing something like the Bible into it and before I knew where I was I was well and truly beaten. Not that I wanted to go to Mass or join the Secular Society or anything like that, you see, I was still a Spiritualist, but I just couldn't get my ideas across, and just for a minute the Catholic convinced me that I was wrong. I don't suppose I'll ever get over it. I hope so though. It'll be a drag if I don't.

"I don't know why I tried to lecture you," Miss Roach said, waiting patiently for her turn on the spliff. "Life is to be lived. Mine is mine and yours is yours. It's a far too short a thing. We've all got to do what we think is best or we aren't even living properly. It's not right to tell someone what to do — it's sort of stealing some of their life away from them."

The spliff started to do its duty. To hell with Miss Roach not being the same sexual type as myself — she didn't look so bad now. I mean when you're close to her it's a different thing altogether; she's warm and soft and all those feminine things and she can get you at it there's no doubt about that.

I put my arm around her and she half-turned and faced me and pressed her breasts against me and they felt bigger and firmer than I had imagined them. When I was kissing her I opened my eyes and saw her eyes tightly closed and sort of quivering and I could tell that she meant it.

There's no point in telling you what happened in bed because I couldn't report to you anything original, but in the morning when I awoke and felt her laying beside me, I wasn't sorry for what had happened. My staying with her hadn't spoilt anything between us, in fact we were closer now than I ever dreamed we would or could be.

"So all is forgiven, Liz?" I said to her.

She didn't say anything but at least she looked up and smiled. She carried on eating her roast beef and said, "Where were you last night? I was very worried this morning when I found you weren't here. I thought something had happened to you."

"You sound more like mum every day," I said, smiling at the same time in case she took offence.

"And what's wrong with mum?" she asked seriously.

"*Nothing*. Relax, Liz, you're too damn serious." I took a mouthful of the stuff that looked like Yorkshire pudding. "I was at a party. I had a few too many drinks and couldn't get home."

She really did start to sound like our mother and look like her too. "You're always telling me I'm much too serious but it's a good thing someone is. If we were all like you I don't know what would happen. We'd all end up in the work-house."

I let it go at that. I was determined not to say one word that might cause an argument let alone a row, as it had cost me all my powers of persuasion to make it up to her as it was. I even had to ask her forgiveness, which is a pretty humiliating thing when it's your sister at the receiving end. She didn't come round easily either. I got the impression that she enjoyed it all. That she got her kicks seeing me humble and even a bit weak before her, telling her I was sorry and that I was the biggest bastard God ever gave life to. And when I realised I was past her annoyance and temper and pride, she wouldn't come out of it and tell me she'd forgotten all about it. No, she kept it going and told me that I purposely waited until there was someone else on the scene before I showed her up, so I had to keep rubbing my nose in the dirt telling her she had every right in the world to be mad, and that it would never happen again and I ought to be ashamed of myself; and in the end she told me that although she'd forgiven me she could never forget it, as I was her brother and blood flows thicker than water, but I was only a boy, not the man I kidded myself I was, and once or twice I felt like asking her who the hell did she think *she* was, the Queen or something? And I'd take everything back because I wasn't really sorry at all, but I managed to restrain myself. You've got to give way sometimes, I suppose. Especially when you're dealing with someone like Liz. She's the last person who'd admit she was wrong, even if she was the wrongest person that ever lived. You'd never get a confession out of her; not Liz. But don't let me try to kid you, I knew it was my fault really. When I thought about it I realised what I'd said to her was a bit much, especially when she was on the baby-making one as well.

To prove she had no more hard feelings she cooked Sunday lunch for me. Of course, it had to be roast beef and Yorkshire pudding. When I told her I was against eating roast beef on a Sunday she couldn't understand me at all. I love roast beef but I told her it would be a good idea if we ate *anything* today and kept the roast dinner for tomorrow as it made me sick to think that everyone was eating the same thing at the same time as me because it was the thing to do. Then she went and made things worse by telling me Sunday wouldn't be Sunday if she didn't have her Sunday lunch, and what the hell was I talking about? I let it go at that.

She cooked it lousy anyway. The meat all shrivelled up. It was the driest roast beef that I'd ever tasted and the Yorkshire pudding was undescribable. I forced myself to eat it and I even smiled at the same time. I didn't dare complain in case she started it all off again.

"Mum phoned last night," she told me, struggling to cut her meat at the same time.

"Really? How are they getting on?"

"Not so good. Their roof leaks or something, and it poured with rain last night there as well. So they had to put a bucket under the dripping water and that meant they couldn't get much sleep. Young George fixed it for them in the end. He's a very clever fellow, don't you think?"

"Too clever, if you ask me."

She scooped up the hard, dry peas on to her fork. "That's what makes me so annoyed with you. Everyone in the whole wide world is completely useless — except you. What's wrong with Young George, anyway?"

"He's a future zombie," I answered.

"A what?"

"A future zombie. A slave to tradition. A part of the great ugly machine of life. A bowler-hatted man. A civilian soldier. A person in a queue. Do you know what's going to happen to him? He'll be made a chief clerk at his office in about twenty-five years' time. He'll get married and have about four kids, and when his wife has had them she'll grow fat and ugly. They'll go to the pictures and the local once a week, he'll go to a football match every Saturday afternoon, he'll follow up the TV serial religiously, he'll get drunk as a lord and smoke a cigar at Christmas, but only at Christmas, mind you, he'll have sex every Sunday morning when he and the Mrs have a lay in, and when he reaches forty he'll realise that what he's doing is exactly the same things as he was when he was thirty, except he'll have a few more stomach ulcers."

"But what's wrong with all that? He'll be happy."

"You might as well say that a peasant in China is happy with his one bowl of rice a day, just because he's used to it."

"It's the same thing."

"It's *not* the same thing. Young George won't be living his own life. He'll be living a life that's been handed down to him—that's been left him in a will. He won't think or act for himself, in fact he won't even think at all. He'll be driving a car that has dual-control, but he won't be able to fight against the other steering wheel."

She stopped eating her tribal dish, put her knife and fork down, and sat there staring at me.

"What's the matter?" I asked.

"I'm beginning to realise the reason why you carry on like you do. It's your birth sign. Aquarius, isn't it? Let me see. You're a dreamer and a revolutionist. You'd probably make a faithful socialist because you have to fight for some dream or cause. Charles Dickens was an Aquarian. You're probably a bit of a mystic as well."

"Remind me to cross your palm with silver sometime. But also remember that I'm a student of the occult myself."

I was just about to set forth on a long and complicated spiel to explain to my sister that I was on the border of Capricorn as well which would make all the difference to my personality and make up, when the telephone rang.

It was Bunty. She asked me why I'd been neglecting her and that I should be ashamed of myself as it was nearly three weeks since I'd turned her on to the pleasure of my company.

"I've been very busy, I really have," I told her.

"Selling hats?" she asked sarcastically.

"No," I said, sounding very important. "I've finished with men's greasy headwear once and for all."

"Congratulations. Why not tell me all about it?"

So I arranged to meet her in the U Club, just off Knightsbridge, that night.

I'd been there a few times before with her, and although I promised myself that I'd never be seen there again, I'd always broken it as Bunty liked it so much.

It just wasn't me.

I'd soon discovered that Bunty liked to show off. She had a ball in places like the U, where she could talk a little louder than the rest, and keep saying that dreadful word darling, and it was usually to me because she was on a really weird one as far as I was concerned. Dig this. She was in her glory when she could be seen in a restaurant or club with yours truly, who looked so very young compared with her, so that she could make a fuss of me and hold my hand for all to see, and introduce me as a *very* good friend of hers that has *lots* of talent — (for *what* I've never found out) and end up telling the club that we were going home.

I didn't mind. I let her have a ball. After all I owed a lot to her as far as my education was concerned. Apart from the charver stakes she'd shown me the so-called smart set, which was far from smart in my opinion. Bloody untidy, I'd call most of them. A load of con men and prostitutes, if you ask me. Most of them didn't know what they wanted and when they got it they didn't know what to do with it. They all seemed frustrated somehow, including Bunty herself. All the women seemed as if they hadn't had a bit for a year and all the men couldn't make up their mind if they were queer or not. They were suburbanites with money. The so-called intellectuals were the worst. When meeting them for the first time they'd ask you a couple of test questions, quite casually, about the latest and longest psychological novel, which was in their world considered very hip, but I used to get them really at it and tell them, quite truthfully, that I hadn't even heard of it. They'd look very awkward for a moment, I suppose they were a bit embarrassed for me, but when they dug that I wasn't ashamed of it in the least, then they'd relax. For being so truthful I think they even liked me. When I told them I couldn't dig the Shakespeare scene either it knocked them right out. I told them I was always a bit suspicious of anyone that had too many murders in their plot. They got me down. It seems to me that if the happenings were beginning to drag a little, they'd liven things up with a nice juicy murder. People don't go around murdering everyone they dislike, like these writer chaps expect you to believe. It's not natural.

"Who was on the phone?" Liz asked me, putting my apple tart and custard on the table.

"A friend."

"You seem to have lots of social engagements lately. What's happening all of a sudden?"

"A million things, Liz. I wish I could tell you. I've nearly managed it and I'm so excited," I said, getting carried away.

"Nearly managed what?" she asked, giving me one of her motherly looks.

"To escape from all this."

"All what? This house, you mean?"

"Not particularly. Just everything that holds a person back from living."

"I'll never understand you," Liz said.

She understood me, all right. I'm sure of it. She knew how I felt—I even think she felt the same way herself. I felt like grabbing her and shaking some sense into her. To tell her she still had time to be saved, and then I felt like a preacher pleading with his congregation to give up their present life so that they could make the heaven scene.

Heaven! A cosy pad of your own where you could be alone sometimes or have as many visitors as you damn well pleased. Of eating when you're hungry, instead of having to lunch each day at one o'clock and dinner at six-thirty. Working Sunday and having Tuesday or Thursday off. Getting up from bed at three in the morning and going for a walk if you wanted to. Days of drugs and dreams and sex and Jazz. To hell with pensions and a comfortable old age. I'd prefer a comfortable young age.

I came right out with it, without any warning, straight to the point.

"What's your boyfriend like, Liz?" I said quickly.

She was suddenly still, like a lion ready to pounce, then she looked wonderfully relaxed and happy.

"I love him very much," was her reply.

117

"You must do. He's a very lucky fellow. Wouldn't you like to tell me about him? You know you can trust me, Liz," I said very softly.

"There's nothing very much to talk about really. I owe him a lot—he's—well—he's brought me a lot of happiness. But it's all so very strange—like a dream. But then I suppose I'm used to living in a dream world. You see I had it all figured out. Even when I was a little girl. I knew exactly when and where it would happen. He'd be rich and handsome and sweep me off my feet. It was all so clear. But it never happened that way at all. I suppose it never does."

She looked so young and helpless sitting there. Like a little girl that had failed an exam.

"We've got to *make* things happen, Liz. It's the only way."

"There you go again with your nonsense. It's all right for you telling me what to do and not what to do, but you've never been through an experience like this. I'd like to be around when you do and see how you face up to it."

She stopped for a moment and I thought she was going to cry.

"You'll have a big shock when life catches up with you," she went on. "It's fine for you on this obsession that you have at the moment. But when you're a few years older things won't seem the same as they did. You'll have to face up to life one day, and when you do you'll be able to call yourself a man."

"But you've got it all wrong, Liz, you have, honest. It's not a matter of age. I'll never change, I know it. If I thought for one minute that I'd end up like Young George, I'd do myself in without a second thought. We've got to make life what we want it to be—we can as well."

She looked annoyed. "It's all right for you to talk like that. If you're so very clever you can tell me how to change someone's nationality."

"What do you mean?" I asked her.

It came out like a shell exploding. "He's a Jew!"

"What difference does that make?"

"He's Jewish, I tell you. He can't never marry me. His parents wouldn't allow it—they'd disown him. Can't you see it's no use..."

Then she let herself go. Out came those terrible sobs that only women can make. Oh man, how my poor sister cried. She meant it, she really did. And I stood there, over her, all stupid and helpless. I wasn't going to tell you—but I don't mind admitting it now—I nearly cried myself.

"Things will work out, Liz, you'll see. Everything will work out."

Thank God her crying didn't last for too long. She stopped suddenly, like she'd turned the tears off with a tap. She gave her nose a good blow on the handkerchief she fished out of her sleeve, and her wet and puffy face all screwed up. "I must look dreadful," she said strangled-voicedly.

"What a family we are," I said, feeling much better by this time. "We're a load of water heads and worriers. Do you remember when we were both kids? We'd cry our eyes out at the least little thing. We'll never alter."

She was drying her eyes with her handkerchief now, and nearly pressing her face against the mirror so that she could see properly. "Look at my eyes, they're disgusting. Just look at my eyes."

"Your eyes are magnificent. Like cool, blue pools of water, serene and pure and clear."

She gave me a playful push. "Flattery, young man, will get you nowhere."

It's great how women hate to look a mess in front of their opposite sex. Even if it's their own stupid brother they've got to look all right. It's a good thought, though, it wigs me the most.

"It's funny," Liz said, "but I would never have believed a few weeks ago that I could have broken down in front of you like I did without feeling ashamed or embarrassed. I wasn't, you know. I wasn't a bit."

There was a silence but neither of us felt awkward. The atmosphere had changed somehow. There was a feeling in the air that told us that a great barrier had been broken, a barrier that had kept us at arms' length through the years, but now it was no more. I felt that I understood my sister completely, that I had got through to her, and for a moment I was right on her plane digging the scene completely. That I was in the middle of her world of insurance and Frankie Laine and romantic novels, and understanding that the fact of her being pregnant was the most important thing that had ever happened to her. Little old Liz — a mother! My sister, who looked like a kid herself, was going to have a baby! I'd be an uncle! The greatness and importance of it all flowed through me, and I felt like throwing my arms around her and congratulating her for being able to take part in the greatest creative act of life.

"Let's go to a Fun Fair!" I said suddenly.

"Did I hear you right?" my thin sister said to me.

"Let's go to a Fun Fair and swing on swings and eat sticky toffee apples and hold hands in the Tunnel of Love."

"Are you serious?" she asked seriously.

"I'm not serious, but I want to go to a Fun Fair, and you to come with me. Battersea Park it shall be. We'll be there in an hour and have the time of our lives. Let's pretend we're kids again and we've run away from mum, and robbed our money boxes as well."

The look on my relative's face was great, man, all naughty and young and even happy.

"We'd better be going before mum finds out," she said, combing her birdsnest hair into a beehive.

We didn't take much trouble getting ready and looking smart and all that. We wanted to run out of the house as quickly as we could because something was *happening* to us. It might have been the drama and the tears, I don't know, but I had the strangest feeling that I'd probably ever had. Even stranger than the ones dear old Harry the Hare whips on you. I felt half happy, half sad, but I wanted to get out of that house, to head for Baron's Court, and to take my sister with me.

"I hope the neighbours don't see us and tell mum," Liz said, slamming the door behind us.

We walked quickly to the station, not saying a word, but now and again I'd look over to Liz and find her already looking at me, and we'd both start giggling.

"Two tickets to Battersea Pleasure Gardens," I told the ticket clerk.

"There's not a station at the Fun Fair," he told us like an idiot.

"In that case I'll have two tickets to the station *nearest* the Fun Fair," I said.

The spot in the distance came closer, showing itself to be a tube train, crawling like a huge red caterpillar along a leaf of earth and grass and signal boxes.

The peasants in the train eyed us suspiciously. What's your game? I can nearly hear them say. What are you up to? Don't think me and Liz are like you, man with the Down & Co snap brim all fur felt twenty-five shillings hat on. We're devils, we are. We'd drown your cat and set fire to your baby if we didn't like you. We'd do anything we damn well pleased. Liz and me are going to enjoy ourselves, just for an hour if it must be, so you and your kind won't be able to stop us. We're going to forget about you and Young George and Mr Cage and zombie and her lover's parents and the baby in her belly, and there's nothing you can do about it.

"Baron's Court!" a porter shouted.

Passports, please! Don't let them aliens in! It'll be unpatriotic if you do. It'll be treason!

I think we changed trains but I'm not sure, as Liz's silence changed into a swinging chorus of conversation. Of memories and snatches of scenes half-remembered, of holidays at Canvey Island, where as kids we found our heaven for a fortnight, even if it wasn't sand, but mud, but we didn't care. Of birthday parties when we played Ring-a-ring-a-roses, and when we were older, Postman's Knock. Liz with her music lessons; how that girl tried the piano, but never advanced any further than *God Save The Queen*. We were happy then, yes, we were happy. Don't you see what I mean, Liz? We didn't think when we were kids, we *lived*. And we were happy.

Before we knew what had happened, the crazy music was in our ears and the entrance to the Fun Fair was in front of us. We got stuck in the turnstiles and the man who took our sixpences cursed us for laughing at him. We threw ourselves into the laughter and screams, and the cries of the stall-holders, surrendering ourselves to it all, letting it take us where it pleased.

Past the Big Wheel, standing there boasting to the other rides that it was King of the Fun Fair, like a lion does in the jungle. The Ghost Train we went on, clutching each other's hand as we went through the dark passages, all cold and wet and spooky; the skeletons, earning their living, danced before us, and the sudden screams of mechanical murderers made our senses reel like a benzadrine highness. The car smashed against the doors, letting us into the reality of the world, and the light startled us.

The spieler at a side-show, up on a rostrum, introducing the performers like they were just about to appear at a Royal Command performance. He looked real and efficient and even sophisticated, even though his dinner jacket had seen seasons upon seasons of wear, from Dreamland, Margate, to the Central Pier, Blackpool. He told us of the many things that happened on the inside in a cool and not too loud voice: "*This* is the show that you've heard about. *This* is the show that you'll go home tonight and tell *your* friends and neighbours about. *This* is the show that all *London* is talking about. *This* is the show that you heard on 'In Town Tonight', when I told Bryan Johnson of the BBC some of the amazing things that happen on the inside of this theatre. I don't care *who* you are, *where* you've been, or *what* you've seen. I *guarantee* that your eyes have never fell on a side-show that is more different, exciting, and entertaining... The price of admission is one shilling. Twelve copper coins of the realm. Coppers. What *are* coppers? We throw them away..." Then he saw a policeman in the crowd (or pretended he'd just seen him) and wished him a very good afternoon. We didn't go into the show because we knew that the performance on the inside couldn't compete with the performance on the outside.

"Let's have a lemonade," I said to Liz, pulling her into a neon-lit snack bar.

"I want a Cherryade. I've always liked them," she said, pointing to a healthy-looking red bottle that was on the shelf.

We blew down the straws and it frothed up and came to life, and we laughed at the woman with the Robin Hood hat who was looking at us in disgust. Liz put Frankie Laine on the juke box and we started to dance around it, yes, *me* dancing, a made-up-on-the-moment dance, but it was great. Before we knew it there were other people dancing with us, and before the record had finished it seemed that the whole snack bar was filled with young people letting themselves go and joining in. Then an important-looking cat wearing a uniform came in and told us that we weren't allowed to dance there, so we told him that we were sorry and we stopped, and the other people disappeared as quickly as they'd come. We finished our drink on two revolving stools at the counter, and Liz kept twisting around on hers until she worked up quite a speed and felt dizzy, and in the end the woman with the Robin Hood hat on gave us a putrid look, so Liz stuck her tongue out to her which she didn't like at all, so she left the bar grumbling to herself about the manners of the younger generation.

"I'd like to go on the Big Wheel," Liz said. "I want to be right up there for a moment, above it all. Half-way between heaven and earth."

"As high as a kite without having anything to smoke," I joined in.

The attendant, who was very un-gipsy-like, locked the bar that went in front of us so that we couldn't fall out. With a jerk, we were away. Swinging and revolving in a huge circle, high and low. When we reached the top it was crazy, like a sexual climax, then down again to ground level as you swish past the faces of the ants below. High again! With an abstract landscape of colour and noise. Then our ride was finished and we envied the people that were waiting for our seats.

We passed the bar, yes, *passed it*. We didn't need drink because drink would dull our senses and we weren't complaining about the state of our senses, so we didn't need drink. I didn't want a smoke, either. I wouldn't ever smoke again, I promised myself. I'd just sell it and get stinking rich and become a filthy fat capitalist and have a crowd of crazy mixed-up Jazz addicts begging me for a free smoke.

We bought some candy floss, pink and silky, it looked so attractive it seemed a shame to eat it, and I disguised myself by using it as a beard and Liz laughed, and after she'd eaten hers she had a bright pink stain around her mouth and it looked as if she'd just finished a marathon necking session.

"I haven't been to a fair for years," Liz said, wiping her mouth. "Isn't it wonderful? Boy, what escapism. I'll have to come every week."

"You should. It'll do you the world of good," I advised her.

Then she stopped walking and stood quite still. The Noah's Ark started up and the shrill, neurotic music pierced our ears. Liz looked at me with child-like eyes. "It'll never be like this again. Never," she said in a quiet voice.

"Let's go on the bumper cars!" I shouted to her, and grabbed a white car for myself and a red one for Liz. I can even remember the colours. I pressed down on the accelerator and away I went, racing and bumping and turning and laughing, trying to find Liz's car. There it was, all red and shiny, and Liz looking deadly serious, afraid that someone would bump her, and when they did she forced a laugh but she didn't like it all the same.

We had another Cherryade in another snack bar (to hell with the expense!) and this time we seated ourselves at a table and told each other how we were enjoying it all and wasn't the bumper cars smashing and the Ghost Train frightening? A puzzled clutter of conversation with laughter and trying to talk over each other and Liz all eyes and wet lips.

Two fairground types came over and sat next to us. The cat nearest Liz was hardly older than her, with large sensitive eyes that had a showing of mascara on them. His fair hair was combed straight back and his unhealthy white face showed up even paler against his companion's sunbrowned features.

"I couldn't believe it when I found out that you'd taken over the mit-reading box. I thought all palmists were Gipsies," said the suntanned man.

The serious-looking youth eyed him nervously. "Gipsies are out! Remember we're entering the Atomic Age. Punters want science not superstition. I've got the best flash in the whole gaff. Tony Graydon, South Africa's youngest authority on the hand. The old girls fall for it hook, line and sinker. I bag the straight punters for a caser, and the mugs I gazump for what I can get."

"I saw the edge around your pitch this afternoon. You were 'avin' a burster," the other man said.

"I'd better be going back," said South Africa's youngest authority on the hand, gulping down his tea. "Can't afford to lose anything. It's going to be a long winter."

We went into the photographer's saloon to have our photograph taken together, because the only ones we had with both of us on had Canvey Island in the background. The photographer had a well-cut suit on and a smile that never left his face. We had the choice of putting our heads through a number of holes, which would make the picture look as if we were a couple of fat ladies doing the can-can, a nurse with a baby (that would be rubbing things in a bit too far), or two sailors. We chose the sailors, and the photographer told us not to be so serious and cheer up and look as if we were enjoying ourselves and we grinned like a couple of overfed gorillas. Then he asked us if we wanted the small set or the large set, so I asked him how much they were, and he told me that the small set was ten shillings as you get four double weight highly glossed large postcard-sized photographs, but

I told him it was too much money, so he let me have two and charged me a dollar. I still have that photograph.

We walked through the lanes of hoopla and shellfish stalls together with the big-breasted chicks with "Can I do you now, sir?" and "Hot stuff from Paris" splashed across their paper hats, past the patient queue for the motor boats, with a loudspeakered voice telling everyone that their time was up and to bring their boats in, by the House that Jack Built, with its crazy angles pointing in all directions, laughing past the Rotor and its pictures displayed outside showing chicks stuck to the wall with their skirts high above their heads.

Why can't the world be a fairground? We'll make sure we don't fall off the rides but we'll enjoy ourselves just the same. When we're one short of sixty-five at the dart stall we'll not complain, and if we've been sports they'll still give us a prize. We'll come home skint but we shan't worry for we've had our money's worth. What value we've had! Laughter, fun and thrills — things that are hard to find outside the range of this wonderfully idiotic music. And it's all so healthy. I envied those that were employed in it. I wanted to be a part of it, to be amongst it all the time, on the right side of those turnstiles, to lock myself in, never leaving the laughing, happy throng.

As we walked back towards the station, arm in arm, my mind was full of thoughts about Liz and me when we were kids and shit our pants and everything. When we lay together in the cold, damp, Anderson shelter, awake in the middle of the night, hearing each other breathe but afraid to say anything in case our mum gave us a good hiding, while the gunfire cracked and spluttered above our heads. When the sky was full of unknown and terrible things; bombs and planes and shrapnel and barrage balloons... all from the sky. Americans with chewing gum bringing a strange new world of plenty briefly into our lives. Saying good-bye to my best friend who was being evacuated to Wales, but I wasn't going; my mum wouldn't part with me. Fitting our gas masks on for the first time. Screaming the house down... horrible smell of rubber... suffocation... no!

126

The war is over! Everyone get drunk and have street parties, with trestles and jelly and dancing and a microphone on a stage where people sing, but not everyone; some are crying. Fireworks, too. *Pleasant* bangs and lights in the sky. The war is over! Surely we'll all have a banana soon? V.E., V.J., V. everything! Even soldiers returning with V.C.s and V.D.

Liz! You're lumbered like me. Lumbered with this whole rotten world. *We're perfect* if the world will let us be. It's you and I that have to fight, if we don't we haven't a chance. Let's *do* something, Liz. Let's *do* something about you being a Gentile. Let's scream our defiance full-voiced, with all our energy, till we drop to the ground with exhaustion. Don't let them get away with it, Liz! Let me go to the parents of your lover and tell them there's no difference between their son and myself except I haven't had my schnickel cut. Show yourself to the Rabbi and cut your arm so that he can see that your blood is red also. For *Christ's* sake, Liz, don't let them get away with it!

But you won't do a thing, I know you won't. You'll let them do as they damn well please, because you're an ignorant, stupid, masochistic fool. They'll put you here and throw you there but you won't care. They'll piss on you and you'll probably drink it. Wake up, Liz!

And when you're dead, I'll come to your funeral and bring fields of flowers and lay them on your grave, but they won't be of any use to you. I'll be crying but *your* tears will never end. They'll flow into the River of Tears forever. And you'll scream and knock your head against walls because it'll be too late, all over, finished.

You'll be *dead*, Liz!

That's the funniest thing I've heard," Popper said, taking a bite out of his large, creamy, sickly-looking cake. "You at a Fun Fair, and with your sister as well. You're a strange one, Squire, you are. Dancing round the juke box, you say? Lord have mercy! I bet you got your kicks."

"As a matter of fact I did," I said, not feeling in the least bit embarrassed. "Haven't enjoyed myself so much for ages."

"You must have been on a weird one, you really must. You say this happened this afternoon? You don't look too gone to me."

"Haven't had a smoke all day long," I told him with a trace of boastfulness in my voice.

"Really?" my junkie friend said, sounding interested. "What's it now? Bennies, L.S.D., or nems?"

"Are you kidding? I wouldn't touch that stuff if you paid me to. Come now, do I look the type?"

"People don't look the type, they just are. You were either made for it psychologically or you're not."

"I can assure you, I'm not."

He ordered another cream cake and a cup of tea, which he put at least five spoonfuls of sugar into, then relaxed again on the very unrelaxing seat that he'd been sitting on. He looked a lot sharper than he usually did, and it was obvious that he'd been buying new drag: a shining light raincoat that promised to look different in about a week's time, and an imported Yank suit (so he told me), not one of those I've-just-arrived-from-New-York NY looking ones, but a member of the neat and expensive variety usually worn by Stan Kenton or an advertising manager.

"Listen, Squire, don't sound too sure of yourself. You know how people can smell a copper from a mile off? Well, it's the same for me as far as would-be junkies go," Popper said, wiping the cream moustache that he had around his mouth.

"Now we're on the junk. Who mentioned that? I thought you were talking about girls' tablets. Man, don't ever associate the white stuff with me. That's completely out as far as I'm concerned. I'm scared stiff of needles anyway."

"I used to be as well — petrified of the damn things I was. It's fine now — since I've had a bit of practice."

"What's it really like, being a junkie, Pops?" I asked him.

"Don't *you* start. You sound like one of those poxy journalists. Every time you meet one they're on you like a ton of bricks asking a thousand questions. I couldn't even answer them if I tried."

"Why not?"

"Because I can't remember what it was like *before* I was hooked. They ask you stupid bloody questions like, 'How's your sex life?' And I tell them, fine — when I lay off the junk. They get me so mad that I offer to sell them a fix so that they can see what it's all about for themselves. That soon gets rid of them."

By the way, we were in a coffee bar. A dirty Soho one called The Liggery, where the strangest mixture of human beings gathered together to fix up deals that never materialise, to talk about their painting and writing and a whole gang of other things, but I'm afraid they talk more than they create. Dusty had me promise never to pass its broken doors, as a high percentage of the inmates would sell their own crippled Granny for a night's kip or a glass of Merrydown. There was a feeling of suicide every time you went into the place, and something unsafe and frightening to those that weren't on the skippers kick.

"But if I really let them in on the junkie world," Popper continued, "they'd be terribly disappointed. Do you know I even feel that they think it's *romantic*, I mean the ones that don't take in the 'confessions' rubbish. They see it as one long kick, a swinging life of pops and happiness and escapism. It knocks me out, that does. Really, it's nothing more than one big waiting in a quack's waiting-room, and when you get inside, a constant battle for keeping your script. To try and fanny someone that's cuter than you are, who's had years of your type and knows exactly how to deal with them. At first you think you can throw any old cobblers at them, but they know you, man, they know more about the thing than you ever will. And they've got just the right answers for you, too. The head shrinker's your enemy, not the junk. The means of getting it, not when you've got it. And when the horrors poke their ugly face around the corner, they're always asso-ciated with that so-called understanding person that writes on those sexy pieces of paper that you take to John Bell and Croyden."

"It must be a drag," I sympathised, offering him a snout.

"No, it's not, I don't mind. I don't like my doctor, that's true, but that's only because she's so big-headed about eve-rything, and tells me how fortunate I am to live in such an understanding country such as England, where they don't throw their junkies in a padded cell to have a cold turkey, and I ought to kiss her smelly feet for her kindness in let-ting me have some horse to poison myself with. Apart from that, it's fine. I look upon myself as a missionary or a monk or something like that, except my monastery is a little more attractive than theirs."

"It's different to what you read about junkies," I said.

"I thought you had more sense than to believe all that crap that's written about us. The same kind of shit is written about your Charge scene as well. It's not so bad when a doctor or trickcyclist does it, but when the poxy thing's written by someone that's supposed to have indulged, then it's a bloody sight worse. You believe them because they make it sound authentic. And even worse still are the writers that *do* write truth about a lot of things that they know about, but add Charge or the junk into their tale to give it a bit of variety."

"I see what you mean," I said. By this time I was really interested.

"Like I read a book once, called '*I Have Never Had A Min-ute's Peace Since I Became A Drug Fiend Eighty Years Ago.*' Well, it was called something like that, anyway. It was all about this fellow that was to be a preacher, but he managed to get him-self mixed up in bad company, and before you could say pop, he was well and truly hooked on about thirty killer drugs. He stole, lied, and cheated, and even sold his best friend's cat for a fix, and in the end, his girl friend, who reminded me very much of the Angel Gabriel minus the wings, locked him into a room for twenty-four hours. When she eventually opened up the door he emerged completely cured and a thoroughly respectable citizen. I ask you. You might as well buy a Mickey Mouse annual."

I'd never heard him speak like this before. I'd not had much conversation with him in the past as Dusty didn't like me to mix with addicts, but the few times I had been in his company I'd never heard him speak about his habit much, except that now and again he'd boast that the junk had never stopped him eating or sleeping or waking or walking, like it did to most of his clan. He had it under control he told everyone, not the heroin but his life. He wasn't one of those sick people that locked themselves in their pad twenty-four hours a day, or spewed every five minutes, or didn't wash for a week. No, the junk was the master of him, but he was the master of his life.

The Liggery was quite crowded by now, and the smell of sweaty bodies was really strong, I'm not kidding either. Quite horrible, in fact. Anyone wearing a clean shirt was stared at very unfriendly like by the rest who seemed to object to the person's presence even. The female section was as bad as their opposites. A cat must be very kinky to want to climb into bed with those duty dolls. They were hitch-hiking across the continent, pep tablets and trad-dogs, with a uniform of dirty jeans, overgrown sweater, I'm-from-Soho sandals and ballet make-up to prove it. They all had the best of intentions to start with, I'm sure, but we have to understand that all great artists are never successful, so how can they afford to change their under-clothes every week?

Popper's black pin-head eyes darted quickly around the smoky, smelly scene before him, giving everyone a hostile look. "This place stinks!" he suddenly shouted out so all could hear. "Why don't they instal some sanitation in this layabouts' lodging house?" Everyone returned his hostile looks but didn't take offence as it was too much bother for them to do that. "People make me laugh," he said, like he was talking to himself. "They call *me* sick. That's funny, that is. If I'm sick I don't know what you'd call these species of animal life. They're not even human. I'd put my name down for the suicide stakes express post, if their bug found it's way in me. I wouldn't mind if they *did* anything, but they don't. At least I hustle with my prescription and work the poor helpless drug addict one on a few kinky old ladies, but they're static, man, stopped and finished."

It was getting dusk, so the disher-up of tea came from behind the counter bringing his bright ginger beard and heavy body with him and started to put a match to the candles on the plain wooden un-scrubbed tables, so that the customers (I'm referring to about half the people in the place) could try and read their books that I'm sure most of them couldn't understand a word of. I couldn't understand the titles of most of them. Dig this. This will slaughter you. They even had their own astrologer in the place! A grey-haired cat, tall and slim, who if he appeared in *What's My Line?* would be guessed straight away without the panel having to ask him any questions. He does nothing but write in books all the time, looking very busy and wise, checking on charts and looking quite gone, but I'm sorry to have to tell you that I've never yet seen him have a client. Perhaps he's working out where he's going to sleep that night!

"What are you doing here?" I heard a voice behind me say.

I spun around and much to my surprise it was none other than my partner in crime, Dusty Miller.

"I've been trying to get you on the phone all afternoon, where have you been?" he asked me all in one breath.

"To Battersea," I answered him.

"Since when have you been interested in gas works and dogs' homes?" he asked critically.

"Never. Fun Fairs. I've had a ball on the roundabouts and they've the biggest Big Wheel that I've seen in my life."

He seated himself down between Popper and myself and took his best and only shortie overcoat off and threw it on a vacant seat. "I know it's your money and all that," he went on, "but don't come the big rich business tycoon with me. You've got to do your share of the graft as well, you know."

"But I didn't know that we were going to start today," I told him.

"He didn't know that you were going to start today," joined in Popper, who didn't have the faintest idea what we were talking about.

"Start today? We've finished," Dusty said to me, ignoring Popper.

"What do you mean?" I asked him.

"I've sold the lot! The whole pound weight's been got rid of, thanks to me and my efforts on your behalf. Come into the carzy."

I followed him into the place that they call a toilet, which would have been a sanitary inspector's delight if he was in a bad mood, and Dusty straight away pulled a very sexy wad of crisp pound notes out of his pocket. I don't think I'd ever seen so much money, except perhaps when I'd been to the bank for some change for the shop, and seen a clerk counting out lots of luscious lolly in a Charlie Chaplin way.

"Is that ours?" I asked, not being able to take my eyes off that wonderfully inspiring sight.

"Thanks to me, yes. One hundred and twenty-eight pounds, minus seventeen and fourpence expenses. Eight quid an ounce, that's what I got. It went like water in the Sahara Desert as there's been this drought on since Danny quit the scene. Don't think this is going to happen every day because it's not. But the important thing is that we're established. From now on it'll be sure and steady."

"But that's just great. I can hardly believe it," I said, with my mind full of thoughts about how I was going to spend this fortune.

"I had to go over to Miss Roach's pad myself today to pick up, and I didn't appreciate it, I can assure you. If I have to go alone again she's sure to tumble."

"It won't happen again, Dusty. You can count on that," I assured him.

He then counted out thirty-eight pounds which was my share of the profit, giving himself the same and keeping back another fifty to buy a pound weight with so that we could start all over again. He told me that he'd already fixed everything up with Ayo and that he was collecting from him the next day at noon.

I felt like a millionaire. I wanted to go to Cecil Gee and buy half their stock up or something crazy like that. This was two months' wages from Down & Co, Mr Cage, look out! If I meet you now I'm sure to land myself in nick on an assault charge. Oh wonderful, sexy, healthy, handy money! I knew we were always meant for each other. Let's stay friends forever and keep turning each other on to the other's company. I'm happy with you if you feel the same about me. Let's wander through life together and comfort each other. There'll never be another friend like you.

"What do you want? A tea or something?" I asked Dusty as we returned to Popper.

I treated us all to a tea and two cream cakes for Popper, who thanked me no end and asked if I'd come into a fortune or something. I wanted to tell him everything, to brag about it, to flash my dirty great roll of spondoolix to the whole coffee bar, and tell them that you have to be a real hustler to earn loot like this, and to pay for everyone's kip at Rowton House that night. But I restrained myself.

The only thing that is to be recommended at The Liggery is the juke box, I mean the records on the juke box. It has its fair share of razamataz and even a few pops, but it also brags a number of discs that are musical. Popper put on a Parker who was playing a swinging *Dancing in the Dark* with a whole line of violins and harps and things. Blowing mad — wriggling in and out of the strings like an eel — saying to the square lady violinist, "*I'm* technical too and I swing like crazy!" Echoes of the Bird in flight — high in the heavens — telling the world...

"What's happening tonight?" Dusty asked me, admiring the new shirt he'd bought himself from C Gee's.

"Bunty's happening tonight," I told him.

"You're becoming quite a little Romeo in your own quiet way, aren't you? Whatever happened between you and Miss

Roach the other night certainly impressed her. She talked about nothing else but you when I visited her today. How's Bunty and the Spiritualist lark getting on?"

"Spiritualism, did I hear you say? Are you in that game, too?" Popper asked me with his voice full of interest.

"It's not a game. It's a very serious thing," I said.

"A friend of mine's in it as well. He makes a bomb out of it. He even has a black mass every month. Perhaps I can introduce you to him sometime. He's a very good contact as far as the spook one's concerned."

"I'm not interested in black masses," I told my addicted acquaintance.

"I see," he said, "you're only interested in the straight stuff. I bet you get those merry widows really at it when you perform. How's trade?"

"There isn't any trade. I'm not even a practising medium. In fact, the novelty has worn off a bit now. I hardly ever go to a meeting these days."

"Silly boy. Keep it up. There's a fortune to be made in it if you play your cards right."

The buzz of conversation around us was working itself up to quite a noise. The crowd could relax now — the day was falling into night, which was definitely more *them*. Gone was the sun with all its harshness and squint-making. Night was the time for artists to tap the fountain of inspiration — but all these seemed to be doing was sip black coffee. But they could talk better, and talk they did. Discussions on painting and politics and poetry and Jazz were being thrashed out amongst the bare floorboards and filthy cups by bearded children with their minds crammed with being different from the rest.

"Don't give me all that Yankee stars and stripes nonsense," I overheard one angry young man say to another. "They're invading our soil and we're their forty-ninth state. America the unbeatable, that's what's planted in your distorted mind. Just because a musician is a Yank he's great, according to you. If a few of our boys were born in the States they'd be classed as first-grade Jazzists, but because they've a Cockney accent it's taken for granted that they're nothing more than poor imitators. Fuck America, that's what I say!"

A tall, lean youth, with spectacles in front of his shifty eyes, and a pair of suede Cossack boots on his enormous feet, came through the door and surveyed the scene with interest. It looked as if his dowdy, dark duffle-coat that he had slung around him like a shawl, had acted as a blanket on many a park bench, and the dirt on his shirt was caused not by crawling under a car, but he'd forgotten he had to take it off occasionally and wash it; that it was a permanent part of him that was unremovable, like his arms and legs.

He spotted Popper and pushed his way through the maze of tables and chairs and people's long legs. When he reached our table he leaned over me and whispered something in Popper's ear. The junkie's face was expressionless, then suddenly it came to life. He didn't look pleased.

"*Narcotics* you say your friend wants?" he shouted out aloud. "*Narcotics?* What are they? Go and tell your friend to do his grassing elsewhere, or I'll punch your friend's friend right out of this smelly place!"

The booted youth didn't need telling twice. He was out of the coffee bar before you could say 'Copper's nark.'

"It's just occurred to me that there's one very nice thing about being a registered junkie," said Popper, with a smile across his sickly white face.

"What's that?" Dusty said.

"When it's time to pick up the ration, I walk up to a uniformed bogey and ask him the way to the nearest chemist shop as I want to purchase my heroin and other dangerous drugs. The poor fellow just don't know what to do, and I've been whipped along to the station more than once, I can tell you. And when I get there, is that poor bastard policeman's face red when I show the desk sergeant my script? I suggest to the constable that I'm a naughty law breaker, and he falls for it like a ton of bricks."

This really wigged Dusty. He gave out a laugh that made even the most disinterested face look around at him. "What I wouldn't do to be able to make that one," he said in amongst his laughter. "That's what I call crazyotic!"

"Rumour has it that you two have started pushing," Popper said to Dusty and myself quite casually.

"Rumour has it right," Dusty said, sounding very business-like. "We've the music world tied up already, but that's just the start. I have plans to move in properly soon. We'll have the whole town under control before long. We've the Charge and we've the ambition. What more do we want?"

"Tact," Popper replied.

"What do you mean?" Dusty asked, sounding slightly concerned.

"I should keep your ambitions restricted to the musicians if I were you. Don't try and conquer too many fields. Jumbo over there knows about you already, and he's not the sort of cat that will stand by and watch you take any of his business away from him."

Popper was referring to a just about young, nearly old cat sitting in the corner, who was reading a *Superman* comic. He had a clean shirt on and a tie as well, but his hair was long and cut in a Boston style, which by the way went out with Dixieland Jazz. His clothes were of the post-war American style, all flash and larey, ice-blue gabardine, twenty-inch bottom slacks as well. Every now and again he'd glance up from his comic and stare at us in a corny movie way, like he was a spy from a non-existing country. He looked a right villain.

Dusty looked annoyed. "Jumbo's kicked too many people around in the past, but he's not going to do the same to me. There's plenty for everyone."

"That's what Jumbo says," Popper said quietly. "But he wouldn't welcome the sound of your voice when you talk about taking over the whole town. He can be very unpleasant when he wants to be and I wouldn't like to get in his way, I don't mind telling you. The trouble with him is his temper. You know what happened to the shoobly-doo when he tried to hustle in on Jumbo's clubs. He left London and returned to the BWI double quick. Jumbo means business and he's been around longer than most of us. When the Charge hit the scene in a big way in '48, he was there at the off. So take my advice and stay away from him. It'll be a lot healthier."

He finished his tea and prepared to leave. "I've got to get to my quack's before she cuts out. I'll catch up with you later," he said. Then he made tracks to the door, giving everyone a filthy look on the way.

A couple of minutes after he'd left we realised that the black notebook that was ligging on the table must be his, so I picked it up to return it when I saw him next. I looked through it first, as there's nothing more that I enjoy than looking at other people's notebooks and diaries. Nosy bastard, aren't I? I must be the nosiest person I've ever met. But at first I thought that there was nothing written in it, so I was very disappointed, but when I turned to about the middle page, the following was written in untidy handwriting:

Brenda is Dead!
She is no more.
A 1,000,000,000 pops away
perched high on a crooked star
chained to the earth by
too many memories.
Is She a Bishop yet?
Stopped by an acre of hypoforest
and a snowstorm of Snow
trapped by

That was all.

"It doesn't even rhyme," Dusty said. "I don't understand that cat at all. I don't suppose anyone does."

"Who is this Jumbo fellow, anyway?" I asked.

"He's just a dealer, but he thinks he owns all Soho. He's not a bad cat really. Just let's say he's a bit greedy. Can't stand to see anyone else earn a living, that's what's the matter with him. If anyone tries to give him a little competition he gets nasty, and a little violent as well. He's always going into nick, and when he comes out he expects the person who's been serving his clients to cut out completely, to let him carry on where he left off."

"I hope we don't have any trouble with him," I said.

"You leave him to me. If he does cut up rough, I'll deal with him."

"I hope you will—'cause I won't."

Dusty puffed away at his cigarette, looking very sure of himself. "We won't have to wait long before he goes inside again. He can't stay out of that place for long. Then we'll be all right."

"I'd never wish nick on anyone, no matter how much I hated them."

"I'm not wishing it on him. But if he does happen to go inside, we can't see all his customers starving, can we? Whether Jumbo likes it or not."

As if he knew that we were talking about him, he got up from his chair and walked sailor-fashion towards us. Dusty managed to get the first word in. "How's it going for London's original dealer?" he asked him. I wasn't sure if there was a sarcastic ring in his voice or not.

Jumbo threw his heavy body down on to the seat which Popper had vacated. "Not too bad yer know. If it wasn't for a few greedy 'ounds everything would be awright."

"Greedy hounds, Jumbo? Don't tell me people are getting greedy with you? I thought you had this town tied up?"

Jumbo's eyes screwed up and looked at Dusty through splits. "They try, yer know, they try. The troubles is I 'ates gettin' rough, but nar and agin I 'ave to. I can't stand greedy 'ounds, they git on me wick. Oo's yer mate?"

"Just a friend, Jumbo, just a friend."

"Ee looks like a haddict."

Dusty smiled. "A whatict?"

"An addict," Jumbo said. I didn't say a dickey bird. "Can't stand haddicts," he went on. "Dangerous people, them. Get

yer in right shtook," He changed his conversation completely. "Nar look 'ere. I don't want yer muzzelin in on me territory. If yer do there's gonna be trouble, see? And I'd 'ate to
see yer boaf in the orspital."

Dusty sounded kind and benevolent. "Don't worry about
us, Jumbo my old friend, we're not interested in your business, we've got too many worries of our own."

"Make sure yer don't." That was about all. He dragged his
clumsy self away from the table and left us on our ownsomes.

I managed to get myself up from the chair, too. "I'll have
to blow," I told my Dusty friend. "Bunty will be waiting for
me."

"I'll walk down the road with you. I can't stand this place,
anyway."

The Soho streets were just the same. A sameness that never
alters. It has two faces. The day one, with its cosmopolitan
natives looking upon the scene as if it was an ordinary country village, not the notorious place it is. Shopping away in
Berwick Street market, and asking the prices of things before
they buy them. The same thing was happening in other vil-
lages all over the country. "What village do you come from?"
the Salop man would ask the Sohoite. "I live in the village of
Soho," would come the reply, "and I've never once got hit
over the head by a pig-tailed, opium-smoking Chinese gang-
ster, when I go out at night."

You don't notice the natives when its night face greets you.
You notice the daring explorers that come from Yankland
and the world past Baron's Court, who stand on its corners
waiting and praying that something will happen, but it rare-
ly does. And you can feel *their* tenseness in the air.

I started walking towards Bunty, leaving Dusty at the Re-
gent Palace.

I passed through the door of the U Club and Bunty appeared
from nowhere and planted a sloppy gin kiss on my face. Her
arms went around me like a pair of handcuffs. All the faces
looked around and some smiled and I was led into a corner

and pushed down on to a velvet chair before I knew where I was.

By the way, velvet's the thing to have in a place like the U and velvet they've got. Everywhere. Velvet all over the place. Really. Dark red velvet curtains and chairs and drapes and dresses, splashed here and there with a touch of gold; twenty-two carat, of course. Chandeliers as well, we mustn't forget the chandeliers, must we? The stink of cigar smoke and perfume and debutantes, and the cause of the stink as well. Dirty old men and clean young women, copies of last year's *The Queen* and *Punch,* undrunk double brandies that soon get picked up and find an accommodating mouth, tall girls, short girls and call-girls ligging all about the place. The poor people trying to sound rich and the rich people trying to sound poor. Frank Sinatra struggling to make himself heard from a one-speakered unit, but with a constant babble of accents you think only existed in mocking Yank films about the English as his competition. People swearing like troopers but making it sound so *nice.* A herd of multi-coloured poodles, looking like successful prostitutes, running all over the place, pissing up the legs of the chairs, while their owners (some of them look more like poodles than the poodles themselves) laugh it off by telling them they've been naughty little boys and girls.

"Oh darling, I'm *so* glad to get away from that horrible old Mayfair," I heard a frightfully frightful voice behind me say. I think it was a female voice but I'm not sure, as they all sounded the same to me. "Mayfair's absolutely *disgusting* since those—er—*women* have planted themselves on the streets. They ought to do something about it, they really should. It's absolutely *putrid.* I lived there for years, but I just *had to* escape. I've bought myself a *divine* little cottage in the mews just around the corner. It's simply *adorable!* Six beds, two diners and three lavs. Oh darling, Knightsbridge is *delightful.* All the best people live here you know. We get up to all sorts of *naughty* things like having pyjama parties — they're *shocking* – oh dear, yes. We had one last week and

141

young Lorna—you know the one, there's only *one* Lorna—actually stole a bottle of milk from my neighbour's doorstep. I told her it was *criminal,* but she didn't care. She's so *daring.* Of course I have to pay *a fantabulous* rent, but who cares? I can always tap dear Daddy for a few hundred when the wolf comes knocking at the door."

"I know what sort of wolf that is she's speaking about," Bunts said to me.

"What sort?" I asked her.

"Human. The legitimate ponce that flourishes amongst this tribe. I can see him now," she said, building up a picture in her mind. "He's usually young, but old enough to know better, dark hair that's plastered down to his big head, a homosexual background, but at last he's been saved, well, nearly, and he must always be popping across to the continent chasing after another French or Italian girl whom he never gets anywhere with. He must elope at least once a year to Gretna Green, or if the girl can afford it, South America, and his future father-in-law makes his daughter a Ward of Court, which saves him just in time. He must have been a soldier in one part of his infamous career, all the other services are out, and he must call himself an antique dealer, although he probably doesn't know the difference between a piece of Victorian to a piece of G-Plan furniture. He's always brushing with the law, but not for anything serious, just a bouncy cheque or something silly like that, and when he's done his time people look upon him like they did pirates in Elizabeth the First's time, sort of villainous but terribly romantic, and so they have a whip around for him to tide him over until he gets on his feet again to pounce on some other stupid deb."

"You seem to know a lot about it," I said, getting interested.

"I'm not clever. You can't help finding out these things if you hang around here for a while. You complain about suburbia, but there's no difference here. They're in just as big a rut as they are where your dear old mum lives."

"Can I get you a drink?" I asked.

"No, you can't. You sit down there. I'll buy you one. And by the way, where have you *been,* for heaven's sake? You've really been getting me at it. You could have been dead as far as I was concerned. It's very naughty of you, so don't ever let it happen again..." Then she was away to the bar to get the drinks, served by a midget of a queer who was very popular with everyone, and who wore tiny studs in his ears that drew comments from all the customers, which wigged him the most.

Bunty came back and sat next to me but before she could say another word, a woman, looking like some exotic bear because of the Persian lamb coat she was wearing, came over to us and clasped our hands like we were long lost friends whom she'd found after a twenty year search. I'd never seen her before. Some people believe that the owner gets to look like their dog after a few years. If that's a fact, this woman must have kept giant Pekingeses all her life. Her eyes as well. Horrible they were. Bear's body — peke's face. Oh fuck!

"So this is the young man you've been telling me about," with her peke's eyes inspecting me as if I was up for sale. I wasn't sure if she approved or not.

"Yes," Bunty said with pride. "Isn't he a darling?"

I couldn't make up my mind if they were deliberately trying to embarrass me, or whether my being embarrassed never entered their heads.

"I don't think I've had the pleasure of catching up with you before," I said to the peke-bear.

"Oh, what charming language," she said. "Catching up with me, you say? What fun!"

"This is Mrs Featherstonhaugh," Bunty told me. "Mrs Featherstonhaugh, meet my personal, private, angry young man."

Mrs Featherstonhaugh shook my hand again. "Angry young man, eh? A writer? I thought so. You can tell by his eyes."

"I don't write," I told her.

"You should. Everyone that's angry about something should write about it. The printed word is powerful."

I could do nothing but agree with her. About the powerful bit, I mean.

"I'm sorry I couldn't pop into your cocktail party last night, Isabella," Bunty said, sounding as if she couldn't care less about this old bag's cocktail party.

"You missed a treat," Mrs Feather... etc said. "*Everyone* was there. Even Lord Rowland. He's an absolute darling when he wants to be. There's no stopping him once he gets going."

I wondered what Lord Rowland got going *at*.

"Do-Do came as well. Dear, darling Do-Do, she's a dream of a woman, my dear. Secretary to the Prime Minister — mistress to the Leader of the Opposition — all that kind of thing. You can understand what I had to put up with." Without any warning she turned on me. "What are you interested in, Bunty's angry young man?"

I wanted to sound sharp. "Eating neck of lamb and listening to Jazz."

"How cute. It wouldn't be an expensive job fattening you up for Christmas. And Jazz, you say? What fun! I know a young fellow that plays one of those saxophone things. He looks *divine* when he's playing it, and intelligent, too."

"What's his name?" I asked.

"Joe Brown he calls himself. Not a very romantic name I agree. He's one of those coloured gentlemen."

"I know Joe myself," I said. "He's never struck me as being a gentleman, but he's certainly a great alto player. He's about the best alto since the Old Queen died."

"Which Old Queen?" Mrs Featherstonhaugh asked.

"I don't mean Charlie Parker anyway," I said.

Bunty laughed and Feather did the same, but she didn't know what at.

We talked a while. To tell you the truth I don't remember what about, so it's no good making things up, but there's one thing I *can* remember: it was very unimportant. I've always felt that words are unimportant sometimes. The thing

144

is, you've *got* to talk to be popular. That's what most people think, anyway. I don't agree. I can be with someone that I really like to be with and sometimes I don't think chatting about the weather is necessary, but the person I'm with thinks I'm bored or something, just because I don't keep rabbiting all the time. I wish people wouldn't think like that. The point is, you're *with* them. That's the thing that counts. Why can't you relax and enjoy them without a lot of words that don't mean much? Like when I was a kid I had a girl friend that I spent hours with without saying a word to, and neither of us felt awkward. I was terribly serious when I was a kid. When I kissed a girl I went all serious and solemn — not like now. I wish I could meet that girl again. She was great. Her name was Heather and she was the ugliest girl you ever did meet, but she was great. She kissed good too.

Well, anyway, I was polite to Mrs Featherstonhaugh and said 'yes' in the right places, but she soon got me down. She was so unimportant and she knew it. If you're unimportant and *don't* know it, it's not so bad. I couldn't help feeling sorry for her though. I feel sorry for all sorts of people, even if there's no reason to. I'll never change.

In the end we got rid of Mrs Featherstonhaugh and I managed to get Bunty on her own. We had a good chat but the first thing that she told me was that she was dying to get me into bed. I hated her telling me that. I don't know why, I just did. It's not that I didn't want to go to bed with her. I felt sexy and all that but she put me off. I suppose I'm a little old-fashioned and like to fight for it a bit. Not too much, though.

Then the owner of this little circus came over to talk to us and see how many drinks we were ordering. She has a peculiarity too common amongst club owners which always puzzled me. If you made a habit of patronising her club every day and spent a bomb there like some people do, you will never be appreciated, but if you walk in there occasionally and spend just a few shillings, she'd make a fuss of you and treat you with a lot more respect and civility than her regulars. Weird, isn't it?

145

She's a middle-aged woman who tries her damned hardest to look sophisticated, but doesn't quite make it. She possesses a fabulous body for her age, but I've been told that she doesn't look so pretty in the nude, when she discards all those womanly inventions that hide under her top clothes. She must spend a fortune at the hairdressers because nearly every time you see her she has a different, but always exotic hair style, which you can't help thinking is a wig. She'd be attractive if her face wasn't so bloody attentive. She's concentrating all the time on the person she's talking to and I know it's a horrifying thought but you can't help thinking that she can see through you whatever your game. Her name is Maggie Watling-Smith, but the rumour is whispered that the Watling part doesn't belong to her at all. (Isn't she naughty?). But then it would be very unhip, I mean very un-U to be lumbered with a name like plain Maggie Smith. The tale goes that she was cast into nick in her native land of Australia for running a call-girl racket, so after doing her time she came to the Mother Land and went semi-legit in opening this club of hers. I say semi-legit because although her establishment caters only for the *best* people (with a few villains to give the place a bit of colour), there was other things going on (I never found out exactly what they were) that put her in the honest but crooked class.

"It's so nice to see you again," she said to me, staring through a pair of spectacles that I'm sure had the crown jewels set in them. "You're quite a stranger. Where have you been all this time?"

"Around," was all I could think to say.

"And how's the Jazz world? Do you still *dig* it?" then she gave out a stupid giggle because I suppose she found the word 'dig' funny.

"I'm still listening," I said.

"You'll have to make him come and see us more often," she said to Bunty. "We need more handsome faces around."

Bunts started to get carried away. "I'd have him with me all the time if I had my way. I'd even chain him to my bed.

He's very naughty neglecting me like he does. Ought to be ashamed of himself."

I couldn't stand all that. I excused myself and went to the carzy for some fresh air. I sat down on the toilet seat and tried to make up my mind if I should cut out or not. I decided to hang on a little longer as I knew that Bunty would get all neurotic and I couldn't have all that. I'd always wanted to turn her on to the Charge as I was sure she'd turn out a gass if I did, but I couldn't get around to putting her wise to my scene. I don't know why. I just couldn't. I knew she wouldn't look down on it; she'd treat it as a huge joke and a *daring* thing to do, and when I came to think of it I realised that it was all down to her in the first place that I made friends with Harry, and she'd planted the first seeds to rescue me from all that outside and I'd still be at Down & Co now if it hadn't been for her, but somehow I resisted telling her.

I went back in again and had a good look around. Everyone was talking. They stopped for a while to let other people have a little go but they soon carried on again. I pushed my way through the crowd, stroking a few fur coats on the way, and found Bunty still with Maggie Smith and a few others. Bunty was looking like a *Vogue* model, with one foot forward showing the long line of her leg as far as it went. They were talking about themselves. What I mean is, when one of them spoke, the word 'I' was used far more than the word 'and'. Like a line of parrots in a bird talking contest they kept up a constant cackle, with a fair sprinkling of witty remarks usually made at a member of their own sex who wasn't in the present company.

Then I found myself chatting to this bearded cat who told me he lived for music. It was everything, he told me, and he was having a fix at the same time because a Chico Hamilton disc had found its way to the gram, quite by mistake, I can assure you. He was gone on Ravel and brought out a heap of scores from the briefcase he produced from somewhere to prove it, because there was Ravel's name written all over them. He wanted to compose. This cat, I mean. Writing some weird symphony, he was, for symphony orchestra, Jazz band and comb and paper, or something like that. I couldn't understand a word he was talking about but he didn't realise this as it was obvious he was having a ball telling me all about the *great* composers like this cat Ravel I was talking about and another one called Bartok and he thought Johnny Hodges was the greatest horn ever. That was plain enough but he didn't leave it at that. He went through the whole history of music every time he wanted to prove a point. I didn't mind though. He was serious about his ideas and I like serious people. Let's get some drama into life, for goodness sake!

I found myself alone with Bunty again. She was already on the way to being semi-stoned, because I suppose she'd taken set on the gin bottle before she came out.

"You've changed so much since I saw you at Dolly Diamond's circle," she said.

"So much has happened."

"I don't know if I prefer you as you are or like you were."

"I know the person I like best and it's certainly not that fellow six months ago."

"He had a strange and innocent charm about him. He's lost it now."

"Who the hell wants to be innocent? I'm not living in a dream world any longer. Things are *real* now — bright and clear. The place I thought was heaven is now the place that I'm in. I'm right up there, perched next to an angel that's relaxing on a shining white cloud. I'm even on the right hand side of God looking down on all the peasants that are slogging away in hell. And it's great."

"You're sounding very dramatic tonight. It's true what Mrs Featherstonhaugh said. You *should* write."

"Maybe I will. Maybe I'll write a book one day. But if I did they'd never believe me, if the truth had anything to do with it. But if I called it 'The Confessions of a Cocoa Fiend' it would be a best-seller."

"I don't understand a word you're talking about."

"No? Of course you don't."

I heard the bearded composer say to a bored-to-tears looking cat, "Stravinsky's *L'Histoire du Soldat* is another example." Maggie Smith was trying to hide her brandy glass behind the counter because she thought she may be left out of the next round with a full glass in her hand, and a pink poodle mis-aimed and pissed up Mrs Featherstonhaugh's leg.

Bunty was lushing away like mad. She ordered gin and tonic, telling the barman she'd mix her own tonic, so not to pour it out for her, then she poured the tonic into a flower pot. All this was because she didn't like to order a straight gin. "You *are* coming back with me tonight, aren't you?" she asked me, her knee touching mine.

"I'm afraid not, I'm anxious about my sister. I want to be home tonight."

"Not just for a little while? I'm forgetting what you feel like."

I told her it was impossible. When I left Liz at the station she was really upset. I wanted to go back with her but I couldn't. We'd had a ball and I didn't want to go and spoil it all by going back to that house with tear-stained floors. I wanted to help her but I could do nothing. Even her promising to buy only kosher chewing gum wouldn't do any good. I made up my mind to have a talk with her that night and try to *do* something.

Bunty said she'd drive me home, so we cut out, leaving Mrs Featherstonhaugh wiping her dress with a damp cloth.

When we reached the corner of my street Bunty drove into the side of the kerb. Thanks for the lift," I said.

"Don't mention it. I'm only sorry that a lift is all that I can give you."

I put my arms around her gently, but she grabbed me tight and directed a pair of wet lips on to my mouth. Her ginny breath nearly knocked me out. "You're *terrible,*" she said. "I'd like to eat you, eat you all up, all of you, yum-yum, to the last piece."

"You're a horrid old seducer of young boys. I'll report you to the police," I said teasingly. "You took my virginity, now you want to run my life. Bad, naughty old woman."

"Don't call me that," she said a little seriously. "Don't ever call me old, I'll get annoyed."

"I like old women," I said. "I don't feel embarrassed with them. And you're the cause of it, you ought to be ashamed of yourself. Still, I enjoyed being raped by you."

"Liar! You raped *me*. You did, you know you did, tell the truth, come on, you raped *me*!"

"All right, if you say so. Good night. I'm going. I'll bell you." I kissed her gently. "Good night, seducer of the young,"

As I reached the garden gate, brightly painted, and to the side of it a board telling the world that my father was a painter and decorator and he gave estimates free, I noticed that the front room light was on. To those of you who haven't had the misfortune of knowing all about this sacred place in a suburban household, I think I ought to wise you up. The front room is somewhere that you mustn't set foot in if you haven't a very good reason for doing so. It is the holy of holies where all the best furniture is displayed like it was up for sale in a showroom, cleaned and polished every day although it doesn't need it, and talked about as if it was a storehouse for the world's most valuable art treasures. The most prized thing in the room is the piano, which although it shines with polish is never tuned, and when someone that can play comes into the household, they are immediately pushed into the front room and given the honour of playing this musical monstrosity which is regarded as a magical thing and must be talked about with pride, but when the person *is* playing it, nothing swinging could ever be the result even it was the Mad Monk himself pushing down the notes, as the middle C is by now the middle D. The front room is a place which is only used at Christmas or birthdays or some similar orgy, that's why when seeing the light on in it at midnight, it really surprised me.

I quickly walked up the path, pushed the key into the lock, opened the door, and there before me was a woman I'd never laid eyes on before. I informed myself that she couldn't be one of Liz's friends as she wasn't exactly in the same age group as her. She'd be a friend of my mother's, if anything. I didn't like the look of her eyes. They looked frightened.

"Who are you?" she asked me.

"That's just what I was going to ask you," I said, forcing a smile at the same time. "I'm the son of the house," I added, sounding as if my dad owned a castle. "What's happening, anyway? Are you a friend of my mother's?"

She didn't look good, man, in fact I thought she was going to faint or something. She was sweating like mad and her face was as red as an embarrassed virgin's. Her mascara had run and it made black smears around her eyes and she looked as worried as a man that had won the football pools but hadn't posted his coupon. She wore a dirty white apron that bulged in the wrong places with unwanted flesh.

"You must be her brother then?" she managed to get out. Then she said it. "I'm afraid your sister isn't very well. She..."

I didn't wait for any more. I rushed into the front room and there was my Liz half lying on the put-u-up, looking as ill as I'd ever seen anyone look. I thought she was just about to die. Honest, I'm not exaggerating. Her face wasn't just white, it was blue as well (*yes, blue!*) and she'd been crying so her eyes were red and all around them were terrible black rings and I got the horrors like I'd never had them before.

Then I dug the horrible scene around her. On the table by the put-u-up was an ugly black rubber syringe with a bulb-like thing on the end of a tube. Next to that was a bowl of soapy water tinged with the slightest shade of pink, a wad of cotton wool, a bottle of Dettol and a pair of rubber gloves.

When Liz saw me she gave out a moan and started to cry again; loud sobs and strange noises like I'd never had the misfortune to hear before. I rushed over to her and she flung her arms around me and I felt her heart beating wildly against

151

mine and she cried out, "Help me! Please! Oh please help me!"

Then I realised what had happened, but I wouldn't accept it, I couldn't; but it was true.

"Why did you let her do it to you, Liz?" I said, and I felt tears in my eyes. "Whatever made you do it?"

I was still holding her close to me and I looked out of the corner of my eye and there was the woman. "You'd better leave her to me. I know what's best in times like these," she said, sounding very unsure of herself.

I let go of Liz and the next thing I knew I'd punched that woman's rotten face with all the strength I could find. She went sprawling across the room and her head hit against the piano and it gave a flat, organ-like note that sounded strangely horrible. She quickly got up and went tearing out of the room before I could aim another blow at her.

Liz was bent over with pain. I never realised before that you can *see* pain, but there it was all over my sister's face. It was all screwed up and her mouth was open showing her white teeth and gums. She was wearing a nightdress which was exposing one of her tiny breasts, but she didn't care. All she cared about was pain. Shooting, stabbing, crippling, never-ending pain. I led her back to the put-u-up and laid her down on it as gently as I could, then I was out of the room to look for that shitty cunt of a woman. I found her packing away some of her murderous paraphernalia into a small suitcase. "Have you called a doctor?" I shouted to her.

She was half afraid that I was going to kick her in the teeth, so she drew back from me. "No, not yet," she said awkwardly. So I ran to the phone and lifted the receiver. She didn't like that at all. She wasn't afraid of me now because she came right over to me with a very sorry look on her face. "Don't call an ambulance," she begged. They'd bring the police if you do."

"That's exactly what I want them to do. Nothing will give me greater pleasure than to see you carted off by the law."

That did it. She grabbed my arm and shouted in my ear, "Please don't call the police! I did it for your sister! She wanted me to. Please!"

Then I heard Liz calling my name, so I put the receiver down and went back in the room to her. Although she was on the verge of passing out she seemed to know what was going on. At first she begged me not to call an ambulance but I soon made it clear to her that nothing she said or did would stop me from doing so. Although I didn't know too much about this sort of thing, and still don't, come to that, I knew that Liz was in a bad way and would have to see a doctor sooner or later if she didn't die beforehand. In the end she gave way on the condition that I wouldn't tell them the truth but instead make up a story that she'd been pregnant and had fallen down the stairs. The woman was listening to all this very intently and when she realised what the score was she swallowed it and I never saw her again. I belled the ambulance, telling them what had happened (I should say told them what Liz told me to say), and then went back to Liz. "They shan't be long now, Lizabeth. Everything's going to be all right," was all I could think of saying. I held her hand and wiped the perspiration off her forehead with my handkerchief, then said, "We should be at dear old muddy Canvey Island now, you know."

"Playing Bingo and watching the open air concert party," she managed to say.

"I wish we *were* there, Liz."

"I don't."

"Why not?"

"Because I wouldn't have been able to go to Battersea Park with you this afternoon, and I *did* enjoy myself so much."

The minutes dragged like hours and I was calling the Ambulance Service all the lousy names under the sun, but when they did arrive they were so understanding and gentle and kind I knew Liz would be all right now. The driver asked if I would go along with her and before I could get a word in she'd said, "Please come with me. I'll feel better if you're there," so I followed them out to the waiting ambulance and away we went to the hospital.

III

CIRCLE

CANVEY ISLAND HAS A LONELY LOOK. Its prom, its main roads and side streets can be swallowed up by people—yet, it still looks lonely. It tries hard to look like a holiday resort, but fails. There aren't enough buckets and spades and fat ladies on postcards in the shop windows. The people seem to be struggling to have a good holiday; they've got to enjoy themselves because this is the only chance they've got. A whole year of scrimping and scraping so that they can have their precious week. Rain or shine, they've *got* to have a good time, and if they can manage a sun-tan to show off with when they get back, then they don't mind being chained to a machine for another twelve months.

When I think back to my childhood visits, all I can remember is panic. Panic to get ready and pack, panic to catch the train, to get to the beach, to meals, to get a seat on the roundabout, to bed, to get up. And panic to catch the train back again. They must talk about it for the next twelve months because that gives them encouragement to live another twelve months, so that they can get back there next year. When it comes around again you go back to that same bungalow that you've had for twenty years because the lady that owns it is so nice.

My mum's bungalow was called 'Seaview', but you couldn't view the sea because of the sea wall. It was in this bungalow that she received the telegram from the hospital informing her that they had her daughter as a patient, so, as you can guess, both her and her husband came rushing back from their holiday minus a sun-tan, but with the crack-up horrors instead.

I met them at the station to escort them to the hospital, and as I was waiting for them to arrive, I tried to imagine how they'd take it. I thought they'd be doing their nuts a bit, but they turned out surprisingly placid. My mum's face was very white and there were cry-marks around her eyes, but she was very quiet and she didn't even ask me any questions about Liz. My dad seemed much more polite than he usually did, and he had a strange air of authority about him: like he was telling himself that this was the time when a father can act like a father and be the strong pillar of the family.

I'm sorry, but all this seemed rather funny to me. They looked two very comical figures when they got off the train — something like Charlie Chaplin does when he's had a bad time of it. And when we reached the hospital we all sat in the waiting-room for mum and dad to see the Matron so that she could explain everything to them, and it really was a funny scene, my mum doing her knitting — one row and a look at the Matron's door — another row and another look at the door — row, door, row — oh dear! Then a quiet sob soon followed by an 'I-must-be-brave' look. I would have given anything to have been able to have been in that Matron's office with them, but they wouldn't let me in. But it so happened that dear old Matron didn't use that nasty word abortion at all. I don't know if the doctors had dug the scene or not, but anyway, you know how human that clan can be. It was just a case of being up the spout and falling down the stairs.

When we reached home that evening (leaving Liz and her bed covered in fruit, sweets and mags), a fog of depression filled the house and mum gave a Shakespeare-like speech about what a silly little fool Liz was, and why hadn't she confided in her as that's what mothers are for, and who was this brute of a man that put her poor innocent daughter in the family way, and whatever happened we must not breathe a word about it to anyone as the neighbours might find out.

I felt like running out of the house and telling all the neighbours myself. Tell them that my sister was in love, and because she was in love she'd shown it by doing the only natural thing. But now she was in hospital, and she could have died, and if she had died it was only them to blame because it was through them that she'd hired a professional killer to do filthy things to her. My Liz was pure — they weren't. My Liz was human — but they'd made her think like an animal. And I vowed there and then to myself that these ticket-takers must never make me think like that, because if they did I knew I wouldn't have any more respect for myself. But it's not as simple as all that. Nothing is simple. Everything's so damn complicated it doesn't bear thinking about. Everything's ridiculous — even Liz herself — because she was the other part of that woman that had snuffed God's life out like a candle.

I sat there listening to my mother go on and on and I wanted to run, run like mad out of the room and keep on running until I dropped to the ground so tired that all I could do is sleep. Sleep for years and years and perhaps never wake up.

It was no use talking, because if I did I knew there would be a scene. My mother *wanted* a scene so that she could get all her nasty frustrations out of her. She wanted my father to say something — anything that she could have a go at, but he was too cute, he'd lived with her for years and knew her, or perhaps knew people, and then I realised that he wasn't a lunatic after all. At that moment I admired him but I didn't respect him. I admired him because he wasn't saying anything, and the mere fact of his silence told me that he didn't think Liz was a prostitute. (I hate to admit this but that was the feeling I had in my mother's case.) But I didn't respect him because of his silence. I wanted him to stand up to my mother, to shout back, to punch her, even, to knock her to the ground and kick her in the teeth, to inform her that he'd snatched a bit before they were married and to ask her if she didn't enjoy it. But my dad remained silent.

Liz was in hospital a fortnight but I didn't get a chance to see her on her own during that time because mum was at the hospital during every visiting period. I went along with her a couple of times but it was always a very huge dragging-down session. I had the feeling we were visiting her not in a hospital—but a prison for dangerous women criminals. Little was said at these little scenes. Just a few, 'How are you feeling?' from mum, a cold, guilty stare from Liz, and an embarrassed look from me. Horrible, it was.

Then she came out, and it was me that met her, on my own as well, and I pushed her into a cab and stopped it at the first pub and brought her a brandy because she wasn't allowed to drink but I told her that brandy was a medicine so stop worrying. It was great to have her on my own again.

"Well, I really did it this time," she said when I got her seated.

"What do you mean?" I asked, taking a sip of my cider.

"All this. The silly mess I got myself in. Those neighbours have really got themselves something to talk about now."

As you can guess, I felt like punching her on the nose for saying that. But I restrained myself. I just said, "Don't mention the neighbours to me. You know how I feel about them."

"You've got to," she said. "For mum's sake." She looked a little guilty.

"You'll find out different one day."

She sat up higher in her chair, then started to run her finger around the top of her glass in a nervous manner. "I've been out of the hospital for twenty minutes," she said in a low voice, "just twenty minutes," glancing at her watch, "so I'm not in the mood for rows. Let's change the subject." She looked up at me. "I read once," she went on, "that everyone in prison spends the whole of their time in there thinking about themselves. Their lives, their mistakes, their loves. Hospital's something like prison, you know. Not so bad, of course. I thought about a lot of things—including you. Do you know something?"

"What's that?"

"You're my only pal. The only *real* person in my life."

And I felt embarrassed.

"Let's go," I said. "Mum'll be waiting."

When we reached home everyone was coldly polite to everyone else, not like a family somehow, like a meeting between

Churchill and Stalin. Mum and dad tried to act natural, but never put in a very good performance. Liz didn't help things: she had this Joan-of-Arc expression, which changed now and again to a defeated channel swimmer's. I sat there like a silent referee. Everything considered, the evening didn't go off too badly, and in a week things swung back to normal.

But, believe it or not, there was another happening that caused more tears and rows than even Liz's efforts did. That was when I left home. Yes, I packed my bag and made it out of that house once and for all. Don't let me kid you, it wasn't as easy as that by a very long way, but I had put in weeks of planning and preparing, then I whipped it on them.

Firstly I told them I'd left my job. That was as soon as they arrived back from the peasants' paradise, Canvey Island. They were even pleased about it as I told them that I'd managed to secure a very sought-after position as a junior sales rep for a firm of typewriter manufacturers in the city. So every day mum got me off for 'work' and I caught the train and met Dusty in Soho.

The "Dusty Miller Indian Hemp Company Limited" had been doing quite well on the Soho stock exchange, so we'd been picking up a sexy score a week each on the average, pushing ounce weights mostly and leaving the tiny packet trade to the other firms, as that branch of the business is very unhealthy if you want to stay around long and not have porridge for breakfast every morning. We had a nice little round worked up and we were responsible for a lot of the very swinging sounds that were being heard around the Jazz clubs, as we had practically all the musicians' trade to ourselves, thanks to our dear friend Ayo, who was still showing up with that Congo Brand No 1, and never once had he guzumped us with a mixture of bitter leaf, asthma cure and canary seed.

The big drag was getting up so early for 'work' and having to make an appearance again in the evening to tell my mum how many typewriters I'd sold and to eat my din-din up like a good little boy. I kept phoning her up at five-thirty to tell her that because I was saving up for a new suit I would be doing a spot of overtime, and she told all the neighbours that at last I'd found a job that I was interested in. Of course, she was perfectly right. But, man, I wanted to be free. *Really* free, I mean. To have a pad of my own and do as I pleased. I had loot now, so I could afford it, but I was determined not to rush things for a change and to goof as far as my old lady was concerned.

Then I put the second part of my plan into operation. I told her that I'd met a very nice chappy at work who lived by himself because he was an orphan (I knew that this would appeal to my mother's sympathetic nature), and I felt really sorry for him as he was so lonely. She nearly messed things up by offering him a home with us so that she could take over the mothering nonsense, but I quickly told her that he wouldn't dream of doing such a thing as he was *ever* so happy where he was, and anyway it was much handier for him to live where he did.

"As a matter of fact," I told her, "it's ridiculous to live this far out if you work in London. I travel three hours every day on that stuffy tube and it gets me down. Dusty, that's my friend's name, has asked me to share his room with him."

"That's a silly name for a man," she said.

"I suppose it is. He's asked me to share his room, you know."

"Has he?" my mother asked.

Then there was silence.

"Yes, he has. I'm thinking seriously about it, too. It would save all that unnecessary travelling."

My mum carried on with her knitting without saying a word.

"Don't *you* think it's a good idea, mum?" I persisted.

"What?" she asked.

"Sharing a room with my friend in town."

"Don't be so silly," she just said.

"But I'm going to. I've promised him."

She found it all very amusing. "I'd dread to see that room after you've been living in it a week. Why don't you get all those silly ideas out of your head? You're only a baby yet."

"But I'm going to, Mum. I've made up my mind."

She looked slowly up from her knitting and I could see that for the first time she was taking all this seriously. She tried to laugh it off again but when she realised that I meant it she went fucking mad. She did her hysterics act on me and for the first time in my life I heard her use bad language. I don't like remembering this so I won't go into all the morbid details but I can assure you that although I'd prepared myself for the onslaught it was a harder battle than I ever imagined it would be. She tried everything except violence to make me change my mind, but I was determined that whatever happened I'd go through with it. If I goofed this chance, I'd never get another. It wasn't easy, mind you. Seeing your own mother crying and breaking her heart in front of you isn't the best of sights, especially when you know that by just saying a few simple words would make her stop. But I did it. I held on for all I was worth and once I very nearly gave in, but I pulled through it somehow.

The next morning I left. It was like a funeral. There was I, struggling to carry my heavy suitcase through the door, with mum and Liz shedding tears like rain, dad remaining silent in the background and our dog Rinty howling like the Hound of the Baskervilles. Just as I was leaving, Liz called me into the front room without even getting permission.

"Keep in touch," she said in a tear-drenched voice.

"I'm not going to Australia, Liz, old girl. I'll see you every week."

"Thanks for everything," she said, as though she'd never see me again. Then she grabbed me and put a wet kiss on my lips which so surprised me I lost my balance.

So that was that. Although I felt thoroughly miserable, I couldn't help feeling relieved and happy as well. Relieved because it was all over and I was past the door, and happy because I was free from it all. I noticed that Old Mother Manley was peeping out of her curtain at me, and thinking what a horror of a son I'd turned out to be, leaving home and all. Nothing like her darling Young George who'd be ligging around her pad for ever and ever if she has her way. But Mrs Manley can go to hell now — so can all the other Mrs Manleys in the Kingdom of Suburbia. I was immigrating to a new and exciting land where things happen and people are individuals, not just a tribe like you are in prison. But one day I would return driving a modern Yank car that looked like something from Outer Space, with a bank roll so big I'd have to have an accountant to look after it for me, and I'd buy my family a cottage by the sea like they've always dreamed about, and they'd tell me that they knew I'd make it one day, and then I'd go across and see Young George. He'd be going through his month's bills trying to figure out how he'd manage till the next pay cheque came along, and I'd throw some loose notes on the table that I had in my pocket and tell him to keep them as I had too much money anyway.

Two days previously to this, I'd found myself (with the help of Dusty) a gass of a pad just off Warren Street. For those of you who are not privileged to live in London, Warren Street is about twenty minutes' journey by your own two legs from Soho, and I don't have to tell you how handy that is if you miss the last tube or bus and don't feel obliged to wait for the very convenient all-night transport that is provided for night workers, but is used by late night party-goers. I won't exaggerate and tell you that my pad was a palace or anything like that, but it was cosy and looked lived in and not the sort of place that you're eager to get out of, like a lot of bed-sitters that some people are forced to live in. Just a largish room with a bed and the usual furniture, but I had a tiny kitchen and a carzy as well. There was no bath but the public ones were just around the corner. The big advantage was that I was the only person living there as it is above some offices and a tailor's workroom, so after six in the evening I could do as I damn well pleased. The prize thing about it was the roof, which was easily got at and provided a crazy landscape of other people's roofs which you could feast your eyes on for hours and discover untold things of interest, as long as you have enough Pot to notice them. I bought a few pots of paint, the whitest I could find, and poured into them a dash of tinned strawberry juice to give it just the slightest shade of pink, and then had a ball with the paint brush. The next thing was a three-speakered Hi-Fi which put you slap bang into the middle of the rhythm section and enabled you to catch the real high ones that Maynard Ferguson blew out, and Miss Roach presented me with a couple of her weirdest paintings, which on the day that she gave them me I goofed very badly with by hanging them upside down. I even invested in a fitted carpet that cost me a pound a square yard to put the finishing touches to this very swinging paddery. I was all set up.

Miss Roach took up the position as my regular chick, acting, unpaid. I didn't let her smother me, but I'd make a habit of going around to her pad nearly every lunchtime to share her spaghetti and VP and to pick up the necessary Charge, and about once a week I'd take her to a Jazzery to listen to sounds and make a hell of a fuss of her in repayment of using her toilet as a warehouse, which she still didn't know anything about. She had the most valuable carzy in the whole of London!

It was on a Saturday evening some months after I'd established myself in Warren Street that I went down into her bargain basement and found her looking as worried as a junkie who'd just had her prescription scratched. "Thank goodness you've come," she said, pouring me out a large glass of Merrydown and VP mixed. "Dusty's just ran into some trouble. He's in a terrible state. Someone gave him a bitch of a punch-up so he's popped into the chemist to buy some plasters."

Ten minutes later DM came through the door looking very sorry for himself. He had a prize-winning black eye, whose bruise hadn't turned out properly yet, and it promised to be a green one and a yellow one before it was finished, also a cut over the other eye and his face was covered with lumps and bumps and abstract scratches.

"What happened to you?" I said, concerned over the state my old pal was in.

"Don't ask such bloody stupid questions! Can't you see what's happened?" he shouted.

"But who did it, for heaven's sake?" Miss Roach chimed in.

"Jumbo did it," he said quietly.

"Oh fuck!" I said.

"Don't *you* start," he spitted out at me. "I've enough worries without you having a go at me."

I knew it would have to happen sooner or later, but it proved to be sooner. I'd kept on at Dusty not to get involved with him, but you can't tell Dusty anything. If he makes up his mind to do something there's very little you can say or do that will alter it. He had this thing about getting in on the half a Tea trade, which is without doubt the uncoolest thing that anyone could do, and not worth it really because we weren't exactly starving serving up the bigger weights, but he just wasn't satisfied. The only places that you could have it off with the little brown packets were a couple of shady clubs that had never appealed to me, where a mixed bag of smokers ligged, but these places were always served by Jumbo or one of his slaves that were always on the skint one but were always very kindly turned on to a good smoke for risking their neck pushing there. Greedy Dusty Miller had decided that it was about time that he gave Jumbo some clean competition, so having had a good blow to give himself the necessary confidence, he'd gone down to these two dives and spread the good word around that he was holding some Matadi that was twice as high-making as that glorified cow shit that Jolly Jumbo was dealing. His new business venture soon came to an abrupt end. Before he knew what had happened he'd been dragged into the carzy and set about, and the one who'd handed out this sentence was none other than Jumbo himself.

"I don't like the look of it," Dusty said, sticking plasters all over his face so that it made him look like a patchwork quilt.

"Don't worry. It's finished with now. He's given you a good hiding so he'll leave it at that," Miss Roach said in her most sympathetic voice.

"That's what you think," Dusty mumbled. "Jumbo doesn't let things go as easy as that. I'm expecting trouble."

"Perhaps we'd better cool it for a few days," I suggested.

"What sort of partner have I got, for fuck sake? You're the sort of cat that would stand around and let someone piss on you. You'd better get some new ideas into your head double quick. We're not going to get pushed around, d'y hear? Not by Jumbo or anyone. If we back out we're finished. So don't give me any more of that yellow talk."

I was scared stiff. I don't mind admitting it either. It's all very well to put the VC one on now and again, but when you're up against a ruffian like Jumbo, it's no use landing yourself in men's surgical for nothing.

I tried my best to sound brave in front of Miss Roach. "I'm not scared. It's just that things are swinging as they stand and I don't want to go and nause things up by getting mixed up with a cunt like Jumbo."

Miss Roach came to my rescue. "I agree with him," she told Dusty. "Lay off Jumbo and he'll leave you alone. What's the use of unnecessary heroics?"

"I think now's the time to turn the children on," I said, bringing out my personal, private Hemp ration. "We'll have it in the match box. If it don't take us places that way, it never will."

I made the spliff, three skins, and drilled a hole in the match box just big enough for the end to fit in. I then put my hand over one end of the box and puffed at the other end so that the valuable smoke went straight down, non-stop express, to my feet.

I'm pleased to report what I expected to report. After a few good puffs things were a lot more swinging than a few minutes previously. We started to laugh at Dusty's busted face and he looked at himself in the mirror and he couldn't help having a little giggle as well. He told us that all good hustlers get beat up now and again, so who cares? It suited him in a way, we all decided. He looked far more rugged, and there was toughness, which was unnoticeable before, hidden behind those battle-scarred eyes?

We put on a Jelly Roll Morton record (I'd ceased to think of him as a square) and listened a while very quietly and afterwards told each other how much we'd been missing when we thought of him as unhip as Karl Marx. Then Dusty let Diz have a blow on the gram, and he blew nice, having a right go at the drummer, hurrying him along, never letting him rest for a moment. Then his stable companion Charlie Parker gave him a rest and took over, knowing that these sounds were going to be played years and years and years later by cats who still thought of him as the Daddy of them all.

"Listen what Harry did for the Bird," Miss Roach said, smoking the spliff right down to the roach. "Man, you're a gass!" she shouted to the record. "That's it! Whip it on me! Oh fuck — that's it!" "

Dusty fed Weep the guinea pig with the club calendar page of *The Melody Maker* and he really appreciated it, perched up on his two back legs he nibbled away two hundred miles an hour. Even Weep was hip!

Then Miss Roach decided we needed a change of scenery, so she invited us to go along to the supermarket to pick up some shopping. Before we went we had another good smoke which assured us that the goods we were about to buy would be the very best, as we could never get guzumped in a million years if we always felt like this. We were most definitely unguzumpable. We made the street scene and stroked a few dogs and cats on the way and took the mickey out of anyone that took our fancy and we were quite convinced that the uniformed bogey we passed suspected that we were under that naughty stuff that we'd just been smoking. Of course, the ignorant young bastard hadn't the faintest idea, really. The shops looked bright and gay and the people that were in them seemed to be doing everything in a mechanical way. *They* weren't real. They were just put there for our benefit, so that we could get our kicks. And our kicks we got. It took Miss Roach a full five minutes to explain to the zombie behind the bacon counter which sort she wanted, and he gave her some very weird looks indeed. If she'd staggered he'd taken it for granted that she was lushed, she walked straight enough but there was something strange about her all the same, you could practically hear the zombie thinking. What was it? I'd have loved to be able to tell him. Nothing would have sent me up more than to say to him, "It's all down to Harry the Hare, zombie, me old pal. He's there for all if you want him. Why don't you get a bit wised up to the happenings? Before you know it you'll be like us. Living. Living with dear old Harry, who never lets you down. You won't goof too much either. Sure you'll have your moments when everything becomes a bit unreal, and you have to take your fair share of the horrors if you're that way inclined, but then in time you'll be able to appreciate those. Yes, *appreciate* the horrors, believe it or not. I know that's tough to dig when you're ignorant about these things, but it's true. Come with us. We'll make you into a human being yet—if you'll let us!"

We nearly bought the shop up. Everything looked so wonderfully inviting. I hate sardines but the tins looked so gay and attractive (yes, sardine tins!) that they were unresistible. Frozen strawberries and fresh cream which I enjoyed thinking about as much as actually eating them. Neon lighting everywhere, which made me think that this was most certainly a modern world we were living in. What on earth will they get up to next? But the neon light hurt the eyes a bit and made things look even more unreal. Dusty knocked over a pile of tins of baked beans and the clatter of them falling down made everyone turn around and stare and brought a real daggers look from the old zombie behind the bacon counter. We tried picking them up and piling them on top of each other again. This, I might add, was a very stupid thing to do because as soon as we got them going to about four feet high, someone put the tin on the top that broke the camel's back and they all came tumbling down again. In the end zombie came over and told us in a polite zombie way that we'd better leave it to him.

We made it out to the street again and automatically went into the news theatre. Much to our delight it was a Bugs Bunny show and of course I don't have to tell you how much that wigged us. There was Harry on the screen that looked like Super-Super-Cinerama, but in reality it was just the normal size. The colours were as colourful as I'd ever seen colours look. The reds were redder, the blues bluer and we sat down and enjoyed the whole wonderful scene, nearly pissing ourselves with laughter. Then Dusty lit up a spliff which gave me the horrors a bit, because we received some very weird looks from the people sitting around us. They must have thought we were smoking horse shit or contraceptives or something, but we didn't care. Then I lost track of the story of the cartoon because I couldn't focus anything but colour. Colour that you imagine is only in heaven — but that's where we were. If heaven was anything like this and I manage to make it, I'll never once complain to the authorities, I promise. We cut out when the newsreel came on because we knew we would have to go through a load of shitty propaganda about them bad Russians. And one day, when we're not much older, they'll have a go at smashing us to smithereens with bombs and missiles and all that Jazz. But remember we've got America on our side, they'll tell us. And right at that moment (if I'd have been there) I would have shouted back to that screen that if you want America on your side you've got to have Esther Costello as well, because she'll always be with them. 'It doesn't matter about bombs!' I would have shouted. 'If we're going to die soon we'd better make it while we're here. Make it with Harry, Rave and High, so we'll remember it forever more. And Miss Roach and Dusty and me will rabbit about it up There, while you're talking about how you got demolished. And we'll tell you. We'll also tell you about Life: the Life we've seen while you were calling us Teddy Boys and Beatniks and Juvenile Delinquents. But we weren't really. It was that Teddy Boy of a politician that blew you up! But don't believe him — don't believe any of them politicians.

You'd be as mad as they are if you did. They must be mad because if they weren't they wouldn't be politicians. They'd be artists or drug pedlars instead!'

Out again into the street. Cars and buses and people and shops racing by, with hooters blowing and voices shouting that you can pick up the evening papers from them. It was a real effort crossing the road. We couldn't make up our minds which car to be run over by, but by a miracle we made it across to the other side without getting ourselves spread across the road.

I found myself in a taxi with Miss Roach closing all the windows and Dusty lighting another spliff and before long you could hardly see a hand in front of you for smoke. The cab seemed as if it was going at least sixty miles an hour, dodging in and out of the other traffic, and once again we convinced ourselves that our time had come. Miss Roach became really frightened and pleaded with us to tell the driver to slow down but Dusty wasn't having any of it. He was getting his kicks and his sadistic streak came out in him a bit because he was getting poor Miss R really at it, telling her he'd never been in a cab that had been driven so fast, and that if we came out of it alive we must consider ourselves very lucky indeed. Miss Roach buried her face in her hands, not daring to look, just hanging on, praying that death would come quickly.

We survived though, because the next thing I remember wasn't being in heaven or hell, but being in amongst the swinging sounds of the Katz Kradle Jazz Club. I think it was a benefit session for a musician that had swallowed his mouthpiece or something like that because practically all the best names were blowing that night. The place was really packed but Miss Roach went over to a happy-looking cat and told him she wasn't feeling well, so would he give her his seat? She scored on that one because he told her that she most certainly could and would she like him to get her a glass of water or something? But she told him that whisky would be a lot better so he went over to the local, opposite, and brought her back a miniature scotch. Dusty drank half of it.

I suddenly fully realised where we were. "How did we get here?" I asked. "We must have got really carried away."

"Everything's for a purpose, dear friend," Dusty said. "We've come here on a mission of delivery. Bill Higginwell has ordered an ounce so we mustn't let him down. Competition is keen—we must provide the best service in town."

There Bill Higginwell was, up on the stage, blowing fast and furious, and the kids in front of him, some tapping their feet, some nodding their heads and some quite still but with their eyes closed. They were a vital part of the happenings, contributing their piece to the scene, helping the atmosphere no end by clapping and shouting in the right places, but some, alas, just stared around them vacantly trying to figure out what all this fuss was about just because a few fellows were playing trumpets and things.

"We'll go into the musicians' room as soon as they've finished this set," said Dusty, holding on tight to the suspicious-looking brown paper parcel tucked under his arm.

We turned around and there by our side was the governor himself, Harry J. Waxman, Jazz tycoon of London. The man responsible for it all. "Enjoying yourselves?" he asked us, looking very pleased with himself and trying to count the five shillings that were packed into his big basement.

I could tell from the start that Dusty was going to take set on him. "Very much so, Mr Waxman, sir," he told him, nearly bowing at the same time. "There is just one thing, though. May I make a suggestion, sir?"

Harry J. beamed at him. "Of course—of course. Nothing pleases me more than to receive helpful suggestions from our members. After all it's *your* club, you know."

"I wish it was," I thought I heard Miss Roach say under her breath.

"What is this suggestion of yours?" this jolly Jew asked.

"It's a request for a band I like very much. I'm sure they'd play well in your magnificent club."

"I shall be very pleased to present them here. Who are they?"

Dusty thought very quickly. "Mick Hipster and his Hep-cats," was the best name that he could make up on the spur of the moment.

"Oh, *those*. Yes, I'll do my best. What's their name again? I'll just pop it down into my notebook."

We just about managed to hold back our laughter until he'd left us.

Bill Higginwell, leader of the top small group in the country, The Jazz Disciples, stamped his foot and led the others into the last number of the set, an original titled *The Last Session*, which they played in an up-tempo, I'll-beat-you-to-the-last-bar sort of way. The kids lapped it up and when Slide McCormack, the trombone player, swung into a few bars of *Green Grow The Rushes-O* they went berserk.

"You'd better come with me," Dusty said, as he made his way towards the musicians' room. We left Miss Roach holding the shopping.

I'd never passed through the sacred doors of the Katz Kradle musicians' room before, and I don't mind admitting that I felt a certain pride when doing so. It's not as romantic as you'd imagine when you get inside—it's so small that's the trouble, but I didn't care. I was really part of the scene now. The big drug pedlar, that's what I was, supplying this country's top musicians (those that smoke, I mean) with their Pot. For the very first time in my life I felt important. They were relying on *me*, even Bill Higginwell, who I considered blew as good a saxophone as many of the Yank 'stars' that a lot of the kids went crazy about after hearing one of their LPs. He was putting his horn away in his case, being as careful with it as a mother would her child, and when he saw Dusty his face lit up. "What's happening, Mr Miller, man?" he asked quietly. He had a big head, physically, not psychologically, and his arms seemed to reach down past his knees.

"The very same thing, Bill. It's shit hot from the Congo. The best there's been for a very long time."

"There you go! I was hoping you'd say that. The last lot frightened me—it was so good," the marvellous musician said.

"This is the very same thing. By the way, this is my partner," Dusty said, nodding in my direction. "If he ever sees you, it's cool."

Bill H smiled but hardly looked at me. He was more interested in the brown paper parcel that Dusty was holding. He passed it over to him. "Yum-yum—what a sexy sight," he said to us, feeling and smelling it at the same time. "I wonder what weird sounds I'll blow with this around."

On having a second look about me I discovered the room wasn't so small but it was so full up with hats and coats and sheet music and musicianly-looking things that it seemed half its true size. There was a knock on the door and it turned out to be no less than the thing that tries to kid everyone she's human: Ruby. She hadn't seen Dusty and myself before she'd said, "Shall I go home and wait for you there, Bill?" Then she spotted us and her face dropped. "Hello, how's things?" she asked us awkwardly.

Dusty was in just the right mood for her. "Things are fine with us, thanks. How are you? I hear the Fascists are getting themselves really set up down Ladbroke Grove way—have you joined them yet?"

She didn't take offence, in fact she didn't even sound concerned. "I haven't any time for politics. All I have time for is Bill. Isn't that right, Billyboy?"

Dusty didn't give him time to answer. "Has she asked to inspect your family tree, Bill? You never know, you may have a Great-Great-Great-Grandfather that didn't come from Northern Europe. She wouldn't like that, you know."

Poor Bill wasn't interested in Dusty's grievances. He just said, "I take it you two know each other."

"Give us the loot and we'll blow. The air in here's getting contaminated," Dusty said, giving Ruby an X certificate look at the same time.

We returned to Miss Roach who was still holding the shopping. "What a time I've had since you've been away," she told us. "Sir Galahad, who turned me on to the scotch, really took set on me. Very cheeky he was, my dears. Asked me to go home with him. The day I'll part with it for a mouthful of whisky, you can hang the flags out. He's got more chance of being struck by lightning!"

We invested in a Coke because the Charge had made our mouths feel and taste like a sewer, and Harry shouted up that he was hungry too, so we sent him down a cheese sandwich. Dusty sat down next to Miss Roach looking critically at the young faces around him, making a sarcastic comment here and there about someone's drag or a couple petting in the corner or anything else that took his fancy. Then Buttercup was upon us suddenly and Dusty asked him if he was interested in purchasing some Africa's gift to England that we were holding.

"I can afford the Charge," Buttercup told us, "but I can't afford the big feed up I'd have to have after. It makes me so hungry."

So we cut out. We made it across the street to the hippest pub in the neighbourhood, had a cider, then Dusty told me he wanted to introduce me to a new contact he'd met that day, so we left Miss Roach after I'd promised to go back to her pad later to have some supper and so on.

We were half way up Wardour Street when it happened. It was all over so quickly I can hardly tell you about it. But there in front of us were about four or five big yobos who were standing untidily across our path. They took the whole width of the pavement up. We'd nearly reached them and I was just about to step into the road to pass when Dusty said sharply, "Fuck, it's Jumbo!" That's about all I remember except for being punched to the ground and feeling a sharp pain in my stomach, which must have been Jumbo's big foot.

Then I saw a policeman's ugly face staring down at me, and I was helped into an ambulance. The aches and pains that had taken over my body was practically unbearable.

I had a good look around, but Dusty was nowhere to be seen.

The Warren Street sun came flooding through my window, hit the bed, and woke me up. Miss Roach was already half awake and she was staring at me through slits of eyes. She put her arm around me and gave me a dry-lipped kiss. Her body was so hot it was almost unbearable to touch. Her hair was a mess; pieces sticking all over the place as if it couldn't make up its mind which way to go, and the remains of her make-up looked quite comical on her otherwise very white face.

"I'll never drink another glass of vip again as long as I live—so help me. I feel dreadful," she said through a muffled throat. "I'll never be able to get up from this bed. Do you know what I'm going to do when I'm rich and famous? I'll buy a villa miles away from everywhere and lock you in it and stay in bed with you for a month. We'll have our meals and our Charge and our vip brought in to us by slaves."

I had to clear my throat before I could speak. "I thought you just said that you weren't going to drink any more of that poison."

"Only on special occasions. Being in bed with you for a month would be one, I can assure you."

With a great effort I managed to get myself out of bed and go to the food cupboard to pour us some grapefruit juice. Due to the state my mouth was in it tasted a million times better than it usually did. I dared to look at myself in the mirror but I wish I hadn't. Shocks, first thing in the morning, are no good to you, and that's what I got. I'm sure I'd aged about ten years in the last twenty-four hours, and the bruises that I'd received from Jumbo a fortnight previously were at their ugliest stage; browny-yellow they were now, I needed a shave badly and my eyes were a glazed pink. I put my head under the tap and once I was past the first jolt of the icy cold water, I had a ball. It felt as though the water was washing away a hundred old cobwebs that had been growing over

174

my head. I put some trousers on and an old sweater that was lying over a chair.

"What a party that was last night," I said to Miss Roach, who was skipping through one of my true crime mags. "You always said that you'd like to see me paralytic drunk. Did you like what you saw?"

She put the mag down on the bedside table. "I was rather disappointed really. You just passed out and I was so looking forward to you singing and dancing and going berserk like one's supposed to do on such occasions. Perhaps you'll be different next time."

"Don't worry about next time. There won't be one," I said, putting the kettle on the gas. "I think drink's horrible."

"That should be my job—making the coffee, I mean. I'd make a disgusting wife. I suppose I'm just not gifted for those sort of things."

"You'd make a marvellous wife. Let's see now—you wouldn't object to your husband drinking because you're always drunk yourself. You'd educate him about art, because although I can't dig what you get up to with your paint brush, I'm sure you're very talented."

"Why?"

"Because you *look* talented, even if your painting doesn't show it."

"How dare you—it does!"

"Excuse my ignorance. But the main thing that would recommend you for the matrimonial stakes would be your other talent."

"What other talent?"

"In bed!"

"Naughty, wicked little boy!"

I heard Mr Gold, the tailor that has his workshop underneath me, call up to me. It turned out to be that I was wanted on the phone downstairs that he let me use, and much to my surprise, it was my sister Liz on the other end. She told me she was just around the corner and would it be all right for her to pop in and give me a sisterly visit? What could I say?

I couldn't tell her it was impossible as I had a chick in my bed, and the pad was in such a state that she'd probably faint when she came through the door. I think I've already told you what a case she is for tidiness, so it gave me the horrors to think that my sis was coming around at the very worst moment she could have picked. So I put on my most natural voice and told her that it would be wonderful to see her, but to excuse me for receiving her in such an untidy room as I had a little party last night (it hadn't been at my pad really) and I hadn't had time to put things Liz-shape. Then I dashed up the stairs and told Miss Roach to jump out of bed and get dressed as quickly as she possibly could. I hadn't mentioned Miss Roach to Liz.

"Everything happens to me," I said, helping Miss Roach to fasten her bra up at the back.

"What a drag," she said. "I always feel so damn sexy when I have a hangover. I thought you were coming back into bed."

We rushed around at supersonic speed, dressing and clearing up some of the rubbish that was ligging about the place. The room didn't look too bad when we'd finished but Miss Roach certainly looked as if she'd been shacking all night with me; she wasn't dressed as though she'd been for a Sunday morning walk and popped in for a visit.

When Liz arrived she looked her same old self: underfed, unsociable and unhappy. The look that she gave Miss Roach reminded me of one a wife would give her husband's secretary when catching them in a hotel room together. I introduced them and although she told her she was pleased to meet her, it was only because she had to; the expression on her face looked as if she meant quite the opposite. She was wearing her Russian peasant's costume and Miss Roach gave her a good look-over, like women do, and I'm sure I saw a mickey-taking look cross her face.

"I'm so glad you came, Liz, how's things?" I said.

"They're just the same at home. Nothing very different seems to happen. In fact, I'm getting quite fed up with it all."

I couldn't believe my ears. She was talking in a very un-Liz like manner. "That's not like you, Liz. I thought you were happy there."

"It's different now you've left. I know I didn't see much of you but it was a lot better when you were around. The house was always quiet but now it's like a morgue. Mum's always complaining about her nerves — she never stops — she's making mine as bad as hers, and Dad does nothing but write in those dreary books of his and watch television. Even Rinty seems as if he's getting old."

Miss Roach made the coffee and it was quite obvious that she was no stranger to the pad. "Do you take sugar?" she politely asked Liz.

"One," she told her without even saying thank you. "What on earth's happened to your face?" she asked me.

I told her that I'd fallen down the stairs (the same excuse as she'd made to the hospital), but as soon as I'd said it I realised you'd have to be an idiot to take that one in, as no one could acquire those brand of bruises that way.

"As a matter of fact, I've really come here to tell you something that I think will surprise you," Liz went on.

"I hope it's a nice juicy scandal. Has Young George got himself nicked for importuning or something?"

Liz blushed and said, "No, don't be terrible. It's just that I'm joining the army."

"I don't think I heard you right. You're what?" I said.

"I'm joining the army!"

"You're joining the army? She's joining the army — oh man! What? *You*? Are you really?"

"I've been thinking about it for some time now, and at last I've decided on it. I've signed on for three years."

"This we'll have to celebrate," I said, getting up from my chair. "I think I've a bottle of VP hidden somewhere. Get the glasses, Miss Roach. We'll have to drink to this."

Miss Roach said, "None for me, thank you. I never touch the stuff."

I found the necessary jaba juntz and poured three stiff ones out. "Go on, Miss Roach," I said to her. "This is a special occasion. Force one down yourself."

"All right then. Just this once." And she drank it right down in one dirty great swallow.

"You didn't even wait for the toast," I said.

"Oh dear, so I didn't. I must drink a toast—so I'd better have another one!"

"Here's to Liz, and may she end up a general!" I said and down went another glass of plonk.

Liz told us about the plans for her new career, and it was obvious that she was thrilled to bits with it all. It reminded me of the time when I was planning to escape from the things that Liz wanted to get away from. There was excitement in her voice and it made me happy to hear her talk like this. She told me that the drama at home, when she told our mum about it, was even worse than mine. I didn't want to try and imagine it—it must have been awful. But I did it and she was determined to do the same. Mum wasn't even talking to her now but she knew that she'd come around before she left, which was only three days away. I don't know if it was the couple of drinks that Liz had but she seemed to loosen right up and talk like mad and was even friendly to Miss Roach. Before long they were talking together like they'd been firm friends for years. Liz had most definitely changed, even since the last time I'd seen her. It seemed that this army thing had really done the trick—she acted like a person would if they were coming *out* of the army—not going in. I knew that she was going to be happy because when I came to think of it, this was the ideal thing for her. She realised this too. We had a right old laugh and we pulled her leg about what she'd look like in her uniform and how she'd manage square bashing and what her sergeant would look like and a hundred other things.

The girls hid their faces while I changed into one of the five suits that I'd bought myself since I'd changed my job. Liz made some comment that my new job must be good to be able to buy new drag, and I told her, quite truthfully, that it was indeed. Good prospects, too, I thought, if the law didn't give me the sack.

"Let's get out of here," I said. "It's Sunday, the time when people are supposed to go for walks and show off their new hats and have a ball."

But before we had time to leave, Dusty appeared on the scene. As soon as Liz saw him she went quiet again and the sparkle that was in her eyes was turned out, like she needed a new shilling in the meter. "I don't think I have time," she said, putting on her coat. "I'll have to be getting back home. You know how mum nags if you're not in time for Sunday lunch."

It was no use trying to change her mind. I knew Liz too well for that, so I let her go. I took her down the stairs to let her out and when we reached the bottom she pulled me to one side, and said in a very concerned voice: "Take care, little brother of mine. I don't like the look of that friend of yours, there's something about him that's creepy."

"Don't worry about Dusty, he's all right," I told her. "He's been a very good friend to me."

"I'm sorry. I didn't mean to be nasty to him. But remember one thing: keep it in your mind all the time — if any time you want to see me about anything — anything at all — I'm at Guildford Barracks. I leave on Tuesday. Look after yourself." I didn't have time to answer; she was gone.

Dusty Miller was full of enthusiasm. Why? I just didn't know. He was jumping about the place telling us what a lovely day it was and he thought it was wonderful to be alive in such a crazy world as this one we'd been sent to, and Ayo had an even better Charge up his sleeve (or in his toilet), green, great and gone-making, which he'd just bought a pound weight of and we'd soon be living in luxury and why was I so miserable-looking? He really was in a happy mood and he seemed anxious for me to have a smoke which he brought out of his pocket already made up. He lit it and passed it to me straight away. I didn't complain about that.

"What's up, Dusty?" I asked him. "You're in an unusually good mood today."

"Nothing, friend, nothing. Why can't someone be happy if they want to. There's far too many miserable people around as it is."

Miss Roach knew him better than that. "Don't tell me there's not a reason for it," she said, "else I won't believe you. You've something up your sleeve all right."

He sat down in the chair looking very contented indeed, taking his time over his words. "As a matter of fact, there is something. But I'm not going to tell you for a while. I'll just keep you at it for a few hours. There's nothing I enjoy more than keeping people in suspense—it does them good occasionally."

I realised the best way to get this information out of him was to play it cool and not sound concerned. "If that's the way you feel—I don't want to know."

He knew that I was just playing it clever. "Fine. If you don't want to know—I shan't tell you."

"Don't be like that," I pleaded with him. "I can't stand the suspense. Let me have it, Dusty. Don't be such an obstinate bastard."

"All right," he said. Then he paused to light a cigarette. "I've got a very big deal coming off. My friend, we're going into another branch of the business."

I couldn't make head nor tail of what he was talking about. "What do you mean? Another branch of the business?"

"It happened yesterday," he told me slowly. "Quite by accident, too. I met this cat who's a merchant seaman, and he told me that he'd picked up something abroad that he wanted to sell. Of course, nosey Dusty Miller had to have a look at it, and guess what it turned out to be?"

"Fucked if I know," I said.

"Nothing less than five hundred grains of horse!"

"What?" said Miss Roach.

"Heroin, my dear. Enough to make us all rich. It's a chance of a lifetime."

"Are you feeling all right?" I asked him.

I'm feeling marvellous. It's true, man, so help me."

"I don't doubt it's true for one minute. But you're not trying to tell me that you're going to sell that stuff?" I said.

I'm certainly not going to use it myself. One correction. *I'm* not going to sell it. *We* are. You're my partner, remember? And we go halves in everything."

I had to swallow before I could speak. "You can count me out. I know I'm no angel but there's a limit to everything. Listen, Dusty, forget it. The day I sell a fix to anyone you can spit in my face. I suppose you're going to give the kids free samples so that they'll be tomorrow's clientele."

Dusty looked as mad as hell. It was pretty obvious that he'd taken it for granted that I was going to approve of the idea; you could tell by his face. When he dug that I didn't want to know he changed completely—he looked vicious even and his pride was hurt because I hadn't shown any enthusiasm about it. I'd rebelled against him and that was the last thing he expected me to do.

"Do you dig what you're going to miss? This is big loot, not just a few poxy pounds that we pick up on the Charge. This is it, Daddy-O, the big chance we've been waiting for. We *can't* miss this opportunity. It'll never happen again."

"I don't *want* it to happen again," I shouted at him. "I don't want to hear any more about it, even if it means we split up. I wouldn't even touch that rubbish! It's not only dangerous, it's fucking evil! I thought you knew better. Don't you *dig* the junkie scene now, or something? Remember it was you who told me all about it, and showed me, too. You showed me that Popper was one of the lucky ones. You showed me them queueing up at John Bell and Croyden's just before midnight, doing their nuts, waiting for twelve o'clock to chime so that they could pick up their poison and jab dirty needles in their arms and legs that were covered in sores. Spewing all over the gaff and living like animals. Man, you can count me out! I don't want to know!"

Miss Roach remained silent, chewing hungrily at her fingernails.

Dusty wouldn't give up. "You're mad! You're stark, raving bonkers! Why don't you join the Salvation Army, they need new recruits! If a thing's worth doing, it's worth doing properly. Do you think you're doing a favour to society by selling Charge? Ask a policeman—he'll tell you the answer. I'm talking about five hundred pounds—not a kick up the arse! Get wise to yourself, boy, you're a drug pedlar as it stands. That's all the judge is interested in. He won't tell you that you've been a good boy and let you off just because you refused to sell junk. You'll get it as heavy as anyone."

"I don't care about that," I screamed at him. "I'd rather forget about the whole thing if you expect me to help you sell that filth!"

I couldn't stand any more of it. I grabbed my jacket and rushed out of the building to get some fresh air.

On the following Wednesday I received a letter from Bunty. It said:

Sweetie,

I was not only disappointed, but disgusted with you when you didn't turn up for our little get-together the other evening. I've met a cute and cuddly young man of nineteen who's training hard to be a dancer. In fact, he's been working so hard that I've decided to give him a little rest down at Brighton for a few days. He's a dream, my darling, and I'm sure that you'll love everything about him. I'm bound to get my kicks as he's so very ignorant about a lot of things, and I don't mean Jazz.

Bunty.

I had to smile when I read it. And I spent a pleasant half hour trying to imagine what she'd be getting up to in Brighton. It brought a few memories flooding back to me as well. She'd taken me there once, and I felt a right cunt when I had to sign the register as her husband. Of course, everyone at

182

the hotel dug what it was all about, but that's not the point. There's no sense in making yourself look ridiculous by trying to work that one over them, is there? She's not exactly an idiot but she really believed that the hotel staff thought that we were married. She wouldn't play it cool and let everyone forget about it, either. She constantly talked about when we went to the South of France for our honeymoon, putting in all the little details, and she raved for hours about the new house that we were going to buy, and all this was in front of the other guests and we received some very weird looks from them indeed.

We met this old girl down there, she was even older than Bunty, who looked and spoke all kinky and she took a real interest in us, or should I say in me, and Bunty loved it and got this old girl really at it, telling her that I'd never liked young chicks, and she (the old girl, I mean) was just my type, and I got so used to this carry-on that in the end I didn't even blush. Well, anyway, this person, whose name she told us was—wait for it—*Matilda!* (honest), trapped me in her bedroom one day after making some excuse that she wanted to show me a photo of her son who was supposed to look so much like me but turned out to be just about my opposite. When she got me in her boudoir, which stank to high heaven of some poxy smelling perfume, she only tried to make it with me. She came the real nonsense, she did. I don't want to lie and tell you that I'm very fussy, but she was a bit too much. Seventeen stone she was, and a face to match as well. She didn't give up easy, either. Practically chased me around the room, and for giggles I felt like reporting her to the law for attempted rape. But that's not the end. When I went back and told Bunty all this, she wasn't a bit surprised, in fact she knew it was going to happen. I ask you! It's a bit much, isn't it? Then she only turned around and asked me, point blank, mind you, if I'd have some kind of orgy (she called it a party) with the two of them. I'm sorry, I can't stand all that. Not having orgies with two women, I mean, but this hippopotamus of a woman? No! She pestered us all the time we were there and Bunts made arrangements for us to meet her in town when we returned, but I didn't want to know.

The trouble with Bunty is that she gets carried away too much. At this same holiday I was telling you about, we were on the beach frying ourselves up, when this chick, who was quite young and silly-looking, came over to us and asked Bunts if she appeared on TV. Guess what the lying cow told her? Right, first time. And before I knew where I was, *I* was on the tele also, yes, *me*, and I never look at the bloody thing, let alone act on it. Before a few minutes had passed Bunty was on the stage and films as well, but she was leaving the following month for Hollywood as the British entertainment industry ignores true talent and America would give her the break she deserved. Before I realised what had happened she had me carried away as well. It's quite catching, you know, once one person gets started. So there I was telling this poor woman about all the different countries I'd visited and I'd never really been as far as Newcastle. Of course, I'd been to Swaziland, I told her. I nearly got myself eaten by cannibals there. It's hopeless once you get started, you can't stop. But as for myself I don't mind people telling me lies, as long as I know they *are* lies. You've met the same kind of person yourself, you must have. I really get them at it, and land them right in the shit by getting them all complicated, so in the end they don't know where they are.

The trouble with that holiday was that it was pissing down with rain all the time, except for the day we met this lunatic woman on the beach, I was telling you about. And Bunty just wouldn't come home. She kept saying that it was just a passing cloud. A passing cloud! When the whole sky for as far as you could see was full of those dirty black clouds and the sea smashed against the prom like it had the real needle with it. Even when the weather forecast told us there'd be rain for the next six months or so, she wouldn't give up. Not Bunts. Only a passing cloud, she kept saying. Not that I didn't enjoy myself stuck in the hotel room all the time, but even *that* can get a bit boring after a week.

184

We seemed to meet all sorts of crazy people there and when we mentioned that we were interested in Spiritualism that really did it. This old fellow that told us he was seventy really took set on us. He didn't look his age though. He must have been ninety at least. Well, anyway, he told us that he'd been a keen psychic investigator all his life, and that he'd traced his former incarnations for hundreds of years. This I could accept, but when he told us that he'd been King Solomon, Oliver Cromwell, Nell Gwyn and Bluebeard, that was a bit too much to swallow! But I didn't tell him so. No, I got him at it and asked if he could remember any of his past lives. Of course he did. I wouldn't mind having a few memories about being King Solomon myself.

I threw Bunty's letter into the wastepaper basket, put my imitation Crombie shortie on and made it into the street. I had to meet Dusty at Miss Roach's. After that nasty little experience I'd had with him a few days previously he hadn't bothered to come around to see me, and I made up my mind that I wasn't going to chase after him. The Charge was still at its hiding place so I took it for granted that I'd hear from Dusty within a few days. He phoned on the Tuesday. Full of apologies he was, and carried on talking for a full twenty minutes telling me that I was right and that after thinking about it he'd decided that it wasn't a very nice thing to do, after all, and he'd told this sailor cat to keep his junk. I'm not sure if he meant it or not. As far as I knew he could have bought the lousy stuff and started pushing it without my knowing, but I wasn't concerned over that. The important thing was that *my* conscience was clear and that's all I worried about.

If you don't know already, it's a very long walk from Warren Street to Bayswater. It is for a lazy cat like me, anyway. But I walked it. I enjoy walking when I have pleasant things to think about. The night before I'd decided that I was going to save hard, *really* save, I mean, because I wanted to get out of this stinking business that I was in as quickly as I could. I'd already managed over a hundred pounds in that sexy post office book of mine and that was without really trying. From that day on, I'd promised myself, I'd get right down to putting every penny that I possibly could away. Then I'd open a business. I hadn't decided what kind yet, but it didn't really matter. A sweet shop would do — anything, as long as I could tell Dusty Miller to go find himself another partner and to be able to go home to my parents and show them that I hadn't turned out like they'd expected me to (for some weird reason my mother had always predicted that I'd end up on the gallows) and that I'd made it, and would my mum like to come and look after the shop as I knew she'd get her kicks that way. It would have to be in town, not where she lived (I wasn't getting as square as all that), or even in the country would be nice, as long as I had a motor to make the London scene occasionally.

When I did arrive, I was whacked out. My feet were aching from my marathon walk and Miss Roach put a pillow behind my head in a real wife-like fashion and made me a strong black coffee.

"So all's forgiven about the other day, eh mate?" Dusty said, with a smile all over his face.

"Everything's forgotten," said I, rubbing my poor throbbing feet.

"We mustn't let a little thing like that come between us," Dusty said, sounding like a poof. "We've too much to lose."

I was just feeling a little better after taking a dexadrine, which I never indulge in except in moments like those, when there was a loud knock on the door. Some knocks are nice, some are not nice. This was not nice. Miss Roach opened it. It was two tall men. They came in and behind them came four more. I hate to admit this but at that moment I didn't have the faintest idea who they were.

"They're policemen," Miss Roach said quietly, then she sat herself down next to me. She didn't move or say anything else.

I felt sick. I wanted to spew my heart up. So this was it...

I can't tell you what exactly happened for about ten minutes after that. Everything went cloudy, a dark cloud, too, and at one time I remember thinking that I was dreaming but I soon found out I wasn't, then everything went terribly clear. Too clear.

"I'll try the toilet," I heard one of the policemen say.

Then I remember seeing it in the policeman's hand and the smile on his face was one of pleasure. He put it on the table and the table suddenly changed to one in the court, with the Hemp on it as piece of evidence number one.

Miss Roach got up from her chair as though she was hypnotised by it and she walked slowly over to it, not taking her eyes off it for a second. When she reached it, her hands went down and she touched it gently as if she was making sure that it was real.

"It's Charge," she said.

The policemen looked at each other and smiled. I'm the inspector," one of them said. "Why don't you tell me all about it?" He sat down on an armchair, making himself comfortable for the big confession. His eyes weren't what you could call hard, but his lips were thin and it seemed that all the nastiness in him had settled around his mouth. He looked like a policeman. "Why don't you tell me all about it?" he said again.

He wasn't talking to Dusty or myself. He hardly looked at us. He was interested in Miss Roach and Dusty knew it and I knew it and Miss Roach knew it. He didn't rush things. He had plenty of time. He worked around cautiously at first, feeling his way, just testing for a weak link so he could break it apart. He called her 'my dear' a couple of times, but you could tell that he wasn't really on her side.

Then he turned to Dusty. "What's your name?" he asked him.

"Albert Miller," came the reply.

"What do you do for a living?" he barked back at him.

"I'm in my father's scrap metal business, sir."

He pointed a finger straight at me. "And what do you work at?"

"A salesman, sir. Down and Company, the hatters," I heard myself say.

"We'll see what they've got on them. Bring Sergeant Stewmer in."

Sergeant Stewmer was a policewoman. She went over to Miss Roach and patted her sexily all over the body, then told the inspector that she was negative.

How the hell did this happen, anyway? My mind kept asking. Policemen don't just barge into people's rooms without any reason and find a pound weight of Charge in the carzy. Someone must get them up to it. It hit me like a sledgehammer. Jumbo! Fucking shit cunt Jumbo! But it seemed that he'd slipped up all the same. The law had obviously made up its mind who it was going to kill and it didn't look as if it was going to be us.

Miss Roach looked as if she'd been through a marathon brainwashing session. She looked from me to the inspector, from the inspector to Dusty. Like a frightened child that had just seen the danger, she begged for someone's sympathy with eyes that made me shudder. But I knew that my fright could not be compared with hers; a mind of jumbled horrors that suddenly take shape and shock her with the sickening reality of it all. A terrible dream of half light and threatening figures with their hands held out menacingly to her. Of racing hearts and hundred miles an hour pulses. Emptiness and loneliness — nothing else in her barren world. No God even, because you realise, like an electric shock, that He may be on their side as well. You can't surrender yourself to it but you have to go along with it. The chair that you cling to for support is even slipping away from you. Isn't *anyone* on my side? Help!

"This isn't no game," the inspector said, lighting his pipe. "We'll get to the bottom of this in the end, so you might as well come out with it now. It'll be easier for everyone."

One of the other law switched on a blinding two million watt bulbed lamp, that hung down from the ceiling like it was a marker for the centre of the room, and the surprise of it made me jump in the air.

The inspector's face was grim but it was a patient one as well. He adjusted his tie a little straighter and tighter. "How long have you been living here," he asked Miss Roach sharply.

She had difficulty in getting her words out. "Nearly two years."

"How much rent do you pay?" he snapped back at her.

"Five pounds," she managed to get out.

"A week?"

"Yes."

That's rather a lot to pay for a young, single, unemployed girl like you, isn't it?"

"I paint," she said excitedly.

"Do you mean that you *sell* these things?" he asked, looking around the room at her efforts."

"Sometimes," she answered weakly.

"Come on. Surely you're not trying to tell me you earn your living at it," he asked with a sarcastic smile.

She sounded as guilty as hell. "Not *exactly.*"

"Then tell me *exactly* how you do earn your living."

"I receive an allowance from my father."

"We'll have to go into that," he said, looking at her as if she was the world's most gifted liar.

The other law were having the time of their lives pulling everything apart, like they were relatives of a rich geezer that had just snuffed it. Finding all sorts of things they were. Travel brochures — odd stockings — empty perfume bottles — bald paint brushes — half a paper back — and even a packet of french letters that made everyone blush.

"How much did the Hemp cost you?" the inspector spitted out at her.

It took Miss Roach completely by surprise. "Nothing..."

"Nothing? Do you mean someone *gave* it to you?"

"No, I don't! It's not mine I tell you. I've never seen it before."

"It was hidden in *your* toilet, do you understand? We know you smoke and you're in with the crowd, so why not come clean? We're not here to harm you. We're here to do our duty. So why not be a clever girl and tell us all about it so that we can help you?"

"But it's not mine," poor Miss Roach said pleadingly.

I was smoking my head off, lighting one cigarette up after the other, nearly dropping the packet every time I tried to take one out. Puffing nervously away like a steam engine, until my mouth was as dry as sand and I felt sick with it.

"How about this, sir," said a baby-faced lawling, and with an exaggerated gesture he displayed a little brown packet that he'd found in a willow-patterned vase.

"More of it, eh?" the inspector said, taking it all for granted. "Well, what about this?" showing it to Miss Roach, who I'm sure was nearly shitting herself by now.

"All right, so I smoke," she said. "But that doesn't mean I sell the stuff."

"Now who said anything about you selling it? You must think we're very hard people indeed. Just let's say you bought it cheap and you intended to smoke it all to yourself," the inspector said quietly.

"But I didn't!" half shouted Miss R.

The inspector looked just a tiniest bit annoyed. "I'm losing a little of my patience," he told her. "You can tell me lies but don't insult my intelligence. Now I want it straight, do you hear? No messing!"

There was a terrible silence, with the alarm clock by the bed ticking away so loudly that I thought it would deafen me. I know things are accentuated in moments like these, but I swear that silence lasted a full minute. Honest.

"You're a silly girl, you really are," the inspector said, changing his tactics again. "You don't want us to have to take you down to that nasty old police station, do you? It would be far nicer if we could settle it all here. This little room of yours is so cosy, not at all like that draughty, depressing police station."

"I've told you everything I know," was all Miss Roach could say.

Dusty was looking very uninterested at the happenings; he didn't even look nervous, and I wished I was the same. But then I wondered what was *really* going on in Dusty's mind. What were his thoughts about Miss Roach's unenviable position? Whatever they were, I was convinced that Dusty had the situation in hand, and whatever he did it would be the best for us all. He'd always been straight with me. Never once had he ever tried to pull any fast ones as far as the Charge was concerned, or come to that he'd never pulled any strokes on me at all. I suppose his feelings concerning our friend in distress were the same as mine. He'd be thinking the very same thoughts as me; he'd also want to own up to this stupid, fat policeman, and tell him it was us, not Miss Roach, that he should be grilling—that we were the guilty ones, it was our Charge and we'd had a ball while it lasted, we caught a glimpse of the real life so we don't regret it for one minute. I was sure that Dusty felt sorry for Miss Roach like he'd never felt sorry for anyone else in his life before. That he wanted to release her from her suffering and helplessness and darkness; to draw back the curtain and let the light back into her world once again. But Dusty's no fool, he knows what he's doing. He'll come up with an answer soon. But will he? He's taking a bloody long time about it if he is. Come on, Dusty, say something. Say something to the inspector that will make him apologise to Miss Roach for causing so much unnecessary trouble, as it all has been a terrible mistake and it would never happen again.

But whatever happens no one will get time. Everyone says that. I mean, anyone will tell you that for your first Hemp conviction you hardly ever get bird. Probation. That's what they hand out. Lovely probation, where all you have to do is sign your name in a book once a week. There's nothing much wrong with that, is there? Anyone can take that in their stride, even Miss Roach. Being as she's a girl and everything they may not even give her that. They'll probably tell her that she's been a very naughty little girl, and that if she's naughty again she'll land herself in a whole heap of trouble, but this time they're going to be kind and let her off. Won't we have a ball that night! We'll get her block-up like she's never been before, and I'll end up staying the night in her bed and comfort her for all the suffering she's been through.

But supposing they don't let her off and they don't give her probation? Just supposing they tell her that there's been too much of this sort of thing going on lately and they can't take in the story of her having a whole pound weight all to herself, just to smoke, so they'll make an example of her to show others that they can't get away with it, and go and send her to Holloway for a few months, in amongst all those mail bags and cobs of bread and Lesbians. What would I feel like then? Every evening at nine, when I was just going to cut down town, would I think about Miss Roach's cell light being turned off? And when it was Sunday and I was just turning over in bed, would I think of Miss Roach in church, where in the next block they were preparing to hang somebody?

The inspector was knocking his pipe against the grate in the fire and the ash came falling out like dirty, grey snow. "Don't think that I'm trying to make deals with you, but I'll tell you what I'll do. Let's face it. You know that I know that it's your Hemp over there, so let's stop kidding each other. If you tell me all about it I'll put a good word in for you to my superior."

"I can't..." Miss Roach tried to say.

"I haven't finished yet," the criminal catcher butted in. "But if you beat about the bush for another couple of hours, that will make my job a little harder and I wouldn't like that. So if I told my superior *bad* things about you, I'm afraid he might do a few things that *you* wouldn't like I"

"It's no use! I *can't* tell you anything about it!" screamed my poor unfortunate friend.

"Why not?" asked the policeman hopefully.

"Because I don't know anything! It's not mine!"

That's the spirit, Miss Roach, my mind was shouting to her. Keep it up! Don't let them get you down! This is Great Britain. Great Great Great Britain! Its law and justice is respected all over the world. All over the universe if the Martians know what's happening down here. By gad, sir! We couldn't convict an innocent person in this dear, old country of ours. That wouldn't be cricket. Impossible! Keep going, Miss Roach. You're *innocent!*

The baby-faced lawling was watching the drama without an emotion in his mind, taking it all in, not missing a word. Watching a Master at work. A man who knew the business and was a copper when coppers were coppers. But don't despair, baby-faced lawling, your time will come. Soon you'll be out on your own, let loose to nick as many people as you possibly can. You'll have a ball, man. You'll pinch people here and you'll pinch people there, and you'll even be able to handcuff them, and when you take them down to the station, if you really hate them you'll be able to give them a good kick up the arse. And in court you'll be able to tell the judge all about them: what disgusting brutes they are and how they're a menace to society, and the judge will recommend you for being able to let him sentence them to rot away in a stinking prison or perhaps even murder the villains! Take it all in, baby-faced lawling. You'll soon learn!

"Inspector, may I say something, please, sir?" asked Dusty out of the blue.

I knew you'd do it, Dusty, I thought. Good old Dusty! I knew you wouldn't let her take the can back for us. I know we're a couple of bastards, but we're not as mean as all that, are we?

"Isn't it possible," said Dusty slowly and precisely, "that someone else could have put that stuff there? I mean, one of this young lady's friends? It could have been there all the time without her knowing anything about it."

"When I want your advice, I'll ask for it," snarled back the public executioner.

Dusty didn't say any more. He let it go at that. He didn't say a single solitary word more. He didn't say that the friend who had hidden it was himself. He just let it go at that. But then you must remember, Dusty, that the law isn't interested in any of Miss Roach's friends that may have put that Indian Hemp in the toilet. He has his pay packet before him. There it is, as plain as daylight! A girl painter unemployed, paying five pounds a week for one room, who never sells a painting, but keeps little brown packets of that ghastly drug in her willow-patterned vases. Then I dug! I would bet my life that Dusty put that suggestion to the law to shove suspicion away from us. You were so cool when you were talking, Dusty. You were ice-cold. Oh, fuck, Dusty! Don't let them take this girl away!

The room went suddenly cold, or I did, one of the two. I think I started to shiver and I tried to stop myself in case the law suspected something and I would be showing my guilt. A man doesn't shake if he's innocent. Or does he? Look, Miss Roach is shaking like a leaf. Don't shake, Miss Roach. You look as guilty as a hanged man, shaking like that. Hold on! No, not like that! You look guilty!

The inspector nodded in mine and Dusty's direction. "I don't think you two will be needed any more," he said.

Dusty didn't need telling twice, he was by the door in a flash, and I found myself next to him. "Thank you, inspector," said Dusty. "It is getting rather late. My mother will be wondering where I've got to."

"Just one more thing," the inspector said. "Have you ever been in trouble with the police?"

"Oh no, inspector. Not me," Dusty Miller said.

"Never?" the inspector persisted.

"Not even a parking offence," said Dusty with a smile.

"And you?" This time to me.

"No, sir," I said.

"How about you?" he said to Miss Roach. She didn't answer.

"Well?" the inspector asked again.

"I have once — yes — but it was a long time ago."

"What happened?" the inspector asked, as if he knew already.

"I was sent to prison for a month."

The inspector's deep voice frightened me. "What for?"

It was then she said it. "You *know* what for!" she screamed at him. "What do you think, for Christ's sake? For Hemp, of course! Indian fucking Hemp!" Then she burst into tears and threw herself on the bed.

She'd never told me. Never. Not a word about it.

"You two clear out," the inspector said, opening the door for Dusty and myself.

I floated out through the door and up the steep steps of the basement in a dream. Not a very pleasant dream as well. As soon as I reached the top of the steps and could breathe fresh air again, I wondered how I possibly stayed in that room for the length of time that I did, without cracking up. I had behaved myself very well. I hadn't once given any clue to the inspector that I had anything to do with it. Man, I must be getting real cool now. Foxing the law even. That's an achievement in itself. I was like one of those hardened hustlers you see in the Yank films, being given the third degree and not turning a hair. I really felt up about it. I was established, I was. A Soho villain with the face of a baby. They may even call me Baby Face one day, I promised myself. Baby Face, the drug king. Famous all over the world but the police wouldn't be able to touch me. Interpol neither. Feared and respected by every big name in crime. I was a smart one sitting there just now. Cool, calm and collected, with the law around me grilling me as well. Fuck, I was clever!

But they were going to take Miss Roach to the station and charge her with the unlawful possession of Indian Hemp, contrary to the dangerous drugs act of this fine old country of ours. A very serious thing, that. Selling it as well. Poisoning the minds and bodies of poor, defenceless teenagers or some shit like that, they'd tell the magistrate. It may even be a judge as she's been in the same spot before. A month's nick they gave her. What would she get for the second whack? Six, at least. Six months inside for me. Not for herself but me. While I fuck about outside enjoying myself. While I hide Charge in other people's toilets to get them nicked. If I carry on like this I may get *all* my friends nicked in time.

Coming out from the heat of the room, it seemed cold outside. I rubbed my hands together because I thought they were cold but I found that they were numb instead. I felt sick and wanted to sit down but I couldn't; I wanted to get as far away from that house as I possibly could. I wanted to get away from it because I didn't want to see Miss Roach any more. I didn't want to look at her poor, helpless face and see the hopelessness of it. The utter despair; but even more frightening was the surrender of it. Yes, she'd accepted the fact that she'd had it. She'd given up fighting now. Do what you like with me was written all over her face. The law wasn't pleased about this or they weren't sorry. They just took it for granted. Another conviction, that's all they cared. People are people and policemen are policemen. People are to be arrested and policemen are to arrest. Another conviction. Another step up the ladder. Another conviction for the drug department. I'll get promotion yet, thinks the Head of the drug catchers. Seven Hemp convictions last week. Two more than the ponce catchers. Wonderful! Even if I *did* have to plant some on a couple of the bastards. But it didn't matter. They were only dirty, black niggers anyway.

"That was a near thing," Dusty said, as we reached the corner of the street. "I thought we'd had it for a minute."

Had what, Dusty? I thought. To take what was coming to us which would be probation anyway. Do you dig what we did instead? We let someone else, a friend of ours, go to prison for us, and all we'd have to do was probation. What's wrong with signing our names in a book once a week? Can't you write, Dusty? Because if you can't you can put a cross. One cross a week would save our friend, not someone we've never laid eyes on before, from being locked away in a lousy cell for six months, maybe more. For something that we did.

"I'm not sure if we did the right thing," I managed to get out.

Dusty stopped walking and stood quite still. "What do you mean?" he said, with a frightened look upon his face.

"She'll go to nick, Dusty. She'll get time, it's the surest thing in the world."

He forced a smile. "No, she *won't*. She's a *girl*. They'll be lenient With a *girl*, they always are. Probation, that's what she'll get."

"Don't talk fucking mad! She's done bird before for the same thing. She's a certainty for Holloway!"

Dusty's face went deadly serious. Man, it was serious. Not only serious but hard and mean too. Suddenly he wasn't good-old-life-and-soul-of-the-party Dusty. He was a different person entirely. His face screwed up a little and that made it more mean-looking still. "Look, understand this," he said. "You don't sell hats any more in a poxy suburban town. You're a hustler, remember? I made you one. I took you under my wing and showed you everything because I thought you were a sharp cat. Someone like me, who couldn't stand the world past Baron's Court. A different, a someone that could stand on their own two feet and look after themselves. But even more important, a man, regardless of age. I trusted you too because my safety and freedom relied on you every bit as much as it relied on me. So, man, you better not make me doubt you for one minute. You're up to your neck in this just as much as I am, and if you fall I fall, so you better keep right up there where you are."

"Up to our neck in what, Dusty? We're not up to our neck in anything. We'll get probation. You can bet your life we'll get probation."

He looked at me as if I were an idiot. "So we'll get probation. Do you know what that will mean? It'll mean we're out of business. We couldn't sell another half of Tea ever again. I don't know about you, man, but I wouldn't be very pleased about that. I've put a lot of work into this little round of ours and I'm not letting it go as easy as all that. This is just the beginning. There's good times ahead, Daddy-O. Things are only just on the move. In a few months we'll have this whole town eating out of our hands. We'll take over the whole market. Everything all ours; the whole source of it all. Then we'll stop selling for a month and everyone will get a real thirst on and pay double the normal price. Things are just beginning — you'll see."

He looked so smug and confident that I wanted to hit him straight in the middle of his ugly face. He leered at me from behind those thick lenses of his and his eyes looked high although I knew that he hadn't had a smoke. The corners of his mouth turned up and I realised what an unattractive example of manhood he was. Fucking horrible, in fact.

You've got to be hard at this game, I kept reminding myself. No feelings at all; stone cold and heartless. Then you'll get somewhere. Miss Roach is used to bird, anyway. It's not so bad the second time; not like the first, when you go in expecting to find the worst and find it. You'll be all right, Miss Roach. With remission you'll be out before you've even realised you're there.

"Don't you think we ought to go back there and tell them the truth?" I heard myself saying.

Dusty swung around on his heels and looked me straight in the eye with a look I could hardly describe as friendly. It was obvious that his temper was rising but he was doing his best not to show it. But it showed. It was right across his face. His teeth peeped out from behind his lips and for the first time I noticed that he didn't even brush them.

"Don't make me do something that I might regret later," he threatened. "We've been friends and I want to keep it that way. We've got to think this thing out and not jump to hasty decisions. Let's think about it for an hour or so then decide what to do. What about having a little smoke? I had a tola hidden in my sock all the time, and I got the raving horrors I don't mind admitting when the law searched me. Let's have a smoke and then decide what to do."

I knew what a smoke would make me decide. One good blow and I wouldn't even think about going back to that frightening policeman and tell him to take me down to the station, then to court, and then probably to prison. I couldn't face him if I had a smoke, I knew that for sure.

"I think I need a smoke more than I've ever needed one, but it's ridiculous getting high at a time like this. We wouldn't think straight or reason sensibly. This is a serious thing, Dusty. We can't just forget about it by having a smoke."

The wind sprang up from somewhere and it reminded me of the time that Miss Roach and I walked up this street together, hand in hand, on the night of Ayo's party. When I went into her pad and shared her spaghetti and her VP and her bed. And in that same bed that night I told her that I loved her. I knew she couldn't take all that in, but it was great all the same, and just for a short while we pretended that it was true, while we were in each other's arms. But you can't tell *anyone* that you love them even if you don't mean it, can you?

"Let's give her a chance, Dusty," I said to him, "she don't deserve all this. She's too *good*. Let's give her a chance."

"What's the matter with you anyway?" he screamed at me. "What, sort of a cat are you? Wake up, boy! I don't like this business any more than you do, but we've got to face it and do what's best for all of us. Do you realise that the law found that packet of Tea in her vase anyway? She'll get charged now, whatever happens. We couldn't be able to get her off any even if we did own up. You've got to face the facts and realise there's nothing we can do about it."

He carried on walking up the road, ignoring me, but I followed him like a lamb. At that moment I felt that I was helpless on my own. I convinced myself that I couldn't face the law on my Jack Jones even if I wanted to. I needed Dusty with me, to give me confidence and the knowledge that there was someone else in my position. I just couldn't face it by myself.

Dusty took my arm and pulled me to him in a friendly, trusting sort of way. "Do you remember when we started out on this crazy escapade? You thought it was just a dream and it wouldn't work out like the way I planned it. Well, it did. And you were grateful. I supplied you with the key to open the door that you always dreamed of walking through. I did that for you. Now I want you to do something for me."

Yes, he'd opened the door to the 'Hip' world for me all right. He'd shown me everything. I found the things I wanted to find; but now I wanted to find myself.

Suddenly I found there were people all around us. Women doing their shopping and men at work and for the moment I wished that I could change places with any of them. Even if they were nothing more than a crowd of boring frustrated peasants.

"What do you want me to do?" I asked him.

"Just have confidence in me, that's all. I've never let you down yet, have I? I've always stuck by you, so you do the same for me for a change."

"But how about Miss Roach?"

"Now the law have the Charge that was found in her vase, she's a certainty for bird anyway. We'll put a couple of quid away for her every week for when she comes out. She'll appreciate that."

A couple of quid a week. A very cheap price for someone to do your time for you, I thought. A couple of quid a week for hours that seem like days and weeks that seem like an eternity.

"Being charged with a few grams is different than being charged with a pound weight. It'll put months on her sentence," I pleaded with him.

He put on a sickly smile. "Have faith in me, friend, that's all I ask. You must think I'm a right bastard, don't you? I have feelings, too, believe it or not. I don't want to see Miss Roach get time any more than you do. But it's not the first time a young girl has done time and it won't be the last. It's not such a bad place, prison, I mean. They get concerts and film shows and some people even like it. I know a chap that's not happy unless he's inside. No responsibility, regular food, plenty of rest. It's not so terrible as some people imagine."

We crossed the road and entered the tube station. Dusty bought the tickets and practically led me down to the platform. "Come in here a moment," he said, pulling me into the station carzy. Then he vanished into a WC.

My brain was in a whirl and I was so engrossed with my muddled mind that I didn't realise where I was. Thousands of jagged thoughts about Miss Roach and poor Liz and the whole stinking poxed-up world.

The door opened and Dusty came out with an enormous, wicked-looking spliff in his mouth. "That didn't take long to make. Get on this man, it'll do you the world of good."

"No," I said quickly. "I haven't decided yet. I may even go back there after all."

"Have a smoke," he said, showing me how. He blew on it like mad and the red end burned down the spliff like it wanted to get smoked up double quick.

"That's better," Dusty said. "That's a lot better. Dear old Harry never let's you down—never! Harry, you never let us down, old feller me lad, and we're grateful; don't take any notice of this cat standing beside me. He's not really one of us. He just pretends he is. He never was."

We walked out on to the platform and it seemed very strange, because there was no one else on it, except a Spade porter pretending to sweep up. The train came crashing into the station, filling the silent platform with noise. We found a seat by the door. Dusty patted my shoulder and said, "Don't worry, friend, everything's going to be all right." The doors were still open and the hum of the train vibrated around us. Then the doors started to close and it was like something from somewhere dragging me out of my seat and I managed to slip past the closing doors just in time. When I was safe on the platform again I turned around and saw Dusty's horrified face pressed flat against the window of the train.

I ran up the stairs and out of the station as fast as my legs would carry me.

The police station's reception desk was bare and polished. There was a smell of efficiency and misery in the air. The desk sergeant looked bored with his job; a murder investigation would have pleased him more, I'm sure. Probably years ago he had great ambitions about being useful to the public, spurred on with humanistic thoughts — catching murderers and highly-skilled bank robbers — but now he'd realised that all his job consisted of was bringing unhappiness and misery to the ordinary people like himself, that had made mistakes through circumstances that confronted him nearly every day.

"I want to see your Detective-Inspector," I said to him.

He looked at me, trying to guess what I wanted him for. "CID, eh? Why the inspector? What do you want him for?"

I felt a bead of perspiration touch my lips. "I'll tell the inspector."

"You'll tell *me*, if you want to see the inspector."

My legs started to shake under me. I tried desperately to get the words out but I couldn't. "I want to see him... I..."

"Come on, out with it. What do you want him for?"

"I want to ask him what station I have to go to, to catch the train to Guildford,"

"You want to see the *inspector* for *that*?"

"I have a terribly important question to ask my sister. She's in the army there. I must see her. She's the only person that can help me."

The sergeant was past his amazement. He looked at me with the hardest professional expression that he could muster. "You'd better get out of 'ere sharpish, me lad, if you don't want to land yourself in trouble. Go on, 'op it!"

I turned around and started towards the door but he called me back. "It's Victoria Station you'll need. By the way, are you feeling all right? You're not ill or anything, are you?"

"No," I said. "I'm feeling much better now."

Terry Taylor

A NOTE ON THE TEXT

In this 60th anniversary reissue of *Barons Court, All Change*, I used as my initial template the 2011 Five Leaves Publications version of the text that was overseen and approved by the author before his death in 2014. This filled out the swear words, so that 'f--k' in the 1960s editions becomes 'fuck' etc. Another minor change made by the author to the 50th anniversary reissue is to the dedication; again I keep this alteration. Nonetheless, the 2011 edition mostly reflects the editing and related conventions of 60 years ago and stays true to the first published version of the text. So rather than rendering 'girlfriend' as one word as many publishers would today, I have kept it as 'girl friend', as did the Five Leaves edition. Likewise, I have preserved 'gass' with a double s at the end when this refers to something being fun rather than rendering it 'gas'. Similarly I have not updated the spelling of dodgey to dodgy — although the latter is the more widely used contemporary version of this term.

Having talked to Terry Taylor about the novel when he was alive, I know he was consulted about the editing of the text prior to it being first published in 1961. To the best of my knowledge he had very little — perhaps no — contact with the publishing house who put it out in paperback in 1965. Therefore if there are any differences in the text between the 1961 and 1965 editions — I have yet to spot any — it seems likely the author had no say in them. The current version of the text relies on the 1961 and 2011 editions, although I have occasionally also checked this setting against the 1965 paperback.

Where I noticed a minor difference in the text between the 1961 edition and the Five Leaves reissue — for example an unlikely capitalisation of 'It' within a sentence — I followed the setting in the 1961 book. This was because I concluded the odd capitalisation was most likely a typing or scanning error in the reset version. Another switch back to the first edition concerns capitalisation. When Ruby announces "I'M CRACKING UP!" this is in block capitals in both 1960s editions of the novel but not the 2011 reissue. I have restored the capitals because to me this appeared more in keeping with the overall tone of the novel and doesn't seem to be a change the author would have asked for — but it is one he could have missed when checking the reset text.

The paragraphing of the book might be considered idiosyncratic by some professional editors but I see it as a deliberate nod to the stream-of-consciousness style of prose popular within the beat genre. In addition I read the resultant breathlessness as a subtle addition to the book's humour and to the way in which the novel conveys the experience of being stoned. The Five Leaves edition of the book introduced the odd break to longer paragraphs — which makes them easier to read — but I have restored the original layout. In my view this better reflects the author's intentions. I think it likely that Taylor's early sixties editors would have wanted to break up his long paragraphs and that he fought for their preservation. When Terry was alive he spoke to me about differences of opinion between himself and his initial publisher over the book's editing — although I don't recall paragraphing specifically being invoked as a bone of contention. Given that most of the long paragraphs were kept as originally laid out when the book was reset for the 50th anniversary reissue, I am unsure whether the breaks introduced in 2011 were an accident or a conscious editorial decision.

I have strived to keep this text as close a possible to what Terry Taylor would have wanted if I'd been able to consult him about it, while simultaneously preserving its early 1960s flavour. There are only very minor differences of the type indicated above between the various editions of the book. Scholars may want to take note of them, as far as the general reader is concerned they are probably immaterial.

Stewart Home,
London, August 2021.

DENIZEN OF THE DEAD

THE HORRORS OF CLARENDON COURT
EDITED BY STEWART HOME

— WARNING! —

You are about to enter the City of London,
the most evil and corrupt place on the planet!

On the border between the City's Cripplegate ward and south Islington's Bone Hill district stands Clarendon Court AKA The Denizen - an elite and newly built luxury apartment block of 99 flats marketed to property investors.

Exclusive? Yes.
Reassuringly expensive? Yes.
Safe? Undoubtedly not!

There were stories, just rumours, about what went on there. Rumours about perversion, orgies, ghosts, bad feng shui and shockingly unpleasant deaths.

When a gorgeous young nymphomaniac bursts into a Clarendon Court apartment, the whole story of depravity and corruption is revealed.

In this collection of short fiction by today's top writers the Clarendon Court investment flats really are haunted by the ghosts of Cripplegate's wild past, when the hood was notorious for its brothels and the ultra-violent criminals who frequented them.

On top of this there's a problem with the spirits of hundreds of thousands of unhappy souls whose corpses were dumped in both local plague pits and the more recent Golden Lane mega-morgue, a huge Victorian Palace of the Dead.

This anthology is a protest against property speculation and a new take on the genre of haunted house horror fiction. The book itself is a talisman that defends our communities against developers and inside it also features Spell Series by the w.o.n.d.e.r. coven. The symbols of this living spell are a lock and key designed to dismantle the neoliberal project and overdevelopment as represented by The Denizen.

Featuring work from

Paul Ewen, Tariq Goddard, Iphgenia Baal, Chris Petit, Steve Finbow, John King, Chloe Aridjis, Tom McCarthy, Liz Rever, Katrina Palmer, Michael Hampton, Bridget Penney, Stewart Home and many more!

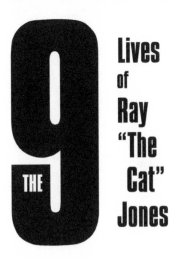

9 Lives of Ray "The Cat" Jones

This is the story of Ray "The Cat" Jones who wanted to become middleweight boxing champion of the world but eventually made his mark as the greatest cat burglar of all time.

– by STEWART HOME –

Ray is a modern-day Robin Hood waging a relentless class war against the rich. From the jewels of movie stars Elizabeth Taylor and Sophia Loren, to the private papers of the Duke of Windsor, paintings by Rubens and Rembrandt, and the furs of the London aristocracy, Ray's carefully targeted burglaries are perfectly planned and thrillingly executed.

A vision of London's underworld from wartime to near present.

The narrative weaves between the clubs of Soho, populated by gangsters and gamblers, to the mansions of Kensington and Hampstead, inhabited by corrupt politicians and millionaires, and on into the dingy cells of the city's prisons.

2021 (originally published 2014) / 5½×8½" / 256 pp

CPSIA information can be obtained
at www.ICGtesting.com
Printed in the USA
LVHW092238051121
702532LV00006B/347

9 781838 218928